"Susanna Solomon's *Montana Rhapsody* had me on the edge of my woven cane seat, paddling like hell to find out what happens next. A thoroughly enjoyable read with an appreciation for romance and wilderness."

—Amanda Eichstaedt, Station Manager of KWMR, West Marin Community Radio

"In a story part *African Queen* and part *Deliverance*, Laura, an exotic dancer from LA, jumps out a second-floor window to escape would-be rapists in Montana and invites herself on a canoe trip where she finds personal growth, a new way of appreciating life, and unexpected love."

—William Goodson, author of *The Blue-Eyed Girl* and *It's Your Body . . . Ask*

"Phrases like 'a fun, true page-turner' and 'engaging romp' come to mind when I try to describe this delightful book. Susanna Solomon has done it again!"

—Ann Steiner, PhD, MFT, Certified Group Psychotherapist, psychotherapist, author, and professional speaker

"*Montana Rhapsody* starts off at a high pitch and never lets down! How can the climax last the entire book? When you are reading about zany, quirky characters, there's no time for ho-hum. This novel zips right along, far surpassing the current of the turbid Missouri—in a holey canoe, no less. This nonstop-action novel is a real page-turner you won't want to miss. Good luck keeping pace with the author and her main character!"

—Sue Potter, educator

"Susanna Solomon's book is full of thrills and surprises. A read you can't put down. I enjoyed every minute of this wild and wonderful story."

—Joan Steidinger, PhD, author of *Sisterhood in Sports: How Female Athletes Collaborate and Compete*

"Susanna Solomon does a masterful job with characterization. From Laura, the pole dancer on the run, to Frank, the chain-smoking tax driver who purposefully hits every pothole, every character in *Montana Rhapsody* is an endearing addition to our literary world."

—Susan Cleek, ELA (English Language Arts) mentor teacher at Hillard Comstock Middle School

"Adventure flows fast with the river in *Montana Rhapsody*, bringing you along in a memorable canoe trip with a vivid cast of characters. Let Susanna Solomon be your guide and delight in the ride."

—Simona Carini, writer, photographer, and cook

"After escaping an overly zealous romantic boss and his side-kicks, Laura Fisher, a pole dancer, finds herself in the wilds of Montana with some wacky people on a canoe trip and finds love. The story is humorous and beautifully scripted."

—Inga Silva, retired trauma nurse and San Jose State University adjunct professor

"You describe it and the river very nicely. And the land around it. You are in fine company. I love the book!"

—Henry Molumphy, librarian, former Officer of the United Nations, and bookseller

MONTANA
RHAPSODY

MONTANA RHAPSODY

A Novel

by

SUSANNA SOLOMON

SHE WRITES PRESS

Published 2018

Print ISBN: 978-1-63152-361-8
E-ISBN: 978-1-63152-362-5
Library of Congress Control Number: 2017956894

For information, address:
She Writes Press
1563 Solano Ave #546
Berkeley, CA 94707

Book design by Stacey Aaronson

She Writes Press is a division of SparkPoint Studio, LLC.

To my children Alissa and Chris.

May they always be drawn to the wilderness.

CHAPTER ONE

⌒

Saturday, 8:00 p.m.
Great Falls, Montana

LAURA

*J*n the dark Laura couldn't see a thing, not the people in the front row, nor the platform under her feet; only the feel of the warm pole in her hand told her where she was, in the middle of the stage of the Big Sky Club, in front of a packed house. The music came on, a low thumping beat and *then* the lights, blinding her. Laura flashed a smile, blonde hair streaming back from under her top hat, butterfly bra and strappy thong sparkling under the spotlights, six-inch heels wrapped around the pole.

The beat picked up and so did she, running her hands up and down the pole, then up and down her thighs in the stocking stroke. She could hear them, those men, over the music, with their grunts and groans while she spun, holding her thighs just so around the pole, and always, always working her hips low and easy, doing her best to stay in synch with the audience, to carry them to a crescendo with the beat. She loved pole dancing. Twirling around the pole felt like flying!

She stopped dancing just before a trickle of sweat slid down her cheek. Her face and chest glistened with perspiration. She just glowed. She swiveled her hips and gave the men in the front row a wink, and the house went dark again. A second later the lights came back up, and she scanned the outstretched hands and moved closer as customers tucked tens and twenties behind the narrow strip of cloth at her hips, bunches at a time, until her thong was brimming with cash.

The bills looked like feathers.

For a small joint the take was better than she'd expected. For the first set of the night it was great. She gathered her cash and ran into her boss backstage.

"You get any hotter, honey, you'll give me a heart attack," he said.

Harry, a weasel-looking guy with deep-set eyes and a sharp, protruding nose, was opinionated, demanding, and cheap. He wiped his forehead with a paper towel, grinned, and held out his hand for his share.

"Later, Harry. That's our deal." Laura beamed her million-dollar smile. A small-time operator in a small town, he'd agreed—in their contract—to get his share when the club went dark at 2:00 a.m.

As for her, this place was doable, not great, but good enough. Anything was better than Mitch and the Flying Horses Club and LA. Anything was better than that sleazeball who was promising marriage and trips to Hawaii, and at the same time banged all the other girls in the scullery while Laura was performing.

Harry, looking disappointed, disappeared backstage.

Marina, one of the other dancers, came down the spiral

stairs and stood in the wings next to Laura, watching the next show. "Good night, eh?" She smoothed the feathers in her headdress and tested her five-inch heels.

"Good crowd for a Tuesday," Laura murmured. She pasted Marina's curls back onto her forehead. "You need more gel, sweetheart."

"This act's a little slow. But they always love the Bluebirds," Marina twittered. "Thanks."

Laura was silent a minute. Compared to LA, the take in Great Falls was pocket change—but with Mom in the retirement home, moving to Montana had been a great idea.

"I wish I could dance like you," Marina cooed.

"You'll get it," Laura said.

"Takes a lot of strength," Marina said. "I work out all the time but it doesn't seem to matter. And that new move of yours, of course, someday, maybe I could."

"Sit-ups, pull-ups, squats, crunches, weights. Use the facilities, here. Grab the pole with your arms, turn upside down, flip your legs right up over your head." Laura had learned that move when she was sixteen, but she wasn't going to tell Marina that. "Men love that one." She took a second glance at Marina's sad little face. "I can teach you if you like. Call me for a time and we'll work it out."

"I was trying last night," Marina said. "How? Like this?" She bent down, extended one leg over her head, and pretended to grab the pole with her hands. "I swore I was going to knock the couch over when I fell on it."

"Practice without heels at first, honey. Better than last week. Give me that call, okay? And in the meanwhile, keep that pole dry."

Marina held up her bottle of alcohol and a rag. "My new best friend, like you," she said and took off for the stage.

Laura heard the applause and ascended the spiral staircase toward the dressing rooms. Her new protégé seemed awkward on the pole, but she had such a young face, and so much joy in her come-hither looks, the guys wouldn't care about much else.

It had been tough moving to Great Falls, packing and driving and unpacking, and she was still tired. Couldn't seem to get ahead. Halfway up the stairs she felt a tap on her arm. Even after ten years of pole dancing and men trying to paw her, she still jumped a mile. It was Harry. Again?

"You're as hot as a sidewalk in Arizona, honey," he said, sweat beading his upper lip. "Wham, bam, thank you ma'am. Wow." His dark brown eyes scanned her body. "Can I get you a drink? Vanilla Stoli, Stormy Weather, or mojito?"

"No thanks." He asked every night and every night she said no. "My feet hurt. I need to rest them before my second set."

"You don't get it, sweetheart," he frowned.

"Some other time." Laura climbed the rest of the stairs and disappeared into her dressing room. She lit a few candles. After the klieg lights on stage, she loved the warmth of soft lights. As she rubbed her sore calves, moaned, and stretched her feet, she heard footsteps outside the dressing-room door. More girls heading downstairs, she figured.

Peering into the mirror and squinting, she pulled off one of her false eyelashes. A small radio played jazz tunes. Her legs were feeling better when she heard pounding on her door.

"In a minute," she hollered.

4

"Darling, sweetheart, I can't live without you." Harry opened the door, came in, and closed it behind him.

Laura started to sweat.

He rested his short frame against the wall.

"Read the contract, Harry. We'll settle later." Wiping a smudge of mascara off her eyelid, she fixed her eyes on him.

"Honey, it's not money I want."

"I've heard that one before."

"You may think that up here in Montana, we're different from your guys in LA. But it's not so."

"Harry, please," she said. "I've got to go back on in ten minutes."

"That's plenty of time. Come on, come give me a little sugar." He reached for her arm.

"I said no." She sidestepped him and flung the door open, pushed him through, and slammed and locked it. The hook and eye on the doorjamb was measly and fastened with a crooked screw. She scanned her dressing-room table for anything she could use as a weapon. Nothing but shit; cleansing cream, brushes, cologne, hair spray, eye shadow, mascara, false eyelash glue, and hairpins. She opened up a few hairpins, shoved her wad of cash in the bottom of the tissue box, and pulled out her nail scissors and set them to the side. Scrounged in her purse. Damn. She'd left her Luger at home.

Five minutes later she heard heavy footsteps just outside. More than one. The door burst open, shattering the jamb. Harry stood there, smiling, arms crossed against his chest, two stagehands flanking him. Mike had a soft face, just a young kid, but Bart looked like a walrus. Tough mustache, short, tufted hair, and a muscle shirt. A thug.

"Honey, you're not supposed to say no to the boss," Bart said.

"He's a sensitive guy," Mike added.

"Hey," Laura answered. "Anticipation is better than the real thing, don't you think? I love to make men crazy." One she could handle, but all three? Mike, the kid, looked weaker than the others . . . but that was probably deceptive. She'd have to take the thug first.

She slipped off one impossibly tall stiletto and wrapped her other hand around some Hold It 'Til You Die hair spray. "Well, then, boys," she said calmly. "If you'll just give me some privacy, I'll be ready to service all three of you."

"Me first." Mike stepped forward.

"Ignore him," Bart said.

Laura kept her eye on Bart.

"The pleasure's all mine, boys," Harry said, pushing past the other two. "Hand your bra to one of the gentlemen. And Bart, smile and be polite. There's a lady present."

Bart stood to the side, grunted, and leaned forward. Mike leaned against the wall and crossed his arms. Harry pressed forward, coming to within six feet of Laura's dressing-room table.

She lunged and drove the stiletto heel into Bart's shoulder, drawing blood, and turned and squeezed the hair spray into Mike's eyes. Mike staggered, bumped into chairs, knocked jars onto the floor. Bart grabbed at the shoe still stuck in his arm.

"Like I said, Laura, no is not an answer." Harry pulled his belt free. "Forget about those guys. I'm ready, eager, and able."

Laura dropped back into her chair and with one shoe on,

drove her heel into Harry's groin, missing his vitals by inches but doing some damage. She felt meat. Roaring with anger, he went for her leg, but she sideswiped him, jumped to her feet, grabbed a hairpin, and stabbed him in the ear.

Harry grabbed his bleeding ear. Outside the corner of her eye Mike blinked back tears and lunged for her. She grabbed a bottle of cologne, broke it on the counter, threw the contents in his eyes, and shoved past him toward the only window.

"Not so fast, sister," Mike yelled and grabbed her arm. She held out the jagged glass, slashed him with a hard right, opened the window, and prayed for a way down.

Six feet below was a balcony and a fire escape. She wrenched Mike's hand off her arm, climbed out the window, and broke her fall on a metal chair. The dark night loomed over her as she pulled the fire escape ladder free, ran down the steep metal stairs, and, dressed in her skimpy bra, a thong, and one shoe, descended to the sidewalk and ran.

CHAPTER TWO

⁄☙

Saturday, 8:30 p.m.

Great Falls

LAURA AND CAMPBELL

*C*ampbell Carr was driving the wrong way down a one-way street in Great Falls, Montana, cursing his car's navigation system, when he heard screaming and a woman, half-naked and wild-eyed, jumped out of a window, ran down a fire escape, and flung herself onto the trunk of his BMW as he drove by. Two men pounded down the stairs after her.

"Drop dead, you asshole!" the woman screamed as a big man ran behind the car and grabbed at her legs.

"Hey!" Campbell yelled. "Hey, both of you! Get off of my car!"

He punched the accelerator.

A red stiletto flew past Campbell's head, hitting the rear-view mirror hard. He flinched, narrowly avoiding a parked car at the corner, turned right, pulled into a driveway, and stopped.

"Not here! Don't stop here. Go! Go! Go!" The girl

8

crawled over the trunk and dropped into his leather passenger seat.

"What are you doing?" he asked. She was smeared with blood. "You hurt?"

"Me? No. But I will be if you don't get a move on!"

"Who the hell are you and who the hell are those guys?" Campbell asked. Two men were gaining on them, pounding their way across the deserted, dark street.

"You want those assholes coming after you too?"

"What's going on here?" Campbell asked, backing up. He was doing his best to stay calm, objective, remembering his mantra. But it kept eluding him. He jammed the car into drive and slammed his foot on the accelerator. They were in an industrial part of Great Falls full of vacant lots and locked warehouses. No place safe to drop her. He drove a mile or two and mashed his brakes when he saw an open 7-Eleven. The two guys had disappeared.

"Okay, sister. Hop on out."

"Sorry," the girl answered quietly, buckling herself in. "We're still too close."

"So, whose blood is it then?"

"That's theirs, not mine." Suddenly she whipped around in her seat and started yelling again. "That's Harry's car. I'd recognize his goddamn red Ford Focus anywhere."

In the rearview mirror Campbell looked back and saw a car gaining on them. "Hold on!" He slid into a hard U-turn, jammed his foot to the floor, and headed straight for the Ford.

"What, are you nuts? Got a death wish or something?"

"I know what I'm doing," he replied. "Get out or be quiet. Which is it going to be?"

"I'm in." Laura scrunched low in her seat.

Campbell fishtailed right by them, into a side street, made another sudden U-turn, and crept up toward the main road. He killed the engine on the dark side of the street where he could keep an eye out for the Ford. His hands were trembling and his chest ached. He took a quick look at the girl. Okay for the moment; at least she wasn't screaming. As for him, his heart was pounding a thousand beats a minute. Not good. Doc Wilson would not be pleased. Neither would Francine. He'd headed into Great Falls for a new camp stove, not to fall into some scene from the movies. He wasn't a race car driver. What the hell did he think he was doing? Playing cops and robbers? He would be late getting back. Francine, a teen, obnoxious and angry already, was going to be pissed.

"So, what's your name and why are you out, at this hour, dressed like that?" he asked finally, once he got his breath back. "A fight? You got in a fight? Where I come from, women don't fight like that."

"And that is?" Laura asked.

"New York."

"You don't know shit from shinola, buddy, but you are kind."

"So, what are you doing, then, costume party?"

"In July? I'm an exotic dancer. My boss and his two pals tried to rape me."

"Dear God."

"That's what I say," Laura said. "You got a jacket or something? I'm freezing."

"In the back."

Laura reached behind her. "Oh shit . . ."

Campbell heard the whine of another car.

He checked his rearview mirror, and punched it. The engine exploded under his command. They blew down the side street in a hail of dark gray smoke and the smell of rubber. A minute later, they were heading north on Highway 87.

"Where are you taking me?"

"I'll help you as far as the Fort Benton police station," Campbell said, shifting into fifth. "Then I'm going to the Union Hotel for a drink, a strong drink, and I'm going to see my daughter, and take off for the river in the morning."

"Where the hell is Fort Benton?"

"An hour out of Great Falls. It's a small river town. My name's Campbell." He waved his hand. "Hello."

"Laura, and thank you," she said.

"You always hang out with guys like that and jump into stranger's cars?"

"No . . . I mean, I don't mean to."

"Not such a good idea, you think? Laura, I could've been a real weirdo."

"You look like a real nice guy to me," she said, admiring his sandy hair, blue chambray shirt, and wide set blue eyes. "Nope, you don't look like a bad guy at all. A real sweetheart."

"Don't go that far," he said. His business associates in New York would never think so. He was nervous, and talking helped. He pulled beyond town and up onto the wide prairie where it was dark and his lights illuminated only a ribbon of road. "Fort Benton is a lot safer than Great Falls, I'd say."

"I appreciate all you've done," she said.

Campbell could hear the tremble in her voice. He cleared his throat. She looked so vulnerable shivering with cold. All that blood; that worried him some. "You're a hell of a fighter." He downshifted around a turn. "So, Laura"—he had to maintain control—"how did you fight off three guys at once?"

"Long story and I don't want to talk about it."

He set the cruise control to seventy-five and looked her over. Good God, what a body! Legs up to her . . . he stopped himself. Hell's bells. She could just as easily be Francine or one of her friends. A thousand times he had told her not to hitchhike. Did she ever listen to him? No.

"I used my best Manolos."

"That right?" He had no idea. "Expensive?"

"Kind of," she said.

"What kind of work do you do when you're not beating up guys?"

"It's a tough business," she said, her voice wobbly. The sobs came from deep inside her, pushing the corners of her mouth down, water seeping into her eyes.

Campbell hadn't seen this much emotion since his last board meeting when old man Jonas had a bone stuck in his throat. He tried to compose himself. Stay safe, he thought. Stay safe and get rid of her. She doesn't matter. Right. He felt like a heartless bastard. Just like Francine always said.

He pulled over, shoved the BMW into park, reached out, and put his arm around her shoulder.

"Your jacket's nice," Laura said, trying her best to fight off tears.

He watched her for a second or two, the fight in her reminding him of his own girl, and he put out his hand again, tentatively, and Laura reached over to him, buried her face in his shirt, and sobbed.

A few minutes later, he smoothed the hair back on her forehead. She smelled like sweat and fear. "So, what's your plan?"

She pulled back and stared through the windshield at the dark sky.

"Get as far away from Great Falls as I can. I had to leave my purse back there, and all my money. I'm up a creek."

"When I get off the river in a few days, I can help you get back on your feet," Campbell said. "Somehow." What was he thinking? He had Francine to take care of, for Chrissakes.

"I'll be long gone by then," she said.

"Right." Then Campbell was silent. She was a cipher. Not someone he needed to know. His life was too complicated as it was.

Five minutes later, they were speeding along the highway. Cattle country. Campbell loved these wide-open spaces and tons of stars. Didn't see anything like them in New York. Rising out of the valley, he took the curves hard and fast in his little speedster. Neat. Car handled like a Lotus. He thought about the river, his canoe trip with Francine. Would she behave this time?

They rose to a plateau and Laura gasped, startling him. "The car! It's still following us. It's them!"

He looked over at her and then checked his rearview mirror. Damn. Bright headlights were closing in on them. He gunned it. He'd always fantasized he was a good driver. The car's engine throttled up, and with a roar of the pistons, he hightailed it out of there, speeding so fast across the prairie that the lights behind them grew smaller and smaller. As they rose up to the highest point on the road, he followed the sign to Fort Benton and dropped down toward the valley below.

He turned onto a dirt road behind a barn, rolled down his window, and listened. The whine of an engine grew behind them, then disappeared. Good. Good and gone. "Pesky little bastards."

"Nothing like revenge to focus the mind. Those guys are both crazy and mean."

"You ever been to Fort Benton? To the Union Hotel?" Campbell broke the silence a few minutes later as they pulled into a parking lot in front of a three-story brick building. "This is as far as I'm going tonight. You're on your own, now."

Laura toyed with the buttons of his jacket that she still wore. "If you don't mind, I'll just come up with you. Call my best friend—or something. I won't be a bother. Just 'til I get back on my feet."

"Like I said, I'm tired," Campbell said. "And I have company. My daughter's with me. Sorry."

"Campbell, but look, it's ten at night, I have no money, no shoes, no clothes, for Chrissakes. Can you get me a room? I'll pay you back."

"I can see the police station from here."

"They'll put me in a cell. Don't you have a pair of pants I can borrow? A shirt? Something? Stella—she's cool, no questions—she'll wire money to the hotel right away. Otherwise I'll be out on the street with those assholes still hunting for me."

He climbed out of his car.

"Please?"

Against his better judgment, Campbell, his heart feeling clumsy, put his arm around Laura and opened the lobby doors into blinding light. He blinked. Someone was coming out the doorway. He stepped aside.

"Dad?" Francine spat. "That you?"

Laura noticed her ragged pair of blue jeans, a blue pajama top with horses on it, flip-flops, short bangs, ponytail, and clouded, hurt face.

Francine looked at her dad and at the girl beside him. She yanked the rubber band from her ponytail with a snap. "Well, that hurt."

Campbell froze. "Francine, I can explain everything."

"Some camp stove you found. Can she cook too?"

"Hey, it's not like that at all, Francine," he muttered, trying to gain ground. "There were these bad guys . . . and . . ." The more he said the worse he felt.

"You're disgusting, Dad," she said, then turned around and marched back inside.

CHAPTER THREE

⌒

Saturday, 10:00 p.m.

Union Hotel, Fort Benton

LAURA, CAMPBELL, AND BETH ANN

"Now, wait a minute. Francine!" Campbell called, but she was already halfway up the stairs. "Damn it all. Come back here!" He placed his hand on the banister.

"Campbell, before you go," Laura said. "All I need is a room and then I'll get out of your way."

Without answering, Campbell rushed up the stairs. Laura ran up to the landing after him and heard pounding as he rose to the third floor above. She turned and came back down. With her skimpy clothes on, at least there was no one in the lobby except for the clerk. She wrapped Campbell's jacket tighter around her.

"Miss?" Laura turned to the girl behind the reception counter. "Could you do me a favor?"

The girl held one hand over her mouth and the other hand just above the bell. She was wearing a crisp white shirt and black vest, two sizes too big.

"I don't normally dress like this, Miss," Laura said. "It was a costume party. I got mugged."

"My manager, Mr. Martins, will not be pleased."

"I just need a room. I'm freezing."

"I could lose my job." The girl held a finger over the buttons of the telephone.

"Just for tonight," Laura said. "It's late and I'm tired."

"My mom told me not to take this job," the clerk said. "It'll be okay, Ma, there's just nice people checking into the hotel." The girl narrowed her eyes. "I don't want to lie to my mom."

"Honey," Laura peered at her nametag. "Beth Ann. That's a nice name."

"You have one minute to get out of the hotel."

"I have a nice mother too," Laura chattered. "Mine's in a rest home. I don't want to lie to her either. Come on, I've got to stay inside. She says, 'Laura honey, you have to be careful. Don't you want to be safe, honey? Don't you want to feel protected?'"

"That's what my boyfriend said, and look what he did to me." Beth Ann pulled up her white sleeve and showed off a blue-purple bruise the shape of a heart. "And he still goes out with my best friend."

"I'm so sorry, Beth Ann." Laura pulled out one manicured finger and touched the bruise. "That must hurt." She paused. "How old are you?"

Beth Ann sniffed.

Laura heard footsteps behind her. Campbell?

"It's a long story," Beth Ann replied.

"Can I borrow some clothes while I listen?" Laura said. "My legs are freezing. Some guys tried to take advantage of me too." Her bare feet were numb.

"I only have a minute," Campbell squeezed around Laura's place at the counter. "Miss, please?"

"Beth Ann," Laura said. "Her name is Beth Ann. I've got this, Campbell."

"You'll need my credit card, regardless," Campbell said, reaching for his wallet.

"Was it him?" Beth Ann asked Laura. She eyed Campbell.

"Miss?" He held out his card.

"No, it wasn't him," Laura whispered to Beth Ann. "He's been great."

Beth Ann smiled and pulled her sleeve back down. "We have a room for you, ma'am. A discount." She pressed Campbell's card back into his hand.

Campbell looked from Laura to Beth Ann and back again. "Everything okay?"

"How's it going upstairs?" Laura asked.

"Not so good."

Beth Ann disappeared and returned a minute later with a paper bag. "All I have are beach clothes. And a little bag of cosmetics, and sunscreen. It gets, like, 110 degrees out here in the summer in July."

"Thanks." Laura took the bag. "You're a doll." She came around the counter to the side, gave Beth Ann a big hug, and held a thumbs-up for Campbell. "See you in the morning, then?"

"Breakfast's at seven," Beth Ann said, putting her earbuds back in her ears.

Laura took the bag and the keys. At last. She was beat.

"Laura," Campbell said, following her and stopping at the landing. "It's not easy for me to ask a favor." He stayed silent a moment.

"I've been tired so long I can't think straight," Laura said.

He tossed his own room keys and caught them. "All I'm asking . . . could you talk to Francine?"

"I'm not so good with kids."

"Better you than me. Room three-oh-one."

"She doesn't know me," Laura said.

"Could you try? I'll be downstairs, here in the bar. She's fourteen, just been a bit moody, doesn't talk to me easily about, you know, girl stuff." Anything for that matter, Campbell thought.

"Girl stuff? I don't know. I'm a pole dancer, not a mom."

He frowned. "Parents and kids, you know . . . this age. It's tough. If you told her what happened, I'm sure she'll understand."

"I'll tell her you're a hell of a driver, will that help?"

"Maybe."

"Probably knows more than you think," Laura said, remembering when she'd been fourteen. The year Dad had left. That had been fun.

Campbell paused. "And before you do, could you put on some clothes?"

Laura laughed. "Sure."

She climbed the two flights of stairs to her room. She'd be gone in the morning as soon as the money came in. She'd call Stella or, what the hell, wire the bank. But then what? Cash a check, but where? She had to remind herself to get up early.

Freshly showered and wearing Beth Ann's sleeveless jersey top and too small shorty-shorts, she went upstairs to the third floor.

"Francine? It's Laura . . . you know, that woman who came in downstairs with your dad?" Laura paused. She heard footsteps. "Could you open the door?"

Someone shuffled on the other side.

"I'm busy," Francine said.

"Your dad . . ." Laura said, then realized that she was talking too loud. "I just need a second."

Francine opened the door, keeping the chain on. "Oh, so you do wear clothes."

"It's a long story."

"It always is," Francine said, looking Laura up and down. "Every year they get younger and younger."

"He saved my life," Laura said.

"Of course he did." Francine squinted. "Now, please leave me and my dad alone." She shut the door.

Laura swore she saw tears in Francine's eyes but couldn't be sure. She was staring at a heavy wooden door while people up and down the hall opened theirs. She held her head high, hung Campbell's jacket on the doorknob.

Back inside her room she called Stella, asked her to ship some clothes and cash to the hotel, and fell asleep as soon as she lay down. Five minutes later she heard pounding on her door.

Hell's bells. She turned over and tried to get back to sleep.

The pounding continued.

"What the hell?" Laura staggered to the door and opened it a little bit. Someone was dressed in khaki pants and a light blue shirt. She focused on a face, an unshaved face, trying to remember. Oh, Campbell. "It's late. I hung your jacket outside your door. Your daughter will talk to you in the morning."

And pigs would fly and her own father would come home and Mom was going to be all right. Sure.

"It's already morning," Campbell said. "I wanted to see if you were all right. Francine and I are about to take off." He strode in and pulled aside thick brown curtains and looked out onto the river below. "Did you make your calls?"

Laura pulled the covers around herself and stood by the window. "Yeah, I should be all right," she lied.

"Well. If you ever get to New York." Campbell held out his card. "Pretty from here, don't you think?"

"It's water," Laura replied.

"There's more than water down there. There's trees . . . and people on the patio having breakfast," Campbell said. "I saw something in the parking lot. Something funny. I told Francine about it and she said lots of people drive red cars."

"What kind of red car?" Laura asked.

"Francine wasn't sure, so I went out to take a look," Campbell said, standing back from the window. "Anyway, I gotta go. Thought you'd like to know."

"Ford?" she asked.

"Those two guys look a little out of place, don't you think?"

From this vantage point even Laura could recognize Bart and his mustache.

"Why would they follow you all the way here?"

"Campbell, ever heard the expression 'Hell hath no fury like a woman scorned'?"

"Of course."

"It's worse with men," Laura said, feeling her mouth go dry. "Is there another exit out of this hotel?"

CHAPTER FOUR

~

Sunday, 9:00 a.m.
Fort Benton

LAURA, CAMPBELL, AND E.B.

*L*aura followed Campbell down a back staircase and into the scullery of the hotel. The dishwashers were hard at work stacking dishes into racks and shoving them into dishwashing machines where steam rose all around them. Beyond, waiters rushed in and out of the swinging doors. Laura hurried, going as fast as she could, hoping to avoid hitting their trays of tomato juice and eggs over easy.

"Those guys will never catch you where we're going," Campbell said as they ran out a back door into a bright, sunshiny day.

Laura blinked against the brightness and tried to catch up with him. He shot down a path underneath broad elms that lined the river where flyers about a revival meeting flapped in the breeze. In Beth Ann's flip-flops she could barely keep up with him.

"Hey, slow down a sec!" she yelled.

"Can't. People are waiting for me." He took off.

She finally caught up with him at the far end of town where he was standing at the top of a ramp beside a group of twenty-year-old girls loading canoes. Two more people—Francine, at the river's edge, was packing a cooler, and a man, twenty feet away, was carrying a canoe over his head.

"Hello, Campbell!" the girls said in unison.

"Good morning, everybody," he cried. "Ready for our trip? Everyone have everything they need? Water, life jackets, lunch?"

"Campbell," Laura touched his arm. "A canoe trip? That's no place for me."

"Can't talk now, Laura."

One of the girls came up and whispered to him.

"Sorry, Nia, you can't bring a suitcase on a canoe. Have you got a duffel bag? Otherwise, E.B. will get one for you."

Nia, a slight Asian woman, frowned and disappeared.

Laura felt out of place. She nudged Campbell. "I can't go . . . canoeing . . . not today, not any day." To her, the boats looked like toys. She dug her hands into the pockets of Beth Ann's shorty-shorts. "Please, I need transportation, a car, a plane, you understand."

"Tell the Indians canoes aren't transportation. That's how they explored Canada. Go see E.B., he'll set you up with everything you need." Campbell busied himself packing canoes. The other girls kept asking him questions.

"Nia, you're teaming up with Alice today."

He slid a canoe into the water. "Jane and Kris, you're all set? How are you doing, Francine?"

She avoided his gaze.

"Okay, great. E.B., good morning, good to see you."
Campbell helped him load. "I have a new partner for you.
Jenny French is sick. It was too late to call. Laura, you'll be
going with E.B."

"Tell her to bring me her gear," E.B. grumbled.

"Sorry, I'm not going anywhere on the water," Laura said.

"Suit yourself," Campbell said. "You can wave to us once
we launch." He set some coolers down. "Too bad. You're going to miss a lovely trip. See? Across the river, how pretty it
is?" He held out his arms. "The Missouri runs wide here, the
color of coffee ice cream. We'll be out for three days." He
cleared his throat. "You'll be fine with us."

A hot wind blew candy wrappers over her feet. "I'm okay
here," she said, a little uneasy.

E.B., a dour-faced man with a John Deere cap, gave Laura
a disinterested look, tipped his cap, and went back to packing
his canoe. Duffle bags and paddles lay in a heap beside his
long legs.

Laura watched them, mesmerized. She'd never been an
outdoor girl. What was the appeal? Mosquitoes? Sleeping on
the ground? Food that tasted like paste? Ticks and spiders?
She shivered, although it was not cold at all.

E.B. came up and stood beside her. "Name's Ezra Benson.
I'm coleader on our trip." He held out his grease-stained fingers. "Sorry, I've been working on my tractor, can't seem to
get the dirt out." He took her hand in a too-tight grip. "Ever
gone canoeing or camping before?" He wore a long-sleeve
khaki-colored shirt, zip-apart khaki pants, and sandals. A
wide-shouldered man, he looked like an extra for some African safari magazine ad.

"Me?" Laura blinked at the early morning light and tugged at the hem of Beth Ann's shorty-shorts. Beth Ann was a much smaller girl, and her shorts barely covered Laura's tush.

"See if this one fits." He held up a life jacket.

It was orange, as big as a semi, and puffy. "I don't need that."

"It's mandatory. Help you if you fall in. They're not called lifejackets for nothing, you know."

"But I'm not going."

"It's a good idea. I've been paddling the Missouri my whole life. Sometimes rivers can be deceiving. It's my job to protect you, keep you safe."

Laura had heard that shit before. She left E.B. and found Campbell loading boats, pulled up close to him, and whispered.

"I can't go with E.B."

"Francine won't give up her seat."

"You don't understand. I can't go with anyone. Not my thing." She held out the life jacket. "Sorry."

"I thought you weren't afraid of anything," Campbell said. "It's just a pissant canoe camping trip, Laura. Class I. Like a bathtub. No thugs chasing you, no racing cars, and no rapids."

Laura looked between him, the river, the fort, the brick buildings in town, and the hotel beyond. "Think they're still there?"

"Step aside," Francine said, shooting a look at Laura. "I need to load." She pushed a canoe into the water.

"No need to be snappy. I never did anything to you," Laura replied.

"And you never will." Francine stepped into her boat.

Everyone was launching their canoes. Laura could hear

Campbell calling her name. E.B. nosed his canoe near shore and waited, paddle in hand, watching her.

Francine sidled up to shore. "Laura, did they tell you anything about canoeing?" she asked. "Thought not. They've got mosquitoes as big as hats out here, and rats, and ticks, and poisonous snakes. And it can be stinking hot."

"Have a great time on the river, everyone. See you later." Laura stepped back off the ramp.

"Ready, Francine?" Campbell asked and climbed into her canoe.

"Bye!" Laura waved.

In front of her, four canoes bobbed five feet offshore. The girls, Francine, E.B., and Campbell churned their paddles in the water, striving to stay near shore and out of the current.

"See you later, then," Campbell said.

The canoeists looked so small out there on the wide river. Laura liked land, safer any day. Behind her she heard two car doors slam.

She turned.

The Ford Focus had pulled into the parking lot.

Laura flew back down the ramp.

"Campbell, come closer!" she screamed. "Let me in! Let me in!"

Behind her she heard boots ringing on wet concrete.

"No girl says no to me!" Mike shouted, running toward her.

Laura leaned over and tried to grab Campbell's canoe.

"Don't do that, you'll swamp us!" Francine said, using her paddle to fend Laura off.

"Don't hit her, Francine," Campbell shouted. "Laura, try E.B.'s boat."

"But he's so far away!" She could hear huffing behind her. E.B.'s canoe was six feet offshore.

"Jump!" Campbell said.

"But I can't swim!"

"No need to panic," E.B. replied, bringing the canoe within two feet of the ramp. "Climb in slowly, Laura."

"Shit, shit, shit!" She bent down and extended one leg.

Footsteps rang on the pavement. With one leg in the boat, she leaned to place the other. And felt something grab her arm.

"Asshole!" She slammed her arm into Mike's, twisted to get away, and flopped into the canoe shoulder first, falling on a cooler, which hurt. The boat dipped down hard, wobbled, and almost flipped over. It was tough to climb back up and take the seat.

"You'll put a hole in the boat doing that!" E.B. yelled.

Mike jumped into the water after her.

"Get away! Paddle and paddle hard!" she screamed. "Now!" She found a paddle on the bottom of the canoe, sat up, and tried to hit Mike with it.

His fingers closed over a thwart.

"Not so fast, buddy," E.B. said, swatting his hand with his paddle and pushing off into the current.

Laura, frantic, stabbed at the water, making spray fly through the air.

"Laura, go slow, we're safe now. Not so fast," E.B. said once they were ten feet from shore.

"Teach me some other time." She dug in.

"Easy, easy."

Her strokes made the canoe turn to shore where it stopped five feet away from a pile of rocks.

"Not again!" Laura yelled.

She paddled backward. The canoe shuddered and didn't move.

"I wouldn't do that, if I were you," E.B. said.

"Excuse me?"

"We're on a rock."

She grasped both sides of the canoe.

Bart waded into the river, Mike beside him.

"Get it *off!*"

"Face forward or you'll dump us."

Laura felt like meat.

E.B. maneuvered the canoe around the rock. The canoe moved another ten feet.

"So who are those guys, Laura? Friends of yours?"

"Not really." Laura twisted her paddle in the water to make them go faster.

The canoe spun down the river, totally out of control.

"Stop paddling," E.B. said, "unless, of course, you want to say hello to your friends again?"

Above the hills beyond, a vast expanse of blue studded with white clouds made her feel very small.

CHAPTER FIVE

~

Sunday, 9:30 a.m.

on the river

LAURA AND E.B.

*T*he shore and the river went by in a blur as they did 360s down the river. Laura tried to take a stroke, but the canoe kept spinning.

Behind them the little town had disappeared and Mike with it. She shifted her focus to the water and tried to calm down. As if she could. Ahead of them, the other canoes were a hundred yards down, and as small as specks. Was that how she looked from shore? A speck? She hoped so, but small as she was, she wasn't small enough. For all she knew, Mike and Bart would follow along on the shore and pick them off the first time they landed. "Is there a road out here?" she asked. She scanned the dun-colored hills and endless countryside.

"In the Missouri River Breaks?" E.B. laughed. "This is wilderness. We'll soon be in canyon country, and no one drives into canyon country, unless they're crazy, drunk, or both. Like those guys chasing you? Why were they chasing you?"

"Just some assholes," she said. "They think I took some

money of theirs, but I didn't." That was far from the truth, but it would have to do.

"You have interesting friends," E.B. said.

"Like I said, they're not my friends."

"All right, then," he said. "So, again, this is all you see. No houses, no roads at all, sometimes a homesteader's cabin. That's why we come. Enjoy it."

Enjoy it? She couldn't turn to look behind her; the sun was beating on her head; she missed her sunglasses, purse, keys, cell phone, Stella, and all her clothes; and she was in a boat in the middle of a river with a man she barely knew.

"They can't follow you unless they have a boat. Did you see them with a boat?" E.B. asked.

"I don't think so," she answered, looking back very carefully. "I don't see much of anything."

"That's the way it's supposed to be. So, Laura," E.B. said, "watch me a sec, see if you can use the paddle the same way I can. Easy turning around, please. Ready now? Slowly, slowly."

She eyed him over her shoulder. Jesus, the shore was a long way away. What if they went over? She tightened her grip on the paddle.

"Try to relax. Just easy moves. That's better, thank you. You know any strokes?"

Strokes? Oh yeah, she knew strokes. The stocking stroke, the caress stroke, the inside and outside spins. Nope, telling him any of that would not be good.

"Uh, not really," she mumbled. She put her paddle in the river and pulled back. Water flew in the air.

"Lesson one. Leave the water in the river." He laughed.

Laura slipped her hand in, expecting cold. It was surprisingly warm. Cliffs moved by, cows grazed on the shore, and trees fluttered in the breeze. One stroke at a time. Stay in the boat and keep paddling. And say over and over, you're safe. But she didn't feel safe.

"All right, let's pick it up a bit. Time to catch up with Campbell and everyone else."

She tried to put more strength in her stroke.

"Better. Now don't shove the blade all the way in. Hold the paddle perpendicular to the water."

She tried; that felt awkward.

"Use your shoulders, your back, not your arms."

Her shoulders? What? Not move her arms? Why not? She pivoted from the waist, feeling like a moron. "Like this?" Paddling had to be easier than dancing on the pole any day.

"Keep the paddle on your right. Otherwise, you make us zigzag. I can steer from here."

"Gee whiz, E.B., I'm doing the best I can." She turned and glared at him.

The canoe rolled to the left. She panicked and leaned the other way, and it rolled to the right. Tipping farther, farther. Laura grabbed the boat with both hands and screamed. Water poured inside.

The canoe bobbed back up, sharp and tidy as a soldier.

"Learn something? Don't turn around so fast in a canoe! You almost dumped us!"

"Oh thank God." Laura clutched her life jacket, her face white. She felt something missing. Oh shit. "My paddle!" It was bobbing five feet away. She reached for it.

"Don't you dare reach for it. You'll dump us again. Haven't you ever gone canoeing before?"

"Um, I've done other things," she mumbled. "But not really . . ."

"I'll bring us closer."

"It's just right there." Laura leaned farther, her belly on the rail, her arm outstretched.

"Like I said, please, please don't move!"

She sat back, as low as she could go, and held on to the canoe with both hands. "In a bad mood or are you always like this?"

"I can't remember." He moved the canoe slowly and surely toward the paddle. "Okay, stay still."

"Smart aleck," she muttered under her breath.

"What'd you say?" E.B. grunted as he made the canoe turn around. "When I say so—and only when I say so—pick it up. All right?"

When they were practically on top of the paddle, E.B. said go and Laura closed her hands around the handle. She tucked it inside the canoe where it would be safe.

A few minutes later they were back in the current, moving sideways down the river.

"Aren't you going to take a stroke? It's a lot easier if both of us are doing it," he said. "It's like sex, Laura."

"Are you making fun of me?"

"As a farmer, that's the best attempt at a sense of humor I've ever had. Haven't you ever heard of tippy canoes?"

"I thought that was a joke."

"Not a joke in my book."

"We're lucky we didn't drown. I didn't know." She adjusted the straps on her life jacket and took a few strokes. Damn thing was just not tight enough.

"Big mistake number one is letting go of the paddle."

Big mistake number one was moving to Montana. Life would be way better if she'd never left LA. "You could have warned me."

"About what? The 'friends' chasing you or the fact that you're in canoe? They wobble. Get over it. Just who are those guys, anyway?"

Big mistake number two, getting into this canoe.

He took a deep breath. "Okay. Paddle a bit to keep us going straight, if you will. No sudden moves."

Clouds of gnats flew into her eyes and mosquitoes peppered her arms. There were more hells in the great outdoors than working in a strip club any old day. "You have anything for the bugs?"

"Try some bug goop." He tossed her a small bottle, then another. "And some vanilla extract—that'll keep the gnats away. You'll smell like cake, but it works great."

She smoothed sticky stuff on her arms and face, and dabbed vanilla under her ears and on her neck like perfume. Weird combination. "You use the bug goop and the vanilla and sunscreen all at once? Why don't they make all-in-one?"

"Keep your eye out. If you spot riffles—logs just below the surface of the water—let me know. In the meanwhile, help bail. We're coming in for a ten-minute break."

"But what about catching up with the others?" Laura asked.

"They stop too. And they should be waiting for us. We won't be more than a few minutes or so behind them."

They bumped the shore hard. Marsh grass as far as she could see.

"Good enough," she muttered, stood up, and felt the ground dissolve under her foot.

"Grab the painter."

She tried to pull her foot up, but the mud sucked at her flip-flop. She pressed her other foot down.

"Like I said, grab the painter."

She felt a rising sense of panic. Both feet were stuck. "What's that?"

"It's the only rope on the boat."

"You could have told me." Shit, the boat was drifting away. "E.B., hold up. Come back!"

"Everything? Do I have to tell you everything?"

"It's not funny," Laura said, trying to extract herself out of the mud.

"All you have to do is grab the rope when I come in again, okay?"

She reached forward, took the line from the bow, pulled him in, and, with the canoe under her, was able to pull her feet and her flip-flops out of the mud. She sat down on the bow of the canoe. "I thought the mud would never let go."

"Sometimes it doesn't."

"And people die out here?"

"Not really, not from mud, anyway. Not in a while." He busied himself with taking off his paddling gloves. "Have some water." He offered her a bottle.

"All this excitement." She took a long drink. "I need to go. Where should I . . .?" Not much around but bent, broken cornstalks and endless vistas.

He got out and pulled the canoe hard up on shore. "Take your time. I won't look."

She slipped a little getting up on the dirt. Caked mud covered the bottom of her shoes, making them slip.

"Do your business and come back."

She took another step and stared at a broad expanse of stubble and earth.

"Not a good idea to go so far in the cornfield, Laura," his voice gentle again, at her ear. How had he come so close so fast?

"I don't need any help."

"No? Suit yourself. We do have ticks out here."

"Ticks? How am I supposed to . . . you know?"

"Squat as high as you can."

"You're kidding me!"

"Not so used to nature, are you?" E.B. turned away.

Doing her best to keep her balance, Laura pulled down Beth Ann's shorts. Just don't fall down, she told herself. Easy, easy. Halfway through her business, she stared at her legs, strong and sure like always; good thing she practiced her squats at home. But there was something wrong. Little specks of mud clung to her calves. Her legs were covered with them. No reason to be so filthy so early in the trip. Standing up again, she pulled up her pants, then bent down to knock them off. But they did something strange. They were moving!

⌐

CHAPTER SIX

Sunday, 11:00 a.m.

on the river

E.B. AND LAURA

"Don't make such a big deal out of it. Just brush the ticks off before they dig in."

"How can you live here with all these bugs?" Laura cried, frantically wiping her legs. "Whatever for?"

"Don't tell my mom you don't like Montana. She wouldn't like to hear that." E.B. shoved the canoe back into the current. He could ask her where she lived and make an argument out of it, but he had no desire. City people. The less he talked to them the better.

He loved the river, the fresh air, the countless birds taking off when they drew near, the endless vistas, the sweep of his paddle through the water. The feel of the canoe under him, moving on, moving forward around every bend, everything new, sweet, clean. Better than the ranch, any day, every day.

He stroked evenly and wondered what Berniece was doing. She didn't like the water, but she'd come paddling once and she'd been pretty good. Way better than Laura who was thrashing around in the bow. Berniece didn't thrash. She was sensible. She made turkey soup the day after Thanksgiving, sewed quilts, and never complained. He kept up an even rhythm, which soothed his ragged nerves. Maybe after two months, she'd discover that the preacher she'd run off with—that Stanley Cornelius III—was an asshole. He brightened. He could hope, couldn't he? Maybe she was already at home, at the ranch, putting up jam, humming to herself at the kitchen window, wondering where he was.

"E.B.?" Laura asked, breaking his concentration. "Everyone in Montana have a gun? You one of those NRA people?"

"You ever gone hunting? Is that one of those things you like to do?" He missed going out with Milt, their broken rifles slung over their shoulders, the early-morning mist hugging the ground, the silence of the air.

"Me, no, but I wish." She took a stroke. "Maybe it's time I learned how."

"Maybe I'll teach you sometime," he sighed. He remembered Campbell's words: "It's your job to please the customers, E.B." If he couldn't stay civil, he could stay silent like he usually did. He imagined Berniece, hand poised above the phone, pulling back a wisp of hair from her forehead, taking his freshly killed ducks with her other hand.

The idea made his heart hurt. His stomach didn't feel so good either. And something odd was flickering across his eye. When he looked for it, the shadow disappeared and wobbling around made him dizzy. He blinked but it wouldn't go away. His father had had cataracts; was he getting them too?

"Guns make me nervous," Laura said. "My girlfriend Stella was held up. Pistol, sidearm, AK-15. What you got?"

"A rifle. Remington thirty-four, my grandpa's, single-shot."

"Single-shot in LA wouldn't do much."

"No, I suppose not."

No answer but a bob of her head. That was a start, wasn't it? "LA. That where you live?"

Another nod. Laura was something else. Blonde hair, legs to everywhere, soft white skin. She tossed her hair over her shoulder with abandon. Berniece wouldn't like the fact that he looked at Laura. Even when they were together, she used to grumble when he gazed at other women. What would she say now? He dipped his hat, scooped up a hatful of water, and poured it over his head. The cold water dribbled over his shoulders, chest, and back. Yes. Better.

"You see any other boats?"

"Nothing out here but us chickens, E.B."

In the middle of a long stretch of river, his stomach took a turn for the worse. He held his gut, and the cramps passed. He'd have to head to shore and soon. He put on some heat.

"If you don't mind, I'm going to sleep in the boat tonight. No ticks there," Laura said.

"The hull is hard and it's cold. Besides what are you going to do with the thwarts? Crawl under them?"

"These things crossing the canoe? They're not removable?"

E.B. laughed. "You'll be all right sharing a tent with me. If that doesn't suit your fancy, you can bunk with Francine. She probably won't mind."

"I'm not sharing a tent with her. She wouldn't like it."

"Francine doesn't like anyone. Okay, then. Ask Campbell if you can share his four-man. It's big."

"Wish I'd brought my own," Laura grumbled.

"You own a tent?"

"Uh, no," Laura said.

E.B. grinned. "So, where did you meet Campbell?" They were getting along, sort of. Better than her yelling at him any day.

"At the Union Hotel. Last night. At the bar."

"Ah." He hadn't that kind of time. Kind of wished he had. Picking up women in bars was not really his thing though.

"So, about sleeping outside? Are there wolves here?" Laura asked.

"Some. Yes. A few. They don't come down to the river, usually."

Laura took some long, even strokes. "Hey, E.B., how's my form?"

"Fine," he lied. She was doing it all wrong, holding the paddle out to the side like a wing, flicking water up in the air, and occasionally digging the blade in too deep, slowing them down. He'd teach her later. For the moment the only thing he felt like coddling was his stomach. Tight cramps flickered across his belly like a sharp knife turning and churning then going away. He wondered if it was the All You Can Eat Platter at the Fish 'N' Fry. Harold had said everything was fresh, you know, fresh frozen, he had said. Right.

If Berniece was really back in the kitchen, how would she know he was all right? He hadn't left a note. He pulled on the paddle again, wishing he could call home.

He bet Laura didn't even know how to boil coffee. He took a deep breath and a long pull with his paddle. The physical sensation made him feel as if he was at least doing something right. That damn Laura, still messing with her hair. He strained with each stroke, but thought better of asking her to help out.

Watching her blonde hair flying in the breeze made his stomach feel better. No fluttering sensations this time. The sun was warm on his head and shoulders. He took off his John Deere cap and raised his face to the sun. A hawk flew overhead and headed to the bluffs on the other side of the river.

"Hey, Laura. See those trees? Those are cottonwoods. Listen. They make this wonderful murmuring noise. You know that Cole Porter tune 'Don't Fence Me In'?"

"Never heard of it." Laura tucked her knees under her chin. "Frontier country in the movies doesn't look anything like this."

"That's 'cause the movies are made in the Monument Valley. The west is big country." E.B. took a drink of water. "I noticed you haven't been drinking enough. I gave you a full water bottle, didn't I?"

"I'm not thirsty." Laura finger combed her hair. "I haven't even broken a sweat."

"That doesn't matter. You're out in the sun, you're exercising, you need water. Unless you want to get dehydrated?"

"This is exercise?" she asked, taking a stroke. "Since when?"

"Even in Westerns, they drink from time to time," he suggested.

"Yeah, I guess. Whiskey, though."

He laughed. So she did have a sense of humor. There was hope.

He took a few solid strokes and let the canoe glide. The boat moved just the way he wanted. Watching the skies, the birds, the cliffs, the bluffs, and the swallows dancing—it made him feel a little better. Maybe when he got home, if Berniece was there, he'd rebuild. Who was he kidding? Berniece wasn't coming back.

He could smell Laura's perfume, lightly sweet, not cloying like the ladies in the line at the Pak 'N' Pay. She sat quiet for a while. Maybe she was getting used to the boat. He stared at the birds. He should talk to her about books, but couldn't remember when he'd last read one.

"Hey, E.B., you ever watch movies?"

"You bet. Gary Cooper, Jimmy Cagney, Orson Welles, to name a few," he said, thinking of *High Noon, Angels with Dirty Faces, The Third Man.* "Great, great flicks—heroes as big as yesterday, and a code of right and wrong." The old movies made him forget about Berniece. Forget about the cold house and empty rooms.

"Gary who?" she asked. "And who were those others? Never heard of 'em."

"Cooper, Gary Cooper. Big Western star."

"Okay, my turn," she laughed. "Owen Wilson, Ben Stiller, Wallace and Gromit."

"Who's Gromit?"

"A dog, a clay dog. Everyone's heard of Wallace and Gromit."

Hurt and bewildered, he waited a few minutes, watching birds peck on the shore. "You intentionally trying to give me a bad time, or what?"

"No. Not really. Sorry."

It sounded like she actually meant it.

"It's pretty country out here, don't you think? Even

though it's not in the movies," he said, looking for something conciliatory, and intelligent, to say.

"Pretty?" she answered. "Land's kind of bleak. There aren't any trees, the grass is dead, and I don't see any cows. What do you do out here on a farm?"

Three generations of Bensons surged in E.B.'s blood. The land pleased him—or used to. Even without Berniece, his body belonged to the land. It owned him. He could actually feel the earth course through his veins, his muscles, his heart. The smell of sweet grass in the spring, the steady grind of the combine over winter wheat, the crunch of snow under his boots, the hoar frost freezing the trees, the warm glow of sunshine on his head. Berniece felt it too; that's what he loved most about her. He reminded himself that Laura was a city girl and didn't know anything. He pulled over for a break.

She stared at him, her eyes wide, just like the new mare he'd just purchased from Ralph at the Feed 'N' Seed. She stood up, stepped onto shore, and stretched.

He ran his eyes over Laura's legs, scanning flawless skin and enjoying the view. He saw what looked like a dark mole. "This ever bother you?"

"Does what bother me? The mosquitoes? The heat? The canoe? Paddling?"

"The mole at the back of your thigh. Does it bother you when you sit for a long time?"

"I don't have any moles on my thighs!"

He touched the black round shape, feeling it wobble.

"Got a match?" he asked, then remembered. "Tweezers?"

"I don't care what you do to me, E.B., just get the fucker off."

"Easy-peasy, hold still." He tightened his grip over the speck, pinched his fingers, rotated, and pulled.

He held the tick out to her. "I got it all," he indicated. "Even the head. If you don't get the head out, sometimes it'll become infected."

She looked at his face, then back at his fingers. Tiny legs wiggled next to his thumb.

"Another reason I hate Montana."

"By the size of it, it's been there a couple of hours." He flicked it into the water. "They can carry Lyme disease, among other things. I had to go to the hospital for an infection one time."

"Thanks," she muttered, her voice hollow. "I didn't feel a thing."

She looked at him with those big mare eyes, brown and luscious and wonderful.

"Like I said, I can be useful."

"Next time I'm peeing in the water." She stepped deftly back into the canoe.

"Not really a good idea. Stay on the sand," he added. "Ready?"

"Not quite." She tucked her hand into Beth Ann's cosmetic bag and pulled out a little tube, trying to thank him in some way. She oozed some onto her hand. "Want some sunscreen?" She held out a tube of Elizabeth Arden SPF Five. She poured a little glob of it into his hand before he could say no. "Your cheeks are looking red."

It wasn't from sunburn. He looked at the glob, then back at her.

"I already have a tan."

"E.B., you need to protect your skin. It's your best feature."

His face reddened even more. He smoothed on the goop, and, feeling greasy, launched the canoe.

Moving around a bend and peering downriver to search for the others, E.B. took even, slow, steady strokes. He loved the feel of the paddle in his hand, the hush-hush-hush of mergansers taking off, the glide of the canoe, the girl in the bow—everything would be perfect if not for the hurt in his gut. Nausea? Something else? Heatstroke?

Down at the end of a straight stretch, E.B. saw some color in the distance, something red against the white cliffs. It looked like Campbell's red canoe. Full of hope he tried to lift his arm, but it wouldn't obey. A flush of heat rose up his neck, making him dizzy. His blade hit the water at an angle. The shaft rotated in his hands. His gut was going to bust.

He shook his head. It was like someone had put a blanket over his senses. He weaved around on the seat, trying to stay upright. Trying to stay focused. It was either that goddamn fish or he was dehydrated. All he could see was one little white dot. The river, the shore, and Laura disappeared as the paddle slipped from his hands.

*

CHAPTER SEVEN

Sunday, noon
on the river

LAURA AND E.B.

eeling the canoe veering to the right, Laura pulled
back on her paddle. The canoe kept heading to the
bank. She took another pull. Nothing going. The stupid boat felt like she did after dancing all night, slow and stiff
and unresponsive. What the hell? They did a full 360 until
she stabbed at the water a few times. The canoe shuddered
and slid down the river sideways.

She listened for the sound of E.B.'s paddle, but there was
no dip, slide, or swish from behind her. If she turned around
too quick to check on him, she could dump them both. Concentrate, girl. This is no different from what you do on the
pole. What's next in this routine?

She ran through his instructions step by step, put all her
weight into it, and dug in. For a second it was perfect; the
front of the canoe rotated to the left. She took another
stroke, but then it went to the right. Fat lot of good that did.
She couldn't steer for shit.

They sped up as the current caught them around a turn. A moment later, the boat drifted toward a rocky shore.

Turning her head ever so slowly, she saw E.B. resting, his paddle in his lap, head down. Eyes closed.

"E.B., come on. Help me out here," she asked. "Pick up your paddle and do something."

"What's going on?" he moaned.

"I can't steer this piece of shit by myself."

"Yes, you can, just try . . . I can't, right now," he mumbled.

The canoe crept closer, fifteen feet from the rocks, now ten.

"I need help NOW!" She pulled back on the paddle hard. The canoe drifted close enough to touch land.

"Just put your paddle in and pull. Hard."

"Nothing's happening. We're going aground. Please."

"Leave me alone."

The canoe touched the rocks.

Laura yelled, "Ezra Benson!"

He didn't respond.

She pushed off with her paddle. The boat drifted onward, hugging the shore. She took a stroke with her right hand, then another with her left. Zigzagging, the canoe slid along ten feet from shore.

"Jesus Christ. What's the matter with you?"

"I knew you could do it," he said. "You're doing fine."

"Do what? Keep us going in one direction? Are you kidding?" Above her, swallows called, as if to mock her. Their chatter filled the air. She felt a little bad. "Are you all right back there?"

No answer. Had he fainted? Had a heart attack? How the hell was she supposed to do CPR? She struggled to remember what she'd seen on TV. Compression, compaction? She had no idea. The canoe skidded across the water like a pair of new shoes on a slick floor. "Come on, you big useless dick."

A gust of wind caught E.B.'s hat. She watched it spin in a circle, then float away.

"Don't you want your hat?"

The canoe drifted toward an island.

"What hat?"

Laura eyed a beach ahead. If only she could pull over there. The canoe shuddered, stalled, and spun. She took another deep, full stroke. The canoe slid sideways.

"Stupid goddamn boat!"

The shore was twenty feet away, then ten. The canoe slammed into something and knocked her out of her seat. She landed on the bottom of the boat.

"Fuck!" She wrenched her shoulder climbing back up to her seat. Then she checked on E.B. He was leaning over his knees.

"E.B. You alive back there?"

"I don't know what to do about these cows, Milt. They seem off today."

"Cows? What cows! E.B., wake up! You dreaming?"

"Check the bilges, Captain Kirk, I think we've gone aground."

Was he making fun of her again? Or completely crazy? Whatever it was, she couldn't help him here. The canoe held still as water rushed around them. The shore, a pole distance away, could just as well have been on Mars. She slid her hands into the water, trying to free whatever stopped them while keeping an eye on the fast-moving river. Branches and twigs broke off, but the canoe held fast. She leaned over farther, water pouring over her arms. The canoe shifted under her.

She wasn't going to die out here. Fuck no. Praying the canoe wouldn't take off without her, she kicked off her flip-flops, grabbed the painter, and, holding onto the sides of the canoe, carefully and slowly eased herself over the side.

Dropping in, she let her legs drift down until she felt something squishy and disgusting with her toes and stood up. She sunk in mud up to her ankles. The water was up to her chin. Holding the painter in her teeth, she moved around the canoe, trying to find out what held it in place. The current pulled at her clothes.

The boat was hung up on a branch.

"Hey, E.B.! Can you give me a hand here?"

Oh God. He was leaning over so far, she thought he'd fall over, into the river. Then what would she do? She eased her hand up over the front of the dumbass canoe. Holding the rope in one hand and bracing herself in the muck below, she dipped her head under and with one hand slipped the canoe free.

Fuck!

"Help!"

The boat was pulling away.

Digging into the mud with her toes, she grabbed the line with both hands, river bottom sucking at her feet and threatening to pull her in with every step. Nine feet away, eight. "Come on you stupid pile of crap." The boat was heavy.

Seven feet, six. She was up to her waist now. Five, four. She pulled harder. Suddenly, the boat rushed at her and pushed her backward into the muck. The water was up to her shoulders.

E.B. laughed.

"So. You're alive?"

"Not really."

His face was the color of milk. He was all still and quiet, like the dead man they'd found in the front row one night after a show.

"You all right?"

He stirred, straightened, and stood up. Wobbling from side to side, he stepped around her, sitting on her butt in the water, and marched to shore.

"E.B.?"

"Stay there."

A moment later, he threw up.

"Whoa," she said. "Feeling better now?" She tied the boat to a branch, got to her feet, wiped mud off her hands onto her once-white shorts, and gripped his shoulder. The puke stunk but he was near. And they were safe.

"Goddamn Fish 'N' Fry. Or it was the heat or something. Good God."

She watched him wipe his mouth on his sleeve.

"Thought my stomach would cave in."

"And I thought you had a heart attack."

"Me? No, ticker's ready for a parade. Can you get me some water?" He paused. "You did good, Laura, steering by yourself."

Beaming, she walked toward the canoe, trying to avoid looking at the mess he'd left.

She leaned in, unzipped the yellow duffle, put her hand around a water bottle, pulled it out, and noticed something strange.

"Hey, E.B.," she said. "Is there supposed to be this much water in the boat?"

CHAPTER EIGHT

&

Sunday, 2:00 p.m.

Slaughter River Campground

CAMPBELL AND FRANCINE

Campbell paced on shore, pecking at his cell phone. No sign of E.B. or Laura or their little red canoe. No cell phone service either. It was getting on toward the middle of the afternoon and time to make camp. Were they stuck somewhere? Lost their paddles? Had Laura fallen in? He threw a few items into his canoe and headed off to tell his daughter his plans.

He found her dozing under the shade of a cottonwood tree.

"Hey, kiddo, keep an eye on the others. I'll be back in an hour—I've got to go back and find E.B. and Laura."

"Suit yourself."

"You hear me, Francine?"

"Yeah, yeah, I got it, Dad." She turned over and closed her eyes.

Feeling a little uncomfortable leaving her in charge, Campbell threw his life jacket, his paddle, and a water bottle

51

into the boat, stepped in, and went to push off. The canoe jammed on something. He shoved harder.

"You're going to break my fingers doing that," Francine said.

"What are you doing here? Stick around. Get some rest."

"Climb into the bow. I'll guide us from the stern. We can go faster together." She yanked the canoe closer, then rolled up her pant legs. "I'm no babysitter."

"What if they need something? Get in trouble?"

"These girls will be fine on their own."

"You don't understand. It's my job. I can't leave them unchaperoned."

"They're all older than I am."

"But not as bright," Campbell said, feeling clever.

"Compliments, eh? Do anything to make me stay? No dice." She popped her gum.

"Don't make this harder than it is." She was getting so tall. "C'mon, you've got to understand. I can't leave them stranded out there."

"Special Dad-daughter trip. You promised."

"We can do stuff later, as soon as I get back." He'd never been good with her.

"Do whatever the hell you want. You always do." She shoved him and the boat away from shore.

"Francine! Don't say things like that! You know they're not true." How and when did their relationship become so strained? His plans for this special trip certainly hadn't included hurting her.

The current pulled him twenty feet downriver, the wrong way, fast. Grabbing his paddle, he turned around and headed upriver toward E.B. and Laura. The going was surprisingly hard. The current wasn't that strong, was it? Still, he could do this. He made up the distance with some effort, and then the canoe slowed down. What the hell? He'd never make it at this rate. He pulled harder and harder. Jason at the gym said he'd been doing great. Damn. He peered forward—and saw some fingers on the gunwale. Francine. In the water.

"What are you doing? Let go! I told you to stay on shore."

"Hi, Dad," she trilled, pulling the bow aside so he could see her grin. "Can't go anywhere? What's the problem?"

"This time, for a change, Francine, how 'bout just doin' what I ask?"

"Not today, not now, and not without me." She laughed, hung off the hull, hair plastered across her forehead, eyes bright.

The current pulled them into the middle of the river, past where the other canoeists were playing cards, past the point where she could still swim to shore.

"For Chrissakes, let me at least get you back on land. You're a pain in the neck, Francine."

"What else is new?" She kicked under the boat and eased them close to a mud bank. She climbed onto some rocks, balanced on both gunwales, water pouring off her, and climbed into the boat.

"Water's warm," she giggled, squeezing water out of her hair.

"Sit down. Sit and behave. Honestly, I don't know what to do with you. We agreed, on the plane, on the trip over, that you'd try."

"Try what? Be cool when you ignore me? That's not part of the plan."

"Francine." He paddled carefully, keeping an eye on her. She used to be such an easygoing girl.

She stood up and walked toward the stern, balancing carefully.

"Sit down!" he shouted. "You'll dump us."

"My turn."

"Get your butt down on that seat!"

"Quit bugging me!" She sat down, fuming. Dad didn't know diddlysquat about canoeing—or poling—for that matter. They could go upriver twice as fast if they were poling, but he didn't know how and he was not patient enough to learn. The current was pulling, maybe, two knots, and they were doing a hard three, one knot over the bottom. Shameful. Paddling alone, it would wipe him out in a hurry.

"We're not getting anywhere fast," Francine said a little too loudly. She always had a kind of loud voice, but liked it that way. People paid attention.

She had tied her hair in a rubber band, back at the neck, the way she liked it, neat, but there were always these stupid hairs floating around her forehead, dropping into her eyes. She used some spit to plaster them back in place. She squinted. A half-mile away and she could still hear the girls' squeaky voices arguing about the cards. Fate worse than death, that. She could have been in the Pine Barrens, riding Midnight, instead of in a crappy canoe with Dad and a bunch of dweebs.

"Hey, Dad? Let me steer. My paddle's got a much bigger blade. I'm stronger than you. I'm younger than you. We'll get there tomorrow at this rate."

"We are not changing places today."

Francine could hear the struggle in his voice. "Tomorrow, you'll forget." He'd grown a puny little beard since the divorce. She agreed with Mom. It made him look like a dork.

"Get a grip. Work with me for a change. You might like it," he said. "Besides, this could be our last trip together."

"Promise?" At fourteen she was already way too old to go on a trip with *him*.

"You're throwing too much water. C'mon, I'll show you," she said.

"Bunk."

She couldn't help it if she was competitive. She wasn't the fastest girl at the Dalton School for nothing. She bit her lip. "Let's change positions out here on the river."

"Knock it off!" he shouted, ending the conversation. His irritating voice coming through the back of her head felt like an ice cream headache. A spider crawled across her knee. Letting it crawl along her arm, she thought about handing it to Dad, but set it on the gunwale instead. He'd probably freak, just like Mom did.

Beyond the canoe, she saw a scuzzy beach, a bunch of straggly trees full of dead limbs, a buff-colored landscape, and hills far in the distance. The sun was blinding.

"New Jersey is prettier than this. They don't call it the Garden State for nothing. Why couldn't I have stayed home? I never wanted to come in the first place."

"We are not discussing this now."

"What about Bolton? I could've stayed in Bolton with Grandpa." She loved Grandpa. He taught her games, like Texas Hold 'Em, and how to bet. They'd spent summers together since she'd been ten. He never got bored or cranky like Dad did.

"Pay attention to the river, and stay up with me," Campbell said. "Try paddling together."

"He's kind to me."

"Not at your own speed, Francine. Try mine. Slow down, you're killing me."

"That's the point." Francine couldn't believe he was so dense. "I'm way faster than you. Grandpa's smart and interesting and fun and he's a lot nicer than you."

"Jesus Christ." Campbell turned the canoe around and ran it into a mud bank with a thud.

"I could have stayed there with him and not come on this stupid trip."

"Grandpa needs to be at Happy Acres," Campbell said. "You know this, Francine. We are not talking about Grandpa, either."

"He was happy in Bolton, just him and the horses and his watercolors. You made him go. Just like you forced me to come on this trip. He hates it there and I hate it here. I could bring him home, take care of him. It would be a lot better than this."

"Hey. I didn't do anything except ask you to go canoeing," he replied. "You like canoeing. You said so yourself."

"You haven't done anything with me since I was eleven and you took me to see the stupid dioramas at the Museum of Natural History. And now, you're trying to make up for it? I'm no fool. You're too late, Dad."

"Just to spend time with you is . . . kind of special."

"As if. As soon as we get to Fort Benton, I'm hitching to Great Falls and flying home. I'm done with your charade."

CHAPTER NINE

⌒

Sunday, 3:00 p.m.
on the river

CAMPBELL AND FRANCINE

"*A*h c'mon, Francine. Be a sport. You don't need to be so negative. I've tried, you know."

No answer. Her collapsed little shoulders told him everything.

He shouldn't have even asked. If she thought his idea of canoeing was lame, wait until he told her about Daisy.

He felt like a traitor.

Ten minutes later, an island seemed to float in the middle of the river, as flat as the water itself with a tiny edge of green. Jesus. He had to tell her and he had to tell her now.

He dug in deep with every stroke, determining where to come in. It was harder than he had anticipated, fighting against a two-knot current. He'd been working out at the 92nd Street Y for nothing. His arms felt like noodles. He took a long stroke, watched Francine's smooth clean paddling, and wished he had her easy way on the water.

In his other life, his city life, business was clean, business was predictable. Clear of this ambiguity, this anger. You want to make a deal, we make a deal. Easy. But this business with Francine, this was hard. He'd been a shitty dad.

"Something bothering you?" he asked.

"Nothing."

He saw a sandy beach ahead. Beyond, rolling hills broadened onto a wide valley. A homesteader's cabin stood askew, its door banging in the wind. He needed a rest. Twenty minutes later he nosed the canoe onto the shore. Stepping out, his sandals crunched pebbles and sand. He narrowed his eyes and adjusted his hat. This would be as good a place as any. But first he had to get her out of her funk.

"Ever see one of these cabins before?" he asked. "You've got to see this place."

She shrugged her shoulders. "What do I care about some rat-infested dump?"

"Come on, take a look."

She stood up slowly, taking weight on her good leg, stretching to hide her pain. Ever since she tore her left ACL in May, her knee hurt like hell. But she wasn't going to let him know; she wasn't going to let anyone know.

"Can you imagine the homesteaders coming here in covered wagons? It's incredible."

"Going back in there with the weeds and shit?" she said. "Ticks and poison oak? Nah. Have a ball. I'm going swimming." She unbuttoned her shirt, showing a tiny red bikini.

"What are you doing wearing something so small?" he asked. "Your mother let you buy that?"

"Dad, all the girls are—"

He cut her off. "A little modesty. That's all I'm asking."

"You must be kidding."

A wind blew down the river, threatening to take his hat. "And it's not a good idea to swim alone." The current was moving fast. "Come on, take a look at this house. Hang around your old man for a little while."

"Half the roof's fallen in." She scratched at a mosquito bite on the back of her hands. "I get history at school. And from Grandpa. I need lessons from you too?"

She stood up on tippy-toes so close that Campbell could feel her vibrate.

"Come on. What has Grandpa ever taught you that's useful? The guy talks to trees. Can you imagine carving a life out here before cars, electricity, iPhones?"

She leaned on her paddle, dug her fingers deep into her pockets, and pulled out her phone. "Damn, my batteries are almost dead. Should've packed the solar charging kit."

A cloud of dust rose and fell, blowing around the cabin. Window frames, long devoid of glass, stared at him with hollow eyes. A rusty plow was set upside down, half-buried in sand. An axle, grass growing around it, leaned against a near wall. Old cans, rusty and full of holes, covered the ground. Broken glass crunched under his feet.

"Pretty neat, huh, Francine?" He scanned the scenery. "We can see for miles—all the formations in the canyon, funny-looking rock pillars with mushroom-type heads, where the harder rock doesn't erode as fast as the softer rock underneath. Francine." He breathed in endless sky, sweet air, listening to grasshoppers hum in the grass.

Did he just hear something? A hiss? The sound of dry

paper, crackling? He knew that sound. He looked down. His daughter's nearly bare feet were brushing tall stalks of grass.

Francine jabbed at her iPhone. Held up one thumb and smiled.

"Turn it off." His voice was low.

"Why? You told me to stop arguing with you."

"Slowly. Back up."

She heard the concern in his voice, with that intonation reserved for crossing streets, hot stoves, danger. She stepped backward and looked down. A snake edged its head out onto the path in front of her. Between her feet and Dad's. All around deeper, thicker grass. Here just a narrow, hardly used pathway leading to the cabin.

"Now, don't move."

She held still, frozen.

He wished he had his paddle; he sure could use it now. The snake was as round as two fingers, neck bigger than its head. A moccasin, a rattler, something big.

They were too far from civilization for her to recover from a bite.

"Very slowly now, trace your steps."

She stepped back, still within easy striking distance from the snake, which was weaving its head back and forth, flicking at the air with its forked tongue.

"Farther."

"Dad, I—"

Campbell unbuckled his life jacket.

"Francine, run!" he whispered.

"But . . . Dad—?"

"Run! Now! Get the fuck out of here!"

Just as she turned to take her first step, he threw his life jacket at the snake.

The second before it hit the ground, inch-long fangs sunk into red nylon and foam.

The snake whipped around the life jacket. The rattle was loud, but not as loud as his heart. This one was a fighter.

He had to get his jacket back, but he didn't want to come any closer. He stood four feet away, jumping around as the snake twisted and turned inside the life jacket. There wasn't even a stick anywhere.

"Give me your paddle."

She hesitated.

"NOW!"

He caught it, stepped back, and smashed the life jacket. Heard a hiss. Smashed it again. Heard a rattle. Being ever so careful, he slipped the blade of the paddle inside the life jacket and felt teeth clatter on the blade.

Then he heard a louder hiss. Coming from the grass? Another snake?

"Move back, Francine!"

He lifted the life jacket with his paddle and, very carefully, shook and twisted it until the life jacket nearly slid off the blade. The snake fell first, onto the overgrown path, then the lifejacket right on top of it. Standing as close as he dared, he eased the paddle through the armhole, and tried again. He lifted the life jacket and the snake. The snake dropped onto the ground. Campbell flicked the life jacket off to the side and smashed the snake.

"Again, Dad!" Francine screamed. "Again and again and again!"

He slammed the blade down, then turned it on edge. Smash! Smash. Smash! Worried about the blade breaking, he turned the paddle up and over and smashed it with the handle, over and over, until the snake was broken open, its lifeless eyes staring at the sky, its tail off to the side.

"Jesus Christ!" He stood, the stained handle in his hands, the paddle over his shoulder, and studied the snake.

"Don't worry. That sucker's dead, Dad."

"Forget about the homesteaders," he said, his voice shaking. "You all right?" He kissed her cheek, holding her tight to him. He shouldn't have taken her back here. She smelled of strawberries and wood smoke and earth.

She pulled back, just a little, then buried her face in his shirt. "Not so bad for an old fart. Cool. One dead snake. One cool Dad."

He fingered the holes in his life jacket, held her close, and breathed in.

Five minutes later they were back in the canoe. Campbell in the bow, Francine in the stern, her strong strokes carrying them forward, downstream, back to camp.

He listened to her, singing off-key behind him. He took a good long stroke and looked back at her. Her fine paddling, the way she held her head up, her skinny frame. A cold sweat was drying on his temples. His body trembled uncontrollably. Close, way too close. Oh God, he hadn't wanted to lose her. He lifted his blade, then stopped mid-stroke.

Tomorrow. Tomorrow he was going to have to introduce her to Daisy. Tomorrow, he was going to ruin everything.

CHAPTER TEN

⌒

Sunday, mid-afternoon
land

E.B. AND LAURA

*L*aura stared into a canoe half-filled with water. "E.B., this sucker's full. I bet it won't even float."

E.B. rubbed his face with his hands, still felt a little queasy, and wished he had some toothpaste. "Say again?"

"I wouldn't mind a cupful, and maybe a little sloshing around my toes would be okay, but . . . hey, if I get in, it's up to my ass. Can you come over here, like right now?"

"Give me a sec." Most guests complained about wet feet, but Laura's new tone, it worried him. She seemed different, somehow, far beyond angry.

Standing up had never seemed so difficult. "Ooof." He was a little wobbly. He cleared his throat. "I appreciate your helping us land. Sorry you got soaked."

"It's not me you should be worried about. Go on, take a look."

E.B. looked at her.

"Not at me, the boat."

"Oh." He watched her march down the shore. Oh my God, what legs. What would Dad say? Laura must have picked up some pebbles because he heard her throw them in behind him. *Plop. Plop. Plop.* He walked over to the canoe.

"See? Just like I told you," she said.

He gazed into the canoe; his bailers, the paddles, and all the gear were floating.

"You're right."

Plop, plop.

"Damn."

Sploosh.

He pulled out the two bailers, and stopped, midair. "No. I'll do this." First right thing he'd done all day. "While I bail, dry off. You look like a . . ."

"A drowned badger?"

"Just about," he said and set to work. A few minutes later she sat on the beach, rubbing her hair. E.B. kept bailing, trying not to look at her. His mind was supposed to be on his work. Right. Dad used to say, "Ezra, you're a dreamer. Concentrate on your studies." But Dad had never laid eyes on Laura.

She'd had a tough morning, but had done well. And she was trying. But God—he closed his eyes a sec—did You have to send me someone so beautiful? It was his fault they'd hit the snag. He shouldn't have eaten that fish. He should've fought his way through the pain. He should've kept up. But, at least he felt a little better. Now he had to empty the canoe, fix the leak, and hustle to find Campbell and Francine before dark. They didn't have much time.

Twenty minutes later he'd made some progress and

stopped to rest. While bailing, he'd stared at the water in the canoe, the river, the hills, the sky—anything but Laura. Trying to concentrate on canoe-type things. Trying to figure out where they were, where Campbell might be.

But he couldn't help it; his eyes kept wandering over to her. She just sparkled, muddy, wet, whatever. He was doomed.

When the canoe was almost empty, she came over to help. She leaned down, facing him. He tried not to stare down the front of her sleeveless top. He'd never thought about Berniece like this when they'd been sharing chores at home.

Working side by side for a while, they established a rhythm, dipping their juice cartons into the mix, their two streams of water flooding into one. When the water was almost gone, he flipped the canoe over. Water poured out onto the short sandy beach, and all their stuff with it.

"This trip could be the best trip I've ever had." Laura grinned. "I mean, the fun never stops, does it? What did you boys say, easy trip, easy as pie? Say, would paddling up Niagara Falls be a hard trip in your book? Where is everyone else, anyway?" She sat back and watched E.B. clean the canoe. "I didn't sign up for this life-and-death business. I get that at work." She remembered all of it, the thugs, that asshole Harry, Campbell just in time. E.B. would think she was joking.

"You still cold?"

She stared off into the distance, shivering. "A little."

He gave her his jacket. "Well, all right, then," he mumbled. "I'll patch the canoe. The others can't be too far." He sponged out the boat. "In five years canoeing this river, we've never been separated. Not like this, anyway. Campbell should have waited up."

"I knew it. The second I stepped offshore things were not looking too good." Laura picked at some grass. "They all just took off." But not the thugs, they had come after her.

"They weren't supposed to." E.B. hunted in his duffle bag for his patch kit.

"When is it supposed to be fun?" She paced the beach. The comforts of civilization, warm clothes, nice beds, streets, even street people, she missed them all. Even LA. And Stella. But not the club. Never the club. "You sure they're no roads around here, E.B.?" Harry could catch them easy, with their boat disabled like this. "Can you pick it up a little?"

"I have to find the hole, fix it as best I can."

"Where the hell are we? It's lonely out here."

"That's what makes it so beautiful," he said gently.

Laura sniffed.

"No reason to be . . . concerned. I got this." He wouldn't use the word "afraid." People in Montana never used the word "afraid." Afraid was when it was forty below, dropping fast, with the cows dying. Even then, he shoved his feelings away. If there was a job to do, "afraid" played no part.

He hunted in his duffle bag for duct tape. Tucked into the side of the hull, away from her, he ran his hands over the smooth surface, looking for a crack or a hole.

"I'll wait, then." Laura filtered green and purple stones through her fingers. "Kind of pretty, aren't they?"

"Argillite. Red if the rocks had oxygen when they were

forming, green if they didn't. The only thing I know about geology," he laughed. He listened to the beat of his heart pound in his ears. He knew she could hear it.

His problem was not with the boat. His problem was with her. The boat—that he could fix. But his body, not so much. Now? Like eighth grade with Mrs. Harrison? Young-ish, like Laura. Blonde, like Laura. Many days, when Mrs. Harrison had said, "Class dismissed," he couldn't stand up. Not then. And surely not now. At least now he had a seventeen-foot-long canoe to hide behind.

"What's with you?" Laura asked. "You look a little strange."

"Nothing," he croaked. "Nothing I can't handle."

"A little green? That your normal color?" She laughed.

"I'll be all right." He focused on his work. With little boat traffic on the river, he'd have to do it right. He couldn't fix the damn hole in the hull if he couldn't find it. He'd been over the whole thing four times.

"Aha." In the middle, at the poor excuse for a keel—a ridge that ran the length of the hull—he found a separation between the ridge and the rest of the body. A hole. Big enough for a baby's pinkie. "Got any gum?"

"At a time like this you feel like chewing gum?" Laura was sunning herself on the beach, feeling better. She leaned forward on her elbows.

E.B. wanted to tell her not to do that. Or to lean over more. Oh God. "Don't be silly. Gum is used to patch the boat." E.B. sat up. "And . . ." Whatever he said wasn't going to help, but he went ahead and said it anyway. "Duct tape," he added brightly.

"What's next? Spit? Underwear? Bananas?" She laughed

as she dug into Beth Ann's bag for gum. "Peppermint, spearmint, or Bubblelicious?"

"Don't be silly." E.B. felt relieved Laura wasn't still angry. "Any kind. Fiberglass canoes are easy to patch. They're strong, light, and durable."

"How's your stomach?" she asked, handing him the peppermint.

"Much better, thanks." As for the rest of me, I'm not telling. He paused, lifting his eyes to her. Big mistake.

"Good." She let her hair fly in the wind.

Oh Jesus. Wouldn't Mack at the Feed 'N' Seed like that view. E.B. shook his head. And God, while you're at it—E.B. smooshed gum into the hole—could you please make her a little less beautiful? And me a little less desperate?

Think! He laid a piece of duct tape over the hole. What about your truck? Think about the truck. When was the last time you gave it an oil change?

Below his belt, his body wanted her close. He lay down another layer of duct tape. He wanted her breath in his ear, his hand smoothing her hair, just like he was smoothing the duct tape over and over. Five layers should do it.

"Then we can go?"

"Of course."

"At the campground, think they'll have dinner ready? I'm starving."

"Should be there within the hour," he choked.

"Another promise or a threat?"

"Campbell's a pretty good cook, generally."

"Generally? Let's hope. Hey, E.B., you said you're from around here?"

E.B. held a piece of duct tape in his mouth. Nodded. He pointed vaguely upriver, in the general direction of his ranch. "You get bored out here? I would. Nothing much to do."

His mother, a second-generation Montanan, would be incensed. She wouldn't be so pleased at his physical state either.

He flipped the canoe over, slid it into the water, and, holding onto the painter, watched it bob. "If you see any water inside, let me know."

She examined the canoe.

"It'll hold, you'll see," he reassured her. The canoe floated just as well as it did before they punctured it. She piled on more and more gear.

"I don't get up normally until eleven when the sun is warm," she said. "That's an old joke. How 'bout you?"

"Me? Every morning I'm up at four," he said, incredulous. "I milk the cows, use the cultivator, repair equipment, run a farm, dig out the road in the winter."

"Doesn't it get cold around here?"

"When it's forty below, if you have a cup of boiling water and throw it in the air, not a drop reaches the ground. It vaporizes."

"No shit." She thought a sec. "People say it's cold in LA when it's fifty."

"A positive?" E.B. asked.

"They don't say that's a positive. They complain."

"Above zero."

"Oh." She leaned her chin on her knees. "Do you ever get lonely?"

He pushed the canoe down. Popped right on up. Good. He didn't want to tell her how lonely. "Twenty below is a warm day. Way too cold for anyone from LA. He put a few bags in the canoe. "But you get used to it. It's not so bad. You get used to everything eventually." He'd never get used to an empty house. He could hear Berniece's footfall everywhere he went.

"It's too busy in LA to be lonely," she said, and stepped into the canoe.

He looked at her, curious. "What do you do for a living, then?" he asked, pushing off.

She ignored his question.

"Hey, E.B.? I saw a sign at Fort Benton. A revival meeting. Coal something. It's not far, right? Isn't that where we're going?"

"In Coal Banks?" E.B. couldn't believe it. "Revival in Coal Banks?" Berniece and that goddamn preacher? Maybe it was some other preacher. Maybe pigs could fly.

"Yeah." Laura ran her hands up and down the paddle. "Like in the movies. Elmer Gantry, remember? Should be kind of fun."

Fun? E.B. took a stroke, and another, faster and faster. If he tried hard enough, maybe he could forget what Laura had just said. Maybe. Oh God, not Berniece. Not that asshole Stanley Cornelius III. He paddled like crazy. He could never get away from her.

"Hey! Slow it down! Slow down!" Laura called.

As if he cared. He dug in again.

"What's the matter now?"

The canoe felt like a slug. Water poured over his feet. He dug in hard and, with all his strength, maneuvered it ashore, slamming the boat onto a rocky shore.

"We can't sink, you said! Easy to fix, you said!" Laura

threw her life jacket at his head, hitting him. "Asshole!" She took off up a bluff.

E.B. sat there, gazing at her disappearing form.

Gum and duct tape had always worked before. He climbed out and threw everything out of the canoe. Under his index finger, he found a softness. A long softness that went a ways down the hull. Good Lord. The goddamn boat had delaminated. Laura was right. It was fixable but not with anything he had. They were screwed.

CHAPTER ELEVEN

❧

Sunday, mid-afternoon
land

E.B. AND LAURA

"*G*oddamn it!" Laura could deal with Harry and his pals, if there was a road, if they'd rented a four-wheel vehicle, if they knew where she was, if, if, if. That was a lot of ifs. But drowning in the middle of a river with a cracked canoe, that would be a sure thing. Damn that E.B. She grabbed her paddle—it would be her only weapon.

Her flip-flops slipped while she fought her way up a muddy bank. *Someone* had to live out here. There had to be a shelter, a house, something, a phone. At the top of the bank she scanned the horizon and saw what looked like a wooden house in a field in a clearing just beyond.

She raced over small shrubs and around rocks, and slid to a stop in front of the wooden building. It was smaller than she'd thought. A quarter-moon had been carved into the wooden door. She peered inside and slammed the door a second later. Damn. In this God-forsaken wilderness of nothingness, the only sign of civilization was a toilet?

The wind blew up, pelting her face with grit, dust, and small pebbles. She squinted in the breeze, holding her hand over her eyes, straining to see as far as she could. Nothing but burnt dry grass and, above her, a huge expanse of blue sky, wider and bigger than anything she'd ever seen. The open space made her feel like a nobody. She'd give away everything she owned for a traffic jam, the sound of honking horns, impatient LA drivers on their way to somewhere.

She was a nobody in the middle of nowhere. In the distance, nothing but empty hills, rolling away forever. Crows called overhead.

She felt like the day Dad had driven down their driveway in his Buick for the last time. She'd been twelve. He'd been arguing with Mom for weeks. Months, years even, if she remembered right. For a month, she'd stood by her open bedroom window, waiting and watching. Mom had told her he'd come back. That she should pray. Fat lot of good that did. Neither of them had seen him since. The heck with him. The heck with all of them. She was on her own, like always.

She looked all around her. If she could just get to the top of a ridge and find a road, then she could see where to go. She stepped forward as sharp grasses needled into her feet.

"Laura!" E.B.'s voice carried on a breeze. What was he yelling at her for? If he wasn't going to get them out of here, she would.

"Shrik, shrik." A call, high and sharp, filled the air.

She stopped, standing quiet, listening. Grizzly bears? A hollowed-eyed monster? Wolves? She tried to think of animals she'd seen on Animal Planet. None of the shows had animal sounds like this. Not hearing anything more, she moved on. Annoying little noise.

"L . . . a . . . uuuu . . . rrrrrr . . . aaaaa!" Again, E.B.'s voice, more faded now. Damn him. She wasn't going back to the river now.

In a few minutes his voice disappeared as she continued to climb. She heard some distant birds, the *zzz zzz zzz* of crickets in the shrubs, and the crunch of her flip-flops on gravel.

Carefully stepping around small bushes as she climbed, she felt like she'd left the river far behind, until she stopped, looked back, and saw the wide expanse of water lapping at the shore. How far had she come? A hundred feet? Fifty? It was pretty much straight up and, for all her workouts, was wiping her out. How did E.B. stand this place?

Grasping her toes tight around the rubber on her flip-flops, she stepped carefully around broken chunks of hard earth, which made for hard going. Out here it was worse than 2:00 a.m. at the club when the few losers in the audience had passed out and all she smelled was stale sweat, spilled beer, and broken dreams. Worse even than the night after Stella was robbed in the parking lot, came to her in tears, and asked for a gun.

"Shrik, shrik." Damn stupid noise. Louder now. What the hell was it? She raised her paddle and grasped her life jacket. Good for her torso but what about her feet? Her naked legs? Ticks lurked in the grass. Snakes, spiders, all kinds of shit.

Get going girl, she thought. Move! But where?

"Shrik!"

She bent down, peering into the bushes and grass. "Come on out, you little dick!"

No sound.

"Coward." She kept going. "If you had courage, you'd show yourself. Piece of crap." She scanned the bushes and grass. Nothing.

The top of the ridge was still a long way off.

What the hell? Out of the corner of her eye something moved. In another direction, something else. "Shrik, shrik, shrik." She whipped around.

The thugs, hiding in the grass? Pretending to be goats? Weasels? Bug-eyed crap-eaters? Trying to scare the shit out of her? If they'd come this far, they'd have surprised her by now. Rats hiding in the grass? Maybe.

She scanned the dirt in front of her toes. Any way she went, she had to go around bushes, wade through the tall grass, and meander around low boulders to get to that ridge. What about trails? Didn't people around here use trails? Roads? Anything? She looked for a depression, a cut in the hill, something to indicate a road, and kept going.

"Shrik, shrik."

She jumped. Hell, that one was close. Little Martian monsters? Badgers? Squirrels? She'd had a lunatic squirrel run up her leg in Griffith Park once. That sure scared the hell out of her. That was then. She wasn't going to let some little pissant rat scare her now. You can do this, girl, she said to herself, and stood up straight. Ignore those little assholes, whatever they are.

"Shrik, shrik." "Shrik, shrik." "Shrik, shrik." The cries came from everywhere.

A little face popped up in the grass. Then another. Another. Hundreds of them. A thousand hungry little devils. About to dig their pointy little teeth into her toes.

She screamed. Every single one disappeared.

Neat! Laura held her breath, then let it out slowly. *I am in control of my little universe. I can do this.* She charged on, listening hard.

Snap.

Snap?

Behind her, a twig broke. A crash in the bushes. What the fuck? Harry? Mike? Here? Mountain lion? Wolf? She could handle the fucking hamsters. And the thugs. She'd tossed them once; she could do that again. She kept walking, as if she didn't hear a thing, but tightened her grip on her paddle.

The footsteps came closer.

Suddenly, she turned and swung her paddle wide.

"Oooof. Jesus, Laura! You didn't have to slug me," E.B. groaned. "What are you doing up here, playing kung fu?" He rubbed his jaw. "I'm trying to help you, for God's sake."

"You scared the hell out of me," she snapped. "I thought someone was about to attack me. Like those guys from Fort Benton."

"Out here?" E.B. scratched his head. "You think anyone could follow you out here? There aren't any roads, for Chrissakes. This is the back of Milt's place. Nothing here but prairie dogs and fat lazy owls. Damn. Don't hit me again or I may hit back."

He looked like she hurt him. "Sorry about that."

"You think you're the only one who wants to get out of here?"

"I bet there's a ranch or something over the ridge," she said.

"Bet? There's nothing over that ridge or the next. It's four miles to Milt's. Can you walk that far?"

"Uh . . ." Laura didn't want to be left alone, but she couldn't walk nearly that far. Not in these dumbass little flip-flops.

"No? All right then. Go back to the boat," E.B. ordered. "And stay there. Drink plenty of water. Do *not* wander off. Think you can do that?" He rubbed his face. "Flag down any boat that comes by. Ask everyone if they've seen the BLM rangers, or if they have a really big patch kit. We need epoxy."

"BLM?"

"Bureau of Land Management. They patrol the river. They could come by today. I've got to get going."

She eyed a distant hill. Her ankles were scratched and bleeding. Four miles? Shit. She'd never walked that far in decent shoes, not if she could help it. Still—being left alone wasn't looking so good either.

"Well?" he asked, his face clouded.

"Come back as soon as you can." Despite her best intentions he was the only hope she had.

E.B. shoved his hat back on his head. "I'll be back when the sun touches those hills over there. See ya." He took off with a slow lope up to the ridge, easily spanning three feet with each stride.

All alone now, Laura watched him go. It was silent, at first. She heard a fluttering of wings and frantically spun around. A bunch of crows landed in some branches behind her. Just like the crows in *The Birds*.

If she wasn't nervous about dancing half-naked for men at 2:00 a.m., why the hell should she be afraid of some dumbass birds? The fucking hamsters had turned out to be smaller than weasels. Prairie dogs, E.B. had called them. Puny little turds. What was the matter with her? Get a grip, girl. She meandered back down to the river, taking her time, trying to figure out how long E.B. would really take.

At least the sun was warm. It felt good. A family of ducks paddled near the shore. She opened up Beth Ann's cosmetic bag and took out a mirror, a comb, a trio of eyeliners, an emergency nail kit. If she started now, they'd be fixed and dry by the time he came back.

Fifteen minutes later, her toenails and fingernails glittering wet in the sun, she didn't feel so confident.

There was no one around. Choking back feelings, she tried to think of the good stuff. What good stuff? Boat, fucked. E.B., hell and gone. Road out of here, none. Campbell and everyone else, disappeared. Was she going to die here?

"Hello?" she called, over and over. Her voice echoed from one side of the river to the other, making her feel like a dork.

Where was everybody? Canoes? Boats? Anyone? The river was empty. And wide.

The hell with that. She threw pebbles into the water, one, two, then a whole bunch. Then stones, then rocks, then the biggest boulders she could handle. They made a resounding *glup glup glup*. And then she heard an echo. Her echo?

She heard another splash. A fish? She'd seen them jumping out in the river earlier. No ripples. A paddle? Someone's canoe? Campbell? She sat up, heard the flutter of wings, and turned. More crows. She was beginning to hate birds.

She reached up and felt stiffness in her arms, stretched her legs, and did some squats. Felt the burn. Make use of all the spare time you have, she always told Stella.

Laura could see her now, late at night, about 2:00 a.m., the last time they were removing eyeliner and shadow with gobs of makeup remover, staring at their puffy eyes in the mirrors under a row of 100-watt lights, telling stories about the customers. Talking about their move to Montana. Laura had pleaded with her, "Come on up. I hear the money's good, no traffic, nice people." But at the last minute, Stella had bailed.

She'd been so right. Moving to Montana had been a disaster. More assholes. They were probably back at the club going through her purse. Having a laugh. Calling Stella? Laura yelled "Damn" as loud as she could and pounded the beach until her feet hurt.

Twenty minutes later the sun had dropped well below the ridge, long after E.B. said he'd be back. "E.B.! Where the hell are you?" Her voice echoed back and forth across the river and faded away, making her feel like an idiot. The evening was cooling down considerably. She thought about following him. Not a real good idea. Where had he gone? She didn't know. What had he said? Wait.

She tucked herself into a quiet corner, out of the wind, cradled her head in her hands, and tried the one thing her mother had told her always worked. Prayer. It couldn't hurt, could it? She closed her eyes and, in a whisper, repeated over and over, "Please, God, are You listening? Can you please, *please*, send someone?" Can I fake it, Mom? Can I fake it and make it real? "Please, just bring him back, please. Whole."

She was praying so hard, she didn't hear the flutter of wings, the flip of a fish jumping in the river, the sigh of wind in the trees, but she did hear something; the slide of a canoe on sand.

CHAPTER TWELVE

⌒

Sunday, afternoon
land

E.B.

E.B. didn't like the feel of leaving Laura alone. She'd be fine if she just stayed put. What was their cardinal rule? Stick together. He knew that. On that account, he'd failed and failed miserably.

He dodged around shrubs on his way up to Milt's, moving as fast as he could, branches and thorns scratching his legs as he went. If he hurried, he could borrow one of Milt's ATVs, maybe even a canoe, and be back on the river within three hours. Still, three hours was way too long in his book. He ran.

He figured they were about four to six river miles downriver from Loma. That would put them on the back side of Milt's five-thousand-acre ranch. A mile away, maybe two, then a mile through the trees. Heading south, he found a deserted dirt track that turned back on itself as it climbed. He negotiated the switchback and studied the river from this new angle. Over the crest, the track narrowed. It would be a struggle with Milt's 1960-era pickup, but if he had an ATV, they'd make it fine. E.B. headed up the next ridge, pulse racing now, the open country bleak and desolate around him. From the top, he saw a valley below, crisscrossed with barbed wire, and in the distance, a tiny streak, a stream of white flowing upward into the blue. At last. One of Milt's outbuildings—good enough.

Sprinting toward the old homesteader's cabin, E.B. sidestepped rusty cans, fifty-five-gallon steel barrels, and an old beat-up truck missing its engine. A winnower, a cultivator, and an old John Deere tractor nudged up around a small corral.

Weeds grew between the wheels and up through the holes in the tractor seat. The front of a white Ford F-350 nudged the rear of a barn. A chain of telephone poles marched down a dirt road right to the cabin. A thin coil of smoke wound up from a broken chimney. Puzzled, E.B. couldn't remember Milt mentioning anything about having a tenant this far out.

He followed the barbed wire fence that stretched down to the barn. An ATV, ticking cool, had been backed up to the cabin door. Relieved, E.B. headed to it. Keys swung from the ignition. Sweet. He stepped cautiously around a coil of razor wire and marched up to the cabin.

"Hello?" The roof of the ramshackle house swayed in the middle like the piebald horse he used to own. Chinks of mortar were missing from between the logs.

Nothing. He stepped closer. "Anyone home?" he yelled, not too loudly, just enough to carry. Wind whistled in a distant set of cottonwood trees. Leaves, scraps of paper, and soda cans tumbled in the wind, coming to rest against the cabin walls and falling in place with other trash.

He banged on the door. Were they deaf or just obstinate? He didn't have all day.

"Quit that racket. You're giving me a headache." A small woman in a blue calico dress slammed the door open. Dust and shreds of tissue flew in the air. "I told them I wasn't going to sell before and I'm not going to sell now."

She looked like his grandmother—small and flinty, collapsed nylons resting on her ankles above a pair of oxblood-colored wingtips.

"I don't mean to bother you, ma'am, but we have a crack in our canoe as long as my arm. Can I use your phone?"

"What do you think I am, Western Union? American Telephone and Telegraph?" She laughed. A few of her front teeth were missing. "Hasn't worked since Mae Johnson gave up the exchange in fifty-four." She studied him. Holding one hand against the doorjamb, the other behind her back, she was half E.B.'s size, with blue eyes and hair wrapped on the top of her head into the shape and size of a doughnut. She squinted as she studied him. "You've got a lot of nerve, coming onto private property."

"Truck, then?" E.B. smoothed his hair. Grandma liked her boys neat and tidy. "Wouldn't be more than an hour, tops," he explained. He scraped mud off his sandals, hopeful and ready to step inside for the keys.

"Can't. Threw a rod. Wasn't that just last week, Harold?"

A grunt came from deep inside the cabin.

The truck was nosed up by the front door, fresh mud splattered on the windshield.

"You remember Melba Fitzhugh?" E.B. guessed. "Loma Elementary, my grandma?"

A flicker of recognition across her face, then a stone stare.

"She cheated for that A."

"She didn't tell me about that," E.B. cooed. "Neighbor to neighbor, can I please borrow your ATV, then? I got a girl down by the river. She's alone and scared. I have to get back there."

"You hard of hearin'?" The old lady shifted something behind her back. "I said no."

E.B. eyed the sagging roof and appliances scattered around the yard. "Tell you what. I'll borrow your ATV, come down here with some friends, raise the roof, clean the place up. We'll return the ATV in the morning."

"Place looks perfect to me," she declared. Her eyes narrowed to slits.

A scrape of a chair on a hardwood floor.

E.B. peered inside, saw a faded yellow-flowered couch, gray from years of use, and heard the mewling of too many cats.

"Gladys, shut the goddamn door. I can't see the TV for the glare."

"I'll be with you in a minute, Harold," she snapped and whipped her head back to face E.B.

"I'm so sorry, ma'am, but can't you see we're in trouble? I wouldn't be here for any other reason, ma'am, as it seems as you like your privacy and all." Something in her hand glinted in the sun.

"You a little slow, boy?"

Before E.B. could answer, she pulled the rifle up and fired, missing his ear by inches. He flew back.

"Harold! Load up, we've got another one!"

Taking protection just outside the doorway, E.B. lunged and grabbed the hot barrel.

"Let it go, you bastard!" Her grip was tighter than a saddle cinch.

E.B. tightened his fingers around the barrel, and, trying not to hurt her, pried the rifle out of her hands and threw it across the yard.

He ran, jumped on the ATV, and turned the key in the ignition. *Whrr, whrr.* The starter turned, but the engine wouldn't kick over. Son of a bitch!

Crack. A rifle shot exploded dirt ten feet away. E.B. crouched down, flattening his body on the seat, and turned the key again. *Whrr, whrr.* Goddamn thing! Go! *Ping.* A shot ricocheted off the tractor seat.

Whrr, whrr. He gave the ATV a little gas, trying not to flood the engine.

Ping. Thwang. A shot hit the hubcap, sending it spinning. "Stupid engine!" E.B. yelled, turning the key again.

Wroom. The engine roared to life.

Ping. A rifle shot hit the road in front of him. He floored the throttle. The tires squealed as he took off, front wheels a few inches off the ground.

More shots rang out. E.B. flattened his body on the seat, wondering how many goddamn rounds she had in that magazine. He swung through a set of gates, headed around the razor wire, cling-clanging over a pile of cans, and spat gravel as he hit the road beyond. Gray smoke billowed out of the engine behind him.

He heard her shots all the way up the hill, the ATV

bouncing and revving as he rode it up, trying not to stall. He took cross-country trails where he could keep the nose down, to keep her from tipping over and throwing him backward. After a while the *pings* and *blams* faded away. He eased off the throttle and climbed the last bit of road to the crest. It looked familiar. Kind of. He thought he remembered the clearing. He let the ATV rumble as he sat, taking his bearings. Sweat dampened his armpits. If the wheels held up, he'd be back with Laura in ten minutes, tops, just when he told her.

He revved the ATV up, memorized his route, and headed down the hill to the track where the shrubs grew in the middle. The undercarriage scraped against clods of hardened gumbo mud.

He eased her down carefully, avoiding ruts as deep as two feet, descending into a gully, full of mud, and accelerated up the other side, spitting earth and gravel as he rose up onto an old ranch road. On the way there was a lot of clatter, rocks and pebbles hitting the undercarriage. He pressed on. He was thankful when the road smoothed out. Couldn't be so far now.

A minute later he heard pings and clicks and clangs from under his seat. That was a bit odd. Then the throttle felt a little funny. He eased back, felt it catch a little, and gave it some gas. He wiped his forehead, and looked back.

All the way up the road, in drops and splatters, was a long line of something wet and black. He climbed off the ATV to check. The line ran all the way up the road and came to rest under the ATV. He dipped a finger and took a sniff. "Ah, shit." It was the distinctive odor of crankcase oil.

He looked under the engine. Oil wept out of a bullet hole in the crankcase with every pump of the piston, its lifeblood draining its life away. Feeling lucky it wasn't a hole in him, E.B. hopped back on the machine and rode it hard before it died.

The sudden silence roared in his ears. He raised his eyes to endless vistas that stretched in all directions. It was going to be a long walk. He just wished he knew which way to go.

CHAPTER THIRTEEN

≈

Sunday, afternoon
land

LAURA

*L*aura knew she'd heard something. A long smoosh on the sand and then quiet. She stayed very still. Birds cackled overhead. Was it a canoe? E.B.? Campbell? Someone else? Something else? When the birds went silent, she listened again. Nothing.

She climbed out of her protected spot, wiped grit out of her eyes and ears, and scanned the beach.

A moment later, there it was again—way off in the distance, around the bend of the beach, beyond those rocks, a soft swish, the same noise they made whenever she and E.B. brought their canoe to shore.

If the sound was E.B. coming in, he'd be calling her name by now. If it was someone else, then who were they? She remembered what Dad used to say when she was scared: "Courage, my little Bean, you can do this." As if. Dad wasn't here now and he hadn't been a lot of help then. Laura paced the shallow beach.

What if it was the guys from the club? What then? Without hair spray and stilettos she felt defenseless, and her fiberglass paddle was next to useless with its flimsy plastic blade. She had to know. Once again she had let herself be scared. Maybe it was some boaters out for a good time? Then she could get some help. She carried her paddle and stayed close to the bushes, purposeful but wary.

Just past the rocks, she saw him. Leggy, broad-shouldered, tall. His face was in shadow. As she edged closer, she gauged the countryside. Empty spaces and not a tree in sight. She switched her paddle to her left hand and picked up a rock with her right. The element of surprise had worked before; she could bean him, if she was lucky, if a lot of things went right. Unless she was going to hurt the only person who could help her? What a dope. She dropped the rock.

A minute later, the man turned around, and the late-afternoon sun illuminated his face. Definitely not E.B. Laura paused, studying him. Not one of the thugs either. She took a breath.

This guy looked like he was born in the woods, face all craggy, beanpole-type body, and loose, easy shoulders. He was leaning over. He waved, but didn't stand up. Fishing, of course. She came up cautiously.

He grinned.

"Sneaking up on Santa Claus, honey?" he asked. "Hoping for a present? Sorry to disappoint you." He rubbed his three-day-old beard.

"You know people who live around here?" Laura asked. "Like a guy named Milt?"

"Here I am, baiting my hook, minding my own business,

dreaming about the movies—you watch movies, honey? I was thinking about Penélope Cruz, when a real honest-to-God movie star shows up, on the bank of the goddamn Missouri no less, right here, in front of me. The Old Man is real, it seems. Mom was right. You ever pray? I've never been very good at it."

"A friend of mine was looking for him."

"All I can say is, thank you, God." He extended his hand. "Good to meet you." His face clouded. "What kind of friend?"

She set the blade of the paddle down. He took her hand and she winced.

"What's the matter, never met a working man before?"

His palm was thick and calloused, and his grip was too tight.

"Soft hands," he sighed, holding hers a little too long.

She noticed the smell of kerosene, and something else. Anchovies? He was studying her.

"Sorry. Bait." He slid his palms on his jeans. "Never seems to come off, no matter how hard I scrub." He stared at her, mouth open. "What's your name, honey?"

She wanted to wipe her palm on the back of Beth Ann's shorty-shorts, but there was too much attention in that area already.

"Moll, Moll Flanders."

"Well, Moll, pleased to meet ya. I'm Tucker, Tucker Claymore."

"Where'd you put in?" She was about to tell him he was the first person she'd seen all day, but what was it that Stella always said? "Lesson One: Don't tell them anything."

"I put in at Wood Bottom," he said.

"Wood what?" she asked. "Are you pulling my leg?"

"It's a landing, sweetheart."

Laura was never going to get used to this place.

"It's around the corner. It's just a little ways off."

"They have a road there?"

"Of sorts." He spat a black stream into the sand. "You alone?"

"Can you take me there?"

"Maybe today, maybe tomorrow, and maybe never. I just got here." He hummed as he dug into his tackle box. "We can have more fun right here, right now."

She wished she was wearing her stilettos.

"You look a little tense. Relax. I'm just messing with you. I can take you over there when I'm, uh, finished here, my little angel." He laughed, then turned his attention to the rod in his hands and starting reeling.

He pulled up a three-foot-long, skinny fish covered with jagged ridges and held it out to her. "Whaddya think?" The fish hung from a bloody hook deep in its gills.

"Horrible-looking thing," she said. Where the hell was E.B.?

"You got that right, sister. This is one piece of shit fish. Good eating and all, but the granddads in this river, the ones I'm looking for, they're six feet long and a hundred years old. I've been searching for one for three years. What kind of friend brings you way out here and leaves you? That's not what I'd do with a girl. What's his name?"

"World Wide Wrestling champion, Fearless Frank." She laughed. "Silly names, I know, but he's a lot of fun. How 'bout you? Ever work out?"

Tucker laughed. "Sure, Monday, Wednesday, and God's day, Sunday. I can do two hundred pounds easy in a clean and jerk. How 'bout him?"

"What kind of fish is this?" Laura had only seen fillets on ice, or sautéed on her plates, hidden by browned panko. "The teeth on that fish look like something out of *River Monsters.*" Lesson Number Two: Humor him.

"It's a shovelnose sturgeon. Been around on earth since the dinosaurs. Older than dirt, like me." He placed the fish on the shore, well away from the water, and as he worked the hook loose with a pair of pliers, he paused, looking her up and down.

"On second thought, I don't think your little friend will like it much if you just take off. Or, are you, you know, parting ways? Surprising the old man and running off with a younger guy? That's cool." He squinted. "Or maybe there's another problem. Your little friend, he could be an asshole. Does he treat you right?"

Leaving me alone on the river, yes, Laura thought. "Pretty much." Lesson Three: Let them think they're heroes. "You been fishing all your life?"

Tucker stabbed his hook into three or four pink bait balls. He ran it over his thick, fat fingers. "He's been gone a while? There's nothing out here but the river and snakes. You like snakes, sweetheart?"

Laura studied that hook. An inch long with a helluva barb. One way in, no way out. Sharper than the hatpin she carried as she walked out to her car at 2:00 a.m. "He should be back in a sec," she lied. Lesson Four: Be smarter than they are. "Snakes—they're not so bad."

"Not unless you see them hanging off your ankle or your arm. Then it's goodbye, sister." He cast his line. "How long have you been waiting?"

She could feel his x-ray gaze boring into every part of her body, easily checking out Beth Ann's too-tight top and shorty-shorts. Lesson Five: Tease them. "About an hour, I guess. It's kind of hot and lonely out here."

The odor of stale tobacco and sweaty socks emanated off his clothes. He reached his hands out in front of him, and, stretching, cracked his knuckles. A tattoo—a black widow spider—ran up his forearm, the bright red hourglass inflating and deflating with the pulse of his veins.

"Where'd you get your tats?"

"Want a cold one?" He bent down, dug through a cooler, and tossed her a Bud. "Place in Vegas, honey, Pete's Wicked Ways."

She caught the beer, cocking her hip the way the guys liked it at the club.

He tipped his beer back.

She studied his canoe. Full and floating. Better than the piece of shit she had. She could head down the river and find Campbell if she had to. And E.B.? He was on his own. Even if he caught up with them later, he'd paddle the rest of the way with Francine, or one of the airheads. Threesomes had never worked for her.

"Ever seen muscles like these?" he asked. The skin around his tiny deep-set eyes crinkled.

"I like a guy with a sense of humor."

Laura watched him, trying to decide when and how to make her move as Tucker dipped his fingers into a white and red tin and popped something in his mouth. He spat, took a sip, and spat again, a long stream of black into the tawny sand. He got up, spat a wad into the sand behind him, grabbed two more beers, and downed them in quick succession. "It's not a bad combo, but you got to do it one at a time. Enough lessons, for now. Come here, sweetheart."

"Maybe later." Lesson Six: Stay in control. His boat was full of junk—empty beer cans, tins, bags of clothes. Some short piece of twine. Nothing but crap. A plastic paddle rested against the seat. Drunk or sober, he could probably outrun her. But swim as fast as she could paddle? No. "Got anything stronger?" she asked.

"Thought you'd never ask, darlin'. Out here every Boy Scout carries what we call 'medicine.'" He bent down, dug through the gear in his boat, and handed her a flask.

She took a big sip—almost fell over. Goddamn, that shit was strong.

"White lightning," he said. "Make it myself."

"My boyfriend keeps talking about the J-stroke, but I don't know how to do it," she said, gathering herself up as best she could. "Can you teach me?"

"Baby, I bet I can teach you whatever you like. But it's sure as hell not going to be about canoeing."

The plastic paddle wouldn't make a dent in his thick head unless she hit him with the edge of the blade.

She watched him run his hand all over his thin, sparse hair.

He looked sideways at her, pointing at the flask. "Knock it back, and you'll stop worrying about that boyfriend of yours. Love the one you're with, that's my motto."

"To your big fish." Laura toasted him, then pretended to take a big sip. "Thanks."

"Smooth, isn't it?"

She sat down beside him and patted him on the shoulder. "Once a stranger, now a friend, Tucker." She handed him back the flask and grinned.

He drank, resting the bottle against his mouth. A dribble ran down his chin. "Enough of this baby. Give us some sugar." He reached over and grabbed her leg.

"You're such a tease," she murmured and pulled away.

A strong breeze shot down the canyon. Laura hoped the dust and grit would blind him. She rubbed the edge of the blade with her thumb. Puny little thing.

He grabbed her around the waist, pulled her toward him, and pressed his mouth on hers.

She pulled back, jumped to her feet, and slammed him with the paddle, the edge of the blade right in the middle of his head.

He opened his eyes in surprise, blood running down his forehead. "Baby, baby, if you wanted foreplay, all you had to do was ask." He grabbed her legs.

She twisted out of his grasp and pushed him. He fell back in the dirt, moaned, got up on his hands and knees, and spat.

She pulled back on the paddle. Before she could hit him again, he lunged, wrestling her to the ground, then reaching for her arms.

Squirming away and up until she was over him, she slammed the paddle down on his head and shoulders, hitting him again and again until he was still.

Keeping her eye on him, she grabbed the bit of twine,

rolled him over onto his face, and tied up his wrists and ankles. Neat and tidy, like she'd been taught at the club. Nearby
a family of crows settled into the branches of a downed tree.

She ran for his canoe, threw in her paddle, and pushed it
toward the water. Damn thing was heavy with all the gear.
No time to empty it now. Watching his breathing, she slid,
pushed, and shoved the canoe into the water with a soft slide,
stepped into the water, got in, grabbed her paddle, and, pulling as hard as she could, moved away from shore.

Barely. Damn. Five feet from the beach the canoe ground
out. She stepped out and pushed. Climbing back in, she
pulled harder on the blade, making progress at last. At ten
feet out the water was only a foot deep. She took another
bunch of strokes, trying not to hit the bottom with the blade.
Each time sliding the paddle in and pulling as hard as she
could, pushing water, trying to get the goddamn canoe to
move a little faster.

On shore, the crows extended their wings.

To her right, a floating log, and beyond it, thirty feet
away, the current flowed. A bunch more strokes to get
around the log would do it. She dug in hard to turn and felt
the canoe slow down. "What the fuck?"

Squawk! Squawk! The crows flew up in a cloud, breaking
over her head.

"Shut up, you dicks!" Laura dug in with her blade, but the
canoe was hung up on the tree. She stood up on her knees
and pushed branches away and took another stroke, twigs
crackling underneath her as the canoe slid past. She was almost around the log—five more strokes would do it. "Now!"
she shouted, feeling free at last, and pulled her paddle

through the water too hard. The canoe headed inland. "No!" She shoved the paddle into the water on the other side, pushed water away, and felt the canoe turn. "Yes! Yes!" she shouted, and aimed toward the middle of the river.

"Going somewhere, sweetheart?" Tucker, standing waist deep in the river, flung out one outstretched hand and grabbed the boat.

CHAPTER FOURTEEN

⌒

Sunday, late afternoon
land

LAURA

"My little bird, you don't want a kiss?" Tucker tightened his fingers on the rail, pushed down, and let water pour into Laura's canoe.

She put her paddle over her shoulder. "Goddamn bastard!"

"You little vixen. Fall for that once and think I'll fall for it again? Some of the world loves smart people, some of them love idiots, and I love you."

Laura swung.

He caught the shaft of the paddle with his free hand and pulled her toward him. "Drunk, bleeding, or confused, honey, I still recognize love when I see it."

"Piece of shit, get away from me!"

"Easy as picking chickens out of a henhouse," he crowed. And tipping the canoe farther, he grabbed her leg, and with one strong move, yanked her into the water.

She dropped into a warm fog, blind, panicked, and felt

herself bob up, her life-jacket up around her ears. She gulped air and went down under again, this time not closing her mouth fast enough. Tasting dirt, she kicked hard and popped up again, the level of water even with her chin. She spat out water, gasped for air, and took her bearings.

"Hey!" she yelled. "Hey, asshole!" He couldn't hear her; he was on shore now.

The current pulled her downriver like a train. She moved her arms and legs but kept hurtling down the middle of the river faster and faster. Had E.B. said anything about rapids? Rocks? More hidden logs? She couldn't fend herself off of anything; she was going too fast.

The shore was sliding along, too far for her to reach. Marsh grass, sand. If only she could reach land. Two hundred feet downriver, rock cliffs came straight down to the water. She was heading straight for them. She lay down on her stomach, put her face in the water, and kicked and stroked as fast as she could right toward the bank, ahead of the cliff. She took a try to go sideways. Found something good. She was still moving downstream faster than she wanted but the shore grew closer. Ever slowly, closer.

Barely able to move inside the bulky life jacket, she kept stroking with her arms and kicking. She kept her eye on that cliff and kicked harder. It seemed to grow over her head, looming there, waiting for her.

A hundred feet from the cliff she felt herself drift. Arms and legs expended, she could feel the fight had gone out of her. She couldn't move this hard much longer.

She wasn't going to go down without one last fight. She kicked hard, harder, felt something different. A fish? A turtle, something squishy? She fought on, found more of it. Something under her toes. Her toes felt a gooey, sticky, slimy softness. The mud sucked at her flip-flops, threatening to take them off. She kept swimming, until both her elbows and knees touched mud.

As wavelets broke over her face, Laura inched her way forward, spitting water. The cliff was fifty feet away, but here marsh grass sucked at her toes. She'd never felt so happy. Twenty feet, fifteen feet to good, hard land. Crawling on her hands and knees, she stood up, a bit unsteady and breathing hard. Under her feet, blessed sand.

"You look like a pissed-off mud guppy."

"What the hell?" Laura turned her head and screamed. That asshole Tucker had followed her the whole way.

"And you used to be so pretty."

If she was going to die, at least it would be on shore. She'd have a better chance of getting in one lick against the asshole before going down.

She eyed him.

"I would've let you use my boat if you'd asked nice," he said, crossing thick arms over a beefy chest. He paused, perusing her body. "Have a few beers, Tucker, huh? A little whisky? Hit me with a paddle? Thought that would feel good? What do you think I am, an idiot?"

Trembling all over, she caught her breath. "Not one of my best ideas, I guess." He towered over her.

"Did you enjoy your swim?"

She tightened her toes over the rubber nub in her flip-flops and grabbed the straps on her life jacket. Two inches of foam provided scant protection. So this is how it ends, she thought, on a godforsaken piece of shit river out in the middle of fucking nowhere.

"You didn't find my bottle of Everclear. That one's yours," he smirked. "Now it's my turn to get you loaded."

"I have an idea," she said, hoping she would think of something and fast.

Tucker looked at her, a mixture of pleasure and pain crossing his face.

Nothing new about that look. She felt like meat every night at the club. Big fucking deal. She knew men. Think, girl, think. She picked up some pebbles and rolled them in the palm of her hand. Her shorts rode up on her tush. Sand and mud streaked the backs of her thighs.

"An idea, eh?" He touched her hair, making her cringe. She wiped her mouth with the back of her hand, leaving a crust of mud on her lip.

He pulled her arm and kissed her, his fish-tasting mouth filling hers. Letting him claw and clutch at her, she looked over his shoulder, and spotted two canoes in the distance.

Never ignore the obvious, Mr. Lee always said.

"Yeah, and it's a good one too," Laura said, hoping her voice held the conviction that would fool him. "Let's talk a walk and see what kinky stuff I have in my boat."

Once E.B.'s canoe was within reach, she turned toward Tucker, gave him a soft, shallow kiss, and, holding her breath, helped him gently onto his back, pressing him down so that the top of his head rested against the canoe. He eyed her, keeping one hand on her arm.

"No more dirty tricks, my little vixen. My turn now."

"I didn't mean to hurt you," she giggled, "but we play this

way in LA. Makes life a bit more exciting, yes?" She smashed her mouth onto his, keeping her tongue well inside her own mouth and her teeth tightly closed. He probed her teeth with his tongue, looking for a way in.

With one hand, she caressed his stubby face and over-sized nose. She smiled, letting her breath warm his face as she eyed the four straps in the canoe E.B. had left on the braces, two just above Tucker's shoulders. Tucker's hands roamed her back, her buns, while she eased one end of the strap loose and slipped it into her hand. She had to move slowly. His hands moved faster.

"I've been looking all my life for someone like you," she whispered. "Caught me off guard, I guess, coming up on me like that."

"I like my girls wet," he mumbled.

She smothered him with kisses and tried not to gag. His rough cheeks rasped her chin.

"Tucker," she mumbled into his ear. "I've always been an S and M type of gal." She ran one hand down his side and slipped it just below and inside the top of his jeans.

He groaned his assent.

"I'll make you a bet. This'll be the best sex you've ever had."

His eyes grew wider.

She burned her lips onto his mouth. His hands took on a desperate air.

"Slow down. Easy, easy," she crooned. Taking one hand, she traced his fingertips, rubbed his left arm, and brought her boobs down to his nose.

He muffled approval.

She eyed the straps, lifted up his arm, all the while crooning and moaning and wiggling, so that his wrist was over one of the braces in the canoe. Moaning false pleasure, she eased his hand back and tied it to the brace, giving the strap ends a good, tight knot. Then doubled it.

"Hey!" Tucker said, trying to tug his hand free.

"Don't you like S and M? I'm a top," she exclaimed, this time letting his tongue touch the tip of her tongue. Any more and she thought she might barf. "And you're a bottom, I surmise?"

He looked puzzled.

"Oh, honey, you're going to like this," she cooed.

He smiled.

Easy, she said to herself. Not too fast. Easy now.

"Didn't I make you a promise, sweetheart? Relax." She stared at his ugly mug, and reached one hand to run through his scruffy hair. "You need some help opening your pants?"

He fumbled with his belt with his free hand, tightening it at first to release the prong of his belt buckle. He thrust his hips to get a better grip when the belt wouldn't come free.

She felt his arousal. "Oh, honey, I can do that for you," she whispered, her breath warm and soft on his ear. "It's part of the game, letting the other person ease your pain."

"But you're tying me up."

"That's the fun of it, don't you think?" She grinned. "I'll release you as soon as you want, all right. Just say 'uncle.'"

Trying not to swallow any of his spit as his tongue explored her molars, she reached behind him to untie the second strap. She shoved her boobs into his face again, feeling him visibly tense up and shudder, and, gently lifting his free

hand away from his belt, she pushed it over his head with
both hands, the strap inches away.

"Uncle!" he yelled.

"Fuck your uncle!" she cried. Lifting up her body, she
dropped her crotch in his face, pressing down hard, and with
two free hands, tied his second hand to the canoe. His arms
were out to the sides like a scene in a porno flick. Waiting
for passion. Waiting for her. He looked like the assholes in
the front row after a show, way beyond stupid.

She sat back, admiring her work.

Tucker kicked his legs.

"Makes it more intense, huh?"

"But I . . . wait. Let at least one hand go!"

"You want me to slap you silly?"

"Come on, let me go. Uncle! Uncle!"

"What's that you said? I didn't hear nothin'." She stood up
and rocked her hips over his, feeling his arousal grow. She
wiggled herself to and fro. "Next game, your rules, okay? This
one's mine."

"Oh brother, oh brother, sweet Jesus," Tucker moaned.
"Open my pants, for God's sake. Open my pants." His face
was slimy with sweat.

She leaned down onto him, gave his nose a brush with
her boob, then sat back.

"If that's what you want, big boy," she said. She scooched
farther back on his body, so she was below his waist. She
fumbled with his belt, slipped it free at last, and held it in her
hands a moment. "Oooh, baby, have you got a surprise for
me!"

"Now. Do me now."

"I told you it would be good, Tucker, didn't I?" She slipped down so she was resting on his knees.

His face was bright red. "Enough games, you bitch! Blow me!"

"Okay, sweetheart," she said.

"If you quit struggling. Really a turn-on, don't you think?" She caressed his face. "Shall I go lower?"

He moaned.

She leaned over his waist and in one quick motion, pulled off his pants. She slipped the belt free, tied it around his ankles, and knotted it tight.

His puny member was no bigger than her thumb.

He beamed, proud.

She tried not to laugh. She backed up and walked away.

"Hey, sweetheart! Come back here!"

"I'll be back in a sec. Gotta get protection."

"Baby? No, don't worry," he pleaded. "I've been tested."

She marched to where his canoe was bobbing at the shore.

"Honey! No, really. Moll!" his voice rose with each of her steps. His words echoed across the river. "Come back, baby!"

She put on her life jacket.

"You bitch! You can't leave me like this!"

She grabbed a paddle and slid his canoe into the river.

"You scum-sucking whore!"

That was it.

She shoved off, climbed into the canoe, and, paddling on alternating sides to make the canoe go straight, headed toward the opposite side of the river.

In the center she felt the current pull her downstream, but she knew how to angle across.

Along the way Tucker shouted expletives behind her.

A hundred yards downstream, she hit land, hard. Her hands trembled too much to hold the paddle. She stepped out onto weak legs, pulled the canoe up onto the bank, and heard something. Something like a person? Come to save her? A white horse? Cavalry? No one had helped her since Dad left, and no one was going to help her now. Get a grip, girl. She stood tall and eyed the shore. Took up the horse posture, from kung fu. Might as well go down swinging.

It wasn't Tucker. His lungs were still plenty healthy, and he hadn't moved. There was something else. Over her head one crow took off, then another, then a whole flock took wing, scaring her like some goddamn scene from Hitchcock's *The Birds*, and she went very quiet.

A few minutes later, she heard something new and strained to listen. It was a twig breaking, a branch breaking, and a far-off sound. Was it a bear? A wolf? Something else?

She tightened her grip on her paddle and peered across the river.

A bird landed softly on the beach and hopped on the sand, looking for grubs. The bird flew up and Laura followed it, all the way up into the sky, and saw something behind it. Something on the ridge top. She squinted. It was a silhouette. A person. She squinted to see better.

Was it E.B? One of Tucker's friends? Or one of the thugs from the club?

CHAPTER FIFTEEN

⌒

Sunday, afternoon
land

E.B.

*A*cross the river and high above the water, E.B. scanned the ridges and hills covered with scrub brush and looked for a way back down. He'd been gone far too long. It looked the same in every direction—empty vistas, broken dead grass, and endless brown hills. He walked back and forth, trying to remember the way. He headed down one path, sure he'd come that way, until he was stopped by tall bracken and a steep cliff. He had to get down and soon.

Nearly tripping over a branch on a narrow game trail, he saw something familiar, the "T" of the carved word "Tevas" from his footprints. Buoyed by the sight, he shot downhill, running faster and faster, and slid to a stop in a grove of cottonwood trees. He could hear the river now. He followed the edge of a cut bank fifteen feet above the water and entered a forest, hearing only birds and the thump of his feet hitting the ground, unsure if he should go upriver or down. He'd go this way for fifteen minutes, then trace his steps. About to turn around, angry with himself for going the wrong way, he heard something new, not the slap of a wave on shore, but a thrashing and crashing. It sounded like an animal.

He barged through the trees, breaking branches and small limbs, all senses focused on the sounds. *Bang, thump, crash, slide.* They were close. Near the beach? Or in the rocks beyond?

"Laura!" he called out.

"Help!"

It was a man's voice!

"Laura!" He jumped over broken tree limbs. What was a man doing here, yelling for help? And where was Laura? Was she all right? He bounded through bushes and ran to the beach. The river was brown and rushing fast. Jesus, was she in the water?

"Help! Get me offa this thing!"

E.B. slid to a stop.

Forty feet away, on the sand, a filthy and scratched man lay on his back, naked from the waist down, his arms strapped to thwarts in E.B.'s canoe, his ankles tied together with a belt.

E.B. was quiet a moment. Someone out here for a religious conversion? He'd heard about people like this but had never seen them.

"Untie me, for Chrissakes," the man pleaded, his voice hoarse. "A bunch of kids—thought they were teaching me a lesson. Some lesson, huh?"

If they did this to him, what had they done to her? "You seen a girl?" E.B. came closer.

"It was a bunch of kids!" the man screamed. "They were trying to kill me. I've been like this for hours. Thank you, Jesus."

"A blonde? About, I don't know, this tall?"

"I don't care about a goddamn girl. Untie me, you asshole."

"Did they mention their names?" E.B. asked, pulling out his penknife. "Tom? Ed? Maybe a guy named Bob Withers? They're a rough bunch on probation for breaking into the Feed 'N' Seed." He bent down.

"There were four of them," the guy spat, "and no one mentioned . . ." He paused. "Ed, yeah, that's right. They kept calling the tall guy Ed."

"Did anyone of them say they'd seen a girl?"

"Hell no. They were too busy pulling down my pants."

E.B. thought a sec. Ed wasn't particularly tall. "They came by drift boat?"

He heard a strange noise in the wind. A crow? No, something else. Higher pitched. He strained to hear. It went away. He bent down to untie the first strap from the thwart. "Too bad they did this to you, bud," he said.

"I was sitting on the bank," the man explained, "fishing, sitting real quiet, working on the grandpa sturgeon I've been chasing for years, minding my own business, and then all of a sudden, bam, there were five of them, on top of me. Could you hurry it up please? I'm dyin' out here. You a local?"

Five? Didn't he just say four? E.B. hesitated, trying to think it through. Yes, there was a rod, and a fish, so that added up. But where the hell was she? He'd asked her to stay put. He looked across the river. Nothing over there but mud and rushes. He swore he'd heard something.

"Loosen my arms, they're killing me. Name's Tucker, Tucker Claymore. Come on." He banged his head on the canoe hull. "I've been like this for hours. My nards are gone, man."

"I don't know any kids who would do this. All of them attacked you at once? Whatever for?" E.B. looked at a maze of hardened knots at the man's wrists. "You don't look like you have a lot of money, if you don't mind my sayin'."

"Shut *up* and untie me. Like I said, five kids and I didn't see any goddamn girl," Tucker spat. "For God's sake."

"Locals—they usually just get drunk and drive off the road." E.B. was floored. "You've seen all those white crosses on the highway?" He bent down and worked another part of the knot free.

"Please! Just cut me loose. Now. Not after I die."

"Must be from Great Falls. Loma kids, they just don't do this," E.B. said as he worked the knot. "She was here when I left. Are you sure you didn't see or hear her?"

"I was fishing. Sitting by myself, fucking fishing."

E.B. scanned the beach, listening. If a bunch of marauding kids were nearby, he needed help. The man's skin was swollen around the knot. He pulled his knife from its sheath, carefully slipped it under the straps, and hesitated. He couldn't see any other canoes or other people around.

The blade flashed in the late afternoon sun.

E.B. sawed back and forth, spilling blood but not wanting to. He released one of Tucker's hands. "That should feel better."

"Finally! Jesus be praised!" Tucker grabbed E.B.'s arm. "They were out of Loma, man," he said, his eyes wild. "All crazy, on speed or something. Shit. I don't know if we can hold them off if they come back." He paused, took a breath. "Do the other one." He looked down at his naked body. "My Johnson is cooked. Shit, man. Have a heart."

E.B. yanked his arm out of the man's iron grip. Sweat and specks of blood slimed his fingers. Could Laura have done this? "Did you provoke them?"

"I didn't do nothing." Tucker reached for the knife.

E.B. pulled back. "Minding your own business, then? Beat you up and leave you naked? Whad'ya do to her?"

"I told you and told you. I didn't see any dumb-ass blonde."

"You kill her?" E.B. asked, bracing the point of the knife against Tucker's chest.

"No! I never hurt her . . ." Tucker sputtered. "She ran when she saw them."

"When she saw them? Or before?" E.B. slid the side of the blade across Tucker's skin. "Where's the girl, asshole?"

"They were after her—so she took off!"

"You're tied to my canoe," E.B. said quietly. "So, where's yours?"

"That's *how* she did it. She stole my boat."

"She's half your size," E.B. said, pressing down just hard enough on Tucker's arm. Strong guy; it felt like wresting a steer. "When was this?"

"Ten minutes, half hour ago, how the fuck am I supposed to know?"

There was that sound again. A wail. Across the river. E.B. stood up to see better.

"Eeeeee . . . Beeee!"

E.B. stared across the river, eyed Tucker at his feet, and looked again. She was waving a bit more frantically now.

Laura was trying to say something, but E.B. couldn't understand. He walked to the edge of the water and gestured for her to yell louder.

Behind him he heard grunting and straining, then a local "Ah!" He turned around and too late saw Tucker fumbling with the belt around his ankles.

"Going somewhere?" E.B. asked and ran at Tucker, knocking him over.

E.B. found himself flying and landed on his back. Wind knocked out of him. Doing his best to catch air, he jumped up to a crouch position.

"Time you worked out, old man," Tucker said and punched E.B., hard, knocking him flat.

E.B., stunned and dizzy, scrabbled to his feet. He caught one of Tucker's arms, twisted it behind his back, and slammed him onto the ground.

Tucker reached out, grabbed a tree branch, and came back swinging.

E.B. backed out of Tucker's reach, but the guy kept at him. E.B. flew behind a tree and heard a thwack as Tucker split the trunk. The branch reverberated in Tucker's hand. E.B. grabbed the branch, twisted hard, and heard an "Ow!" from the other side. The bastard wouldn't let go. He spun the limb and augured Tucker to his knees.

E.B. took a breath and stood over his opponent. "Had enough?"

Tucker laughed, pivoted, and caught E.B. in the back of the hip with his boot.

E.B. went down, hurt, tasting blood.

"Bastard!"

"She was loving it!" Tucker shouted. "She pleaded for more!"

E.B. rose, hip and shoulder sore, and swung.

Tucker fell and E.B. was on top of him, arm cocked, fist clenched. He hit him once on the jaw, but not again. He'd never been a violent man. That would do.

Tucker's nose looked broken; blood was running down his chin and onto his neck.

"She liked it," Tucker said.

E.B. slapped him. "You want to go for broke? Just remember, asshole, I castrate steers before breakfast."

Tucker flinched. He slipped his tongue over split, swollen lips.

E.B.'s head and hip hurt as he stood over Tucker and scanned the river. Laura was in the canoe, heading toward them.

He held out one hand to hold her back. "Wait."

"Can you walk?" he asked Tucker.

Tucker groaned.

"So much the better." E.B. pulled him under the arms and dragged him to a cottonwood tree, making sure to go over rocks and boulders and thorns that were in the way.

E.B. held Tucker to the tree as Laura handed him straps from the canoe. E.B. tied him tight, waist, neck, arms, and feet to the tree. Tucker's body was scratched; bruises and welts covered his skin. The guy was meaty. E.B. had been lucky this time. Finishing the last knot he looked over at Laura.

"You all right?"

She nodded.

"How did you . . .?"

"I hope a branch from the cottonwood tree falls and kills him," she said.

CHAPTER SIXTEEN

Sunday, late afternoon
Slaughter River Campground

CAMPBELL

"Oh, for God's sake," Campbell said as he pulled into the campground where he'd left the other canoeists. Francine hurried ahead. Campbell's knees made cracking sounds as he stood up. The place was a pigsty and wouldn't be if E.B. had been around. Campbell ran into camp, hoping he was wrong.

Goldfish crackers crunched under his feet as he circled the small clearing where empty Triscuit boxes, cookie bags, and used soda cans lay scattered all over the ground. Since his heart attack a year ago, he was supposed to exercise with moderation, Dr. Jensen had said. Yeah, right. Today he'd done a year's worth. His wet clothes clung to him like a shroud.

Five minutes later he'd searched the whole place and found Kris, Jane, Alice, and Nia sitting on a bluff, tossing little twigs into a crackling fire. Francine, perched on a log nearby, had her nose deep into one of Grandpa's philosophy books. She'd settled in fast. His girl—still snarky, still wonderful. And alive, thank God. That snake had been a big one.

Beyond them, nothing but empty plains, barren hills, a few shrubs, and an outhouse with a rickety door hanging from its hinges.

"Well, waddaya know, the prodigal son returns." Jane gave a little snort.

"Anyone seen E.B. and Laura?" Campbell asked, already knowing the answer.

"If everyone had kept together like we were supposed to, we wouldn't be in this mess," Nia spat. "And the answer is no."

"Seen anyone else?" Campbell caught his breath. "BLM rangers? Other canoeists? Anyone with a drift boat?"

"What do you think, we're blind?" Nia asked.

Campbell checked with Francine, who resisted a giggle.

"No one here but us chickens, and we're starving." Alice tossed her Sprite can into the fire. "Glad it wasn't me you left back there. I bet they drowned."

"E.B.'s a good strong swimmer, so I doubt that, Alice," Campbell said. "No need to worry." He was worrying enough for all of them.

"You were gone for hours." Alice flicked back her long black hair. "We thought you'd taken ill."

"On a trip like this? Living on freeze-dried food? Hard to do," Campbell answered. "I told you I'd be back and here I am."

"But you left them," Nia argued. "And us."

Campbell wrenched his mouth into a smile. E.B. and Laura should be setting up camp now, if they were all right. That "if" was a big one. He tried to remember where he'd packed the tents.

"When's dinner?" Nia asked.

"Jesus." He realized he had all the tents. E.B. would have to make do with a tarp, and one sleeping bag, if they had one. They'd freeze. "I'll get started. Everyone set up your gear?"

They scattered. He unrolled the roll-up camping table, set in the legs, and pulled out the stove. This trip had been a nightmare from the start. He should stick to what he knew. New York. Daisy. Paperwork. And he should never have let Laura get in his car. If E.B. had been alone, he would have kept up. Well, that was kind of a mean thought—Campbell kicked over a bucket of water by mistake. They had newbies on the river all the time and took good care of them. Campbell's stomach twisted into knots. He should have waited for them.

"I could use a hand. Francine?"

"Maybe later, Dad."

Campbell looked on as Francine sidled up to dewy-eyed Nia, who was reading, leaning against a tree. What was Francine up to now? He craned his head to listen.

"Are you finished yet?" Francine asked Nia.

"You read romances? Five more pages to go." Nia held out her dog-eared paperback, *Despair in Duluth*. "We've all read it now." The other girls, sitting nearby, nodded their heads.

"I don't have time to read junk like that."

Nia frowned. "Then what'ja ask me for?"

"Fun."

Nia was eight years older, six inches taller, and built, but probably flabby as hell, Campbell thought.

"What is it that you want?" Nia asked. She turned to the other girls, held up her hand, and whispered something.

"You remember kindergarten, don't you, Nia?" Francine stood in the other girl's face. "That's where I learned that it's rude to whisper." She pulled up to her full height of five foot three. "If you share with them, you share with me. Or maybe—think about it, because you never know—out here? To you or one of your friends."

Nia visibly stiffened.

"You got a problem over there, Francine?" Campbell called.

"Everything's just ducky, Dad. We're all getting along like gangbusters." Francine slid up to Nia. "Apologize."

"Francine! Knock it off!"

Nia sneered. "You're worse than your dad and he's so bad, it's laughable."

"You slimeball." Francine tightened her hand into a fist.

"Campbell!" Nia yelled. "Get her to back off. She's trying to kill me!"

"Francine, please." Campbell moved in and dragged her away.

"Get a grip," he whispered. "You can't go around hitting people. These are paying guests. What do you think you're doing?"

"She dissed you, Dad. And made fun of me, too."

"Feel pretty powerful? Picking on a girl twice your size?"

"Let me go and I'll finish her off."

Campbell held her around the waist. "I'll let you go when you stop grinding at the ground like a taxi at a red light."

"You can't stand there and let her get away with shit like this. Makes you look like a wuss."

"You've been suspended twice for fighting at school. You

can't stop now? While we're on vacation?" He released his grip a little. "Give it a rest. Mom said to count to twenty when you get mad like this."

"Mom's not here."

"I am and I'm telling you to wait. I'll let you go when you calm down."

"But Dad," she said. "Those girls? They're all dickheads."

"Suck it up, Francine. Being a grown-up, sometimes, really sucks."

"Eggs. It sucks eggs. Let me go."

"As you wish." Campbell dropped his hands.

She shook off his arms, but held still, trembling.

When did his little girl get so strong? He could hardly hold her anymore.

"I'm okay now," she said and picked up her philosophy book. It was five hundred pages and heavy. He'd told her not to bring it, but what else did she like to read?

"Francine," Campbell said.

"Don't worry, Dad, I'm on page three hundred forty-two. Interesting guy, Kant."

He watched her walk away. A moment later when he saw her approach Nia, he tensed up.

Francine held the book low and slapped it against Nia's leg as she walked by. "Whoops," she grinned. "This is a mother-heavy book, Nia. Would you like to see what grown-ups read?"

Nia, widening her eyes, picked herself up and ran into her tent.

Ten minutes later, Campbell arranged the coolers in a circle so they could all sit together. Everybody dug into the pasta and salad he'd prepared. After supper the sun dropped below the canyon walls and the light was dim. He sank his head into a storage bin, looking for a flashlight, and heard a crackle in the underbrush. It was Francine.

"Better?" he asked, feeling relieved it wasn't one of the other campers.

Without a word, she turned on the stove and set a pot of water to boil. "Tea?" She gave him a funny look. "You okay?"

"Maybe they're resting and will come in later. Maybe he's showing her a homesteader's cabin. Damn it all, Francine, E.B. knows better."

"At camp last summer one of the canoes was late, and the counselors had a fit. This little twerp Larry Peeves broke his arm. We had to go back. Took all day. An infection too, not pretty." She dug into one of the coolers. "E.B. have any antibiotics? Then they should be okay."

"Francine? Don't scare me like that."

"What's for dessert? I'm still hungry."

Campbell searched his pocket for his last Power Bar and tossed it to her. Antibiotics? The first aid kit was in his canoe.

With the others out of sight, this was as good a time as any to tell her about Daisy. "So, Francine"—he swallowed— "this is a real special time . . . dad and daughter . . . you and me . . . Soon you're going to . . . You having a good time . . .?"

"I'm all right," she said, taking a bite.

"No more fights? Your tent set up, kiddo?" Cool air ruffled what was left of his hair. He swallowed. Daisy would be on the river in less than twenty-four hours. At this rate he wouldn't be there to meet her—and she'd be alone. And he had her sleeping bag and coat.

"I don't know why you made me bring my own tent, Dad. We could have shared. Mine's big enough."

"I snore," Campbell said.

"No more than I do," Francine laughed. "You say so yourself."

"There's something I need to tell you."

"Hey!" She turned suddenly. "Did you see that? Antelopes!" She scampered across the grass.

"Francine!" Campbell, in despair, watched her run. He cursed himself. He could have told her about Daisy long before now. Back in New York, or in Great Falls, or in Fort Benton, or on the river, or any old time. The minutes were falling away. Though secretly, he was relieved. He was such a coward.

It was just going to be so much harder in the morning.

The sky in the west turned a dark rose, and Campbell remembered, for a moment, the reason he kept coming to this river and this wilderness. He adjusted his headlamp, picked up dirty plates, utensils, cups, brought everything over to the roll-up table, and set up two pots of boiling water, one hot and soapy, the other rinse water, to which he added a dot of bleach. All he wanted to do was climb into his sleeping bag and crash. He knew better. If he didn't clean up, all the food and pots and pans would attract raccoons, possums, or worse, skunks.

He washed the camping plates and utensils by the light of his headlamp. He looked around and saw flashlight beams splash tent walls. Some of the canoeists were laughing, more than he could imagine after his day. From another he heard snoring—his little girl.

He adjusted the strap on his headlamp, stared into soapy water, and rinsed one dish after another, setting each clean plate on the table to dry, feeling like a failure.

If only he'd waited for E.B. If only he'd gone farther upstream with Francine. If only he'd told Francine about Daisy. If only he'd given Daisy her coat.

Now, they were a day behind. E.B. or Laura could have gotten hurt. Daisy was going to freeze. And when Francine heard that Daisy was coming, she'd be crushed. No way getting around that now. What a stupid fool he'd been.

Daisy had been such a sport about coming. She'd been so happy when he'd promised he'd spoil her. She'd have loved to watch a fire burn and to peer out of his tent in the morning, her soft blonde hair on his cheek, tucking her face onto his neck and shoulders, the raspberry scent of hers warming his heart. Now she'd be afraid, alone, and cold.

Lost in thought, Campbell didn't hear the sound at first. When he did, he froze, his wet hands suspended above the water. The howls and cries that came floating over the water echoed in the hills, causing a too-familiar pain in his chest. They weren't the "high high yip yips" of coyotes but something baser, deeper, and more haunting. Howls and wails. It was wolves, a gang of them. The roaming pack from Loma had entered the Missouri River valley.

He patted the table beside the stove, carefully, trying not to cut himself on the blade of a knife. When his fingers touched smooth metal, he moved them down until he found the handle, closed his fingers, and held the blade at his side. He listened again.

The howling came in waves, one after another, and then

silence—absolute silence. He could hear his heart during the quiet. Another howl, then another.

Across the campground a branch broke. He stayed real still. Another branch, louder this time. He swallowed, hoping the wolves wouldn't go to the tents.

Hearing a crinkle of leaves behind him, he spun and felt something slip. He reached up and tried to grab his headlamp. Too late. It dropped into the water, plunging him and everything else into darkness.

CHAPTER SEVENTEEN

Sunday, earlier that same evening
land

LAURA, E.B., AND TUCKER

"Enough." E.B. touched her wrists. Laura's hands were trembling.

"You let him go, you idiot," she said.

"Hey!" Tucker yelled. "Untie my neck at least! I'm going to die out here!"

Laura's hair was disheveled; her body amped up like a fearful colt. "Are you hurt?" E.B. asked.

"No," she lied. Everything ached. But she wasn't going to tell him that; she wasn't going to tell him anything like that. "He was tied good and fast to that canoe. Next person coming by will let him go. Oh, he'll get loose somehow." She twisted away from him.

"I would hate it if he hurt you," E.B. said.

"'I'll be back in an hour, two, tops,' you said."

"When I got to the top of the ridge . . . I should never have left you," E.B. sputtered.

"You think?"

"Did he come at you first? Or was it the teenagers? How did you get away? How many were there?"

"Ask him," Laura said.

Tucker, noticing they were talking about him, started screaming again.

"Maybe you'll tell me some other time," E.B. said.

"Maybe pigs will fly and cabbies will dance." All she wanted was to be home, in her own bed, Stella's number lighting up her cell phone. "Give it a rest. Just give it a goddamn rest."

E.B. noticed a deep scratch on her arm. "Did the kids do that?"

"Stop asking me dumbass questions." She pushed Tucker's canoe into the river. "Get in."

Tucker's yells filled the air, scaring some birds who were coming in to feed.

"That asshole's not coming near me again."

"Did the kids show up first or was it this guy?"

"Where the hell *were* you?"

He could hear the quiver in her voice.

E.B. moved their gear into Tucker's boat and checked his own. "I'll come back, with Ken, with a fiberglass kit, and patch it. Nothing we can do now."

"Quit dawdling. I can't stand the sight of him."

"Yes, of course." He pushed off into the river and within a few strokes, felt the current pull them. It felt good to be back on the water again and back with her.

"You were gone a long time."

"I found a little cabin," he replied. "Thought it was part of Milt's place. Smoke coming out of the chimney and everything. An old lady answered the door and started shouting at me right away. She went to grade school with my grandma—I thought that would help. I asked to use her phone. She disappeared inside and came out blasting. I stole her ATV, and she shot out the oil pan. I had to run the rest of the way."

"That was you? I thought it was hunters."

"I wish it had been," he said, going quiet. Shit, that old bag had shot him right between his legs. He took a look upriver and watched Tucker and the clearing disappear as they went around a bend and picked up speed.

"Better now?" he asked a few minutes later.

"Let's just get going. I hate this river."

Despite his sore hip E.B. matched his stroke with hers. Whatever he had gone through, she'd had worse. "I don't doubt it," he said. "I would too."

Half an hour later, while the sun's rays pinked canyon walls, E.B. eased back on his paddling. They'd gone around two, three bends, and in all the time she hadn't said a word. He checked his watch. Dusk in the canyon came early. There was no telling where there would be a good landing again. With an expert stroke, he pulled them onto a beach.

"You need to go? Again?"

He couldn't stop looking at her, her sad little shoulders, paddle across her lap, blonde hair streaking across her face. She was more powerful than she looked and full of secrets.

"We need to make camp. This is as good a place as any."

E.B. passed her a bottle of water. Watched her a minute or two. "Drink." What had happened back there? Should he ask? Or should he just wait, like they did with the kids in Sunday School who fidgeted and dawdled when he knew they'd taken off with the chalk?

He put out his hand to touch her.

She recoiled.

"When did you get that scratch? Before or after the kids tied him up?" She defeated a bunch of teens and a grown man? She was a mere slip of a thing.

"I wasn't paying attention," she answered, tipping her head back and swallowing half the water.

The evening enveloped them, hugging trees with a dank mist, touching their flushed faces with cool air.

"We're going to camp here?" Laura asked. The place looked bleak.

"Yes, of course."

"And the others?"

"I'm not sure where they are. We can't look for them now. I don't want to get caught on the water in the dark, Laura."

"There's no place to hide," she whispered.

Owls called from the other side of the river.

She jumped.

"There's a great campground above this cutbank," he said. "And steps, too, see?"

Something slipped into the water nearby, making a swooshing sound. She grabbed his arm.

"It's okay," he said. "It's just an otter. Let's get set up, shall we? While we still have plenty of light?"

He unpacked Tucker's canoe.

"I don't know what's in here," E.B. said. "Up on the bluff, it's safer. I'll hide the canoe. You'll see." He pulled the boat up on shore and climbed the bank. "Come up here, Laura. It's okay now," he said, his voice soothing. "I'm here and I won't leave you."

"I've heard that lie before." Her dad used to say that; he used to say a lot of things that weren't true. She saw his face fall. "It's been kind of a long day."

"Yes, of course, I understand," he answered, hurt but a soldier. He wouldn't mention it again.

She contemplated arguing with him, but was too tired. She watched him gather up gear and take off up the bluff. Suddenly, she was alone. Wavelets slapped the beach. Feeling vulnerable, she grabbed a cooler and an old army bag and beat it up to the bluffs.

A flat plain spread itself out in all directions. Trees stood sentry. Golden light—the last of the day—spread itself along fields of honey-colored grass.

She stood there, uneasy and still. That strange feeling again—E.B.'s kindness.

"E.B.?" she asked, calling to him. She peered into some trees. "You there?"

"You bet, kiddo," he answered. "I'm right here. Take my hand."

Despite her lingering despair, she reached out and felt warmth.

Fifteen minutes later, they hid the canoe behind two shrubs, well out of view of the river. Then they carried up all the rest of Tucker's gear—plastic bags full of clothes and a cooler full of cans.

In the bottom of a tackle box, E.B. found a small flashlight, turned the batteries over, and switched it on. A pinpoint of light stretched out in front of them. He splashed the light onto Laura. She blinked. The little metal mag light was dim, but decent enough to set up a makeshift shelter. In another hefty plastic bag, he found a flannel sleeping bag. It reeked of cigarette smoke, but it was better than nothing.

"Can you find the stove?" he asked.

She bent over into the boxes again. She imagined something big and bulky—like the four-burner stove her mother had on Staten Island. It was as if someone turned out the klieg lights, as if she was staring into the darkness of the audience. Except there was no one there, no one whistling, moaning, sighing. Not a cough or a stir. Frogs croaked in the distance. She dug her hands into a pile of bags, not finding any stove.

"It's okay, I'll find it," E.B. said. "Put on all the clothes you can find. It's going to be chilly tonight."

She dug into a bag patched with duct tape and found a flannel shirt, holes in the back and patches at the elbows. There was an extra pair of jeans, stiff with dirt and grease, as well as some socks, a hat, a bomber jacket. They smelled just like her brother after a basketball game.

She stood up, Tucker's bag of clothes bunched up in her arms, and headed off for some bushes.

"Don't go wandering far. I'm not going to look. "

But he *was* looking.

"Sorry." E.B. searched the army bag. "Hurry before you get any colder. Hypothermia's no joke in cattle country."

She started trying to pull Tucker's jeans over her wet shorts. Grunted a little.

E.B. heard her struggle. "Not that way. You'll freeze. Take everything off—even your whitey-tighties. You're soaked. And hurry, I've got to set up a shelter. I could use your help."

"All of it?" she questioned, peeling off Beth Ann's little

shorty-shorts over goose bumps on her thighs. Even her underwear? She didn't like that idea. She looked at him, unsure, and muttered something low under her breath he wasn't supposed to hear. Feeling fragile, she stepped away, slipped off her flimsy thong, stuffed it into the pocket of her shorts, and pulled on the itchy shirt, the stiff jeans, the huge socks. She stuck the stinky wool cap on her head. She felt like she'd swum in a sewer, but at least she was warmer.

"See that rock over there? Grab this small stuff—this little line. Put it through the grommet and hand it to me," he requested.

She knew he was thinking about her.

Laura grabbed the small rope and looked at the darkening sky.

"Thanks," E.B. said. He set up a lean-to—a tarp stretched over a branch—and carved a trench around the makeshift shelter to keep water out. The wind had come up, threatening rain.

"You think the others are worrying about us?" Laura asked.

"Probably. Somewhat. We'll be fine, have stories to tell Campbell in the morning. We're lucky. We have a way to stay warm and dry. And we have food. Thanks for getting this canoe and all the gear." He tightened the lines around some branches, making a squeaking sound. He stopped a sec. He'd given her all the warm clothes they had. He'd freeze. So?

"Camping is kind of not really what I expected," she said, holding a line for him.

He laughed. "Not quite what I expected, either. Good. Now, matches, please."

She stared at the flimsy structure, then back at E.B., who cocked his head and asked, "Hungry?"

"Oh God, yes," she said, helping him light a small stove the size of a soup can. He balanced everything on top. "Now, please help me find duff for a mattress," he asked, and she followed his moves, as much as she could, gathering leaves and dead grasses on the prairie ground, always wanting to stay near him, and not go into that inky darkness that lay just beyond the blue flame of Tucker's tiny stove. "You've done this before," she said, feeling his heat, his reassuring presence.

They piled a six-inch-tall layer of duff on the ground under the makeshift shelter.

"A trick I learned from my grandfather, who used to sleep with the cattle when he wandered too late to come home."

She watched him. He was being so kind. What was she going to tell Stella? "I met this guy on the river, he dressed me in smelly cowboy clothes, and . . ." Then what? Made sure I was warm. "That all?" Stella would ask. "Yes, Stella, that was all." Her shivers disappeared.

"If you hand me that light, I can gather some firewood," she said a moment later. "Have any paper?"

"Not a good idea. A glow on the bluff would only draw attention to ourselves," E.B. warned, gathering what was left of his voice. It seemed more like a croak to him. He tried not to think about how beautiful she was as he picked up the empty coffee can they'd used as a pot and poured out the noodle water.

He loved listening to the dulcet tones of her voice. Keeping his mind on work usually helped. Some. He laid down the sleeping bag, and didn't pay attention to his rapidly cooling body. He'd given her all the clothing they had. He'd freeze. So? Would Grandpa do any different?

He'd curl up tight. What if he fell for her, big time? She would break his heart and head back to LA, anyway. He concentrated on their water supply. They would have only enough for a slight breakfast, if he could find any coffee.

"Can I do anything else?" Laura offered, sitting with her hands on her knees and watching E.B. in the last dim light.

In her oversized clothes, she looked vulnerable and sweet.

The light flickered out. He guided her to where she should crawl under the lean-to. She lay down where he told her. He unzipped Tucker's sleeping bag; the stench of tobacco, unwashed clothes, and the faint smell of anchovies lingered. E.B. laid it over her, tucking her in and making sure it covered her completely as she lay on her side. Touching her inadvertently, she was toasty warm.

"E.B.?"

"Yeah?"

"You're going to freeze unless you come closer," she said. E.B. lay down and wiggled his way close to Laura, but not touching her, and pulled over a fraction of the sleeping bag to cover himself. He curled up as tight into his own ball as he could, trying not to put his arm on her, trying not to think he was avoiding the most beautiful body he'd ever seen. She was so close. Sweat beaded his upper lip. He felt bad he was not providing her with every comfort of home.

"Let me know you're here, and safe," she said, her voice muffled by the sleeping bag.

E.B. kept back.

"I'm so sorry this trip has been such a disaster," he said, his hot breath blowing on her hair. "When we get back, I'll treat you to a night in the best room at the Union Hotel. It has a fireplace. I've always wanted to stay there." It would be the first time for him too; Berniece had said it was too expensive.

He tucked up close enough to feel Laura's breath on his neck. He swallowed hard. "Laura?" Maybe he could go a little closer? No response. She was fast asleep.

CHAPTER EIGHTEEN

⁀

Monday, 6:00 a.m.
Slaughter River Campground

CAMPBELL AND FRANCINE

*S*ound asleep in his tent and dreaming of Daisy, Campbell felt someone touch his shoulder. He smiled and reached out, but the hand disappeared. He turned over in the dim morning light and reached farther. Finding nobody there, he sat up in a hurry.

"Jumpy, aren't you?" Nia peered through his tent flaps.

"What's the matter? Everyone all right?" The wolves had come into camp?

"How do I turn on the stove?"

Campbell reached into his shoe where he'd placed his watch. Damn. He'd planned to be searching for E.B. and Laura long before now.

"I'm not sure how, and if I do it wrong," Nia went on, "whoosh, there go my eyebrows. That's what you said last night. I kinda like them, even if everyone says they're too bushy."

"It's only six. Have a heart." Campbell turned over. Double

damn. By the afternoon Daisy would be at Coal Banks Landing, and he wouldn't be there. He had their sleeping bags and the jackets, and her favorite hat. She was going to freeze.

"Campbell, I wouldn't be bothering you, if," Nia continued, "if you'd showed me how yesterday, like I asked. But you didn't and I can't and you're not asleep anymore anyway, so why not be a champ and help me out?"

"In a minute. Two." He lay back down and waited until he heard her go away. But there was no sound of footsteps. He bet she was still standing there. He threw on clothes and with effort spoke calmly. "Been up long, Nia?"

"Since five." He watched her rock back on her heels and fold her arms over a lightweight Patagonia jacket. "Nice, this morning," she said. "No wind. Not like yesterday afternoon when it blew like stink."

"I'll make coffee." If he hurried, he could cast off within the hour. Crawling out of his tent, he went to stand up, felt a tightness in his back, and collapsed on one leg.

Nia didn't notice, thank God; she was standing with her back to him, taking photos. Standing up properly, he meandered over to their makeshift galley, reached into an Action Packer, a plastic storage bin, found a coffeepot, dug for filters, and closed his fingers on a pound of freshly ground Jamaican Blue Mountain coffee at the very bottom of the bin. Carefully and slowly he stood up. Nia frowned.

"Got your cup?" he whispered through twinges of back pain.

"I drink tea. Didn't you read the form? I filled it out, twice. I was being so careful, wanting to get everything right."

"No problem, Nia," he whispered. He never read those "food preference" sections on the registration forms. The only thing he read was the experience part, and on that line, everyone lied. "Sorry about that."

She pouted.

He set down the coffee, dug back in the Action Packer, and tossed cans, plastic plates, and utensils onto the overturned lid. Finally he found some tea bags behind the canned soup and tossed them up onto the roll-up table. Looked up at Nia. He shouldn't have.

"Oh dear. Maybe I wasn't being very clear. You got any Earl Grey? I don't drink infusions, unless it's at Tea for Two on Fulton Street down in the Bowery. You know, New York?"

Campbell dropped his head back into the bin. Who packed this piece of shit? Ken? Campbell had told him to organize food better than this. Now cans were mixed with dry packets of lemonade, oatmeal, and soup, and the packets were all torn so his hands were covered in sugar and other crap. He tossed out a bag of lettuce that was already starting to brown. A loaf of bread, a can of tuna, and at last, his hand closed on a tea tin. He squinted at the label—English goddamn fucking tea.

He sat back, and held out a tea bag. A half hour had passed. He hoped she'd take it and go back to bed. He would have.

"Got half 'n' half, and sugar?" she asked. "What else ya got in there?" She peered into the bin over Campbell's shoulder.

"Oatmeal. Cream of Wheat. Instant. Something easy." The wind picked up, wrinkling the once-placid river. Oh Jesus, already?

"But that kind of breakfast isn't what's advertised in the brochure. Home-cooked breakfast, it said."

"Nia, you're right. If you'd read the fine print, that was for one morning, not two," he lied. "If you would, could you be satisfied with something like this? I've got to get back on the river, find E.B. and Laura. Just today, okay?"

"But I'm hungry now, Campbell. You'll be gone all day. We finished all the snacks yesterday. Bacon and eggs for breakfast makes me a nice girl, and not moody or anything like that, and you don't want me to be cranky, do you? My friends say I'm really mean when I'm cranky." She thought a minute. "And the eggs need to be medium." She paused. "You know—when the yolks are still a little runny but the whites are really hard?"

Campbell rubbed his face. He stood up, towering over her slender little frame. He remembered what Ken had told him: "Trip's all about service, Campbell." He winced. His grand plan—buying into Ken's business, having a place to go summers with Francine and Daisy, eventually moving out of New York—everything hinged on this trip going well. And now it was going to shit.

"I'll see what I can do," he said, hitching up his pants. Babysitting, that's all the job was. If he didn't buy into the business, he could still spend summers in Montana, couldn't he? Do something else? Start over?

In the distance, mist rose from the river. He had to hurry.

"Go sit by the river, and I'll call you when I'm ready, 'kay?" That way, at least, she wouldn't be hanging around like a puppy, wanting attention. And he wouldn't have to keep himself from slugging her.

She tightened her lips. "Water has to be really hot."

"Of course," he answered, cranking up the little alcohol stove. If Ken had done what he was supposed to, he would have bought a propane stove like Campbell had asked, but he was too cheap, so all they had was this stupid alcohol stove. It took hours to heat anything. Jesus, he was never going to get out of here.

The sound of Nia's little feet pounding away on the gravel pleased him no end.

Digging for bacon, Campbell missed E.B. With the two of them, breakfast would be a snap. He took a look upriver. Where are you, buddy? You all right?

Back at work he wrestled their heavy as bejeesus water jug so that he could tip it, and, losing his grip, sloshed about a third of it onto his feet. Shit. If he kept this up, they'd have no water before the trip was over. River water, filtered, boiled, or strained, was still too full of pesticides to drink.

"Hey! Couldn't you have kept it down?" Jane asked, coming up on Campbell. "But hey, now like I'm up, I'd like a double cap, soy, light on the foam, please."

Damn, another one, Campbell thought, and set a second pot of water on the stove. "I wish I could, Jane," he muttered, "can't, won't, don't care. Go away." He gritted his teeth.

"You say something?" she asked.

"Nope."

"I'm just kidding about the coffee, Campbell, I know this is no five-star affair."

Campbell kind of wished it was; then he'd have a staff of four. They were working him like a dog with an old bone.

"You guys keep talking this loud, you're going to wake Francine." Nia slid to a stop near Jane.

"You can hear her snoring all over camp," Jane giggled.

My little girl, thought Campbell.

"Can we change partners? I'm tired of paddling with Kris. She's too slow." Jane, standing over him, smoothed her pajamas and flicked back her hair.

"How's Jamaican Blue Mountain?" Campbell said. "Black?"

"Super," Jane laughed. "You know, I was wondering how you could make all that fancy coffee without one of those Italian gizmos."

"Sounds like you've been camping before," Campbell said.

"Me? No," Jane said, "just trying to be sociable. My dad says that's my only weakness."

Startled, Campbell poured all the hot water he'd prepared for Nia into Jane's coffeepot.

"Hey," Nia complained. "That was for me."

"I'll make some more." He refilled the pot and stirred the eggs in the fry pan, eyeing Nia. She was kind of pretty with that little mouth and jet-black hair. But her personality needed work.

"God, I love the river." Jane took a long sip and stared at Campbell. She blinked sleep out of her eyes and peered over the top of her insulated plastic mug. "Been doing this long?"

With more water set to boil, he struggled to open the vacuum-sealed bacon packet. He had to use his hunting knife and stabbed the thick plastic until the strips were free and his hands were greasy. He set the bacon into another fry pan.

Having forgotten to pack paper towels, he wiped his hands on his zip-apart pants, smearing grease everywhere.

Something caught the corner of his eye. Kris was up and out of her tent, wearing silky, sky-blue pajamas and red slippers that flapped while she walked. She looked like she'd been sleeping at the Plaza. Now he'd never launch by eight. Damn and double damn.

The sun climbed up a distant hill.

While the bacon cooked, he searched the ground for his hat. He soon found it, crushed in a ball by the tent, his Ray-Bans just to the side, a little twisted but wearable. He made a mental note to put all his valuables in his shoes when he slept. He shoved his wrinkled hat onto his head, slipped on his sunglasses, and ran back to the stove where the bacon sizzled and smoked.

He turned the heat down.

"Campbell," Kris said, nudging him, her pajamas sleeves fluttering around her wrists. "Where's toast? Sourdough toast. I'm hungry."

"I can't make toast on a Coleman," Campbell replied, pouring hot water into the coffee filter. "Want some?" If he made another pot, that would keep them occupied while he loaded the canoe.

"Shall we break camp, Captain?" Kris asked. "I can be ready in three minutes, tops."

He was about to answer when one of the other girls sidled up to him.

"My dad makes toast when *we* go camping." Alice put her arm around Kris's waist. "He cooks better camping than he does at home. You got a DO?"

"I'm not carrying a Dutch Oven in a canoe. They weigh like twenty-five pounds. Are you crazy?" He cracked a bunch of eggs and threw them in the fry pan, turned the knob under the burner, and then thought a sec. What else did he need to take today? Water. Apple. Jacket. First-aid kit?

"Watch the eggs, will you?" He gathered his life jacket and paddles, refilled a water bottle, and took everything down to the river.

Then he smelled something burning.

It was the bacon. He ran back, turned off the burner, and flipped the charred sides over.

"I can't eat that, it's burnt," Jane complained.

"And I'm a vegetarian." Nia peered into one of the coolers. "What else you got?"

"How about a banana and an apple?" Campbell tried to keep his temper. "You'll find them in the cooler."

"Where's the fresh OJ? I can't drink concentrate." Jane dug in the food bin.

"Sure you can," Campbell answered.

"But it tastes like water."

"Girls, please. Camping is all about doing things a little differently. Everything tastes better outdoors." He gritted his teeth. "Please, go get dressed."

"Before my second cup of coffee?" Jane asked, bewildered.

"I'll make some more," he grumbled. Catering to other people's every whim just felt wrong. How the hell did Ken do this day after day?

After making sure everything was cooking fine, Campbell carried his canoe down to the water. Hearing another voice behind him, he dropped it with a thump, wrenching his shoulder.

"Having another interesting day, Dad? You said you

wanted a change of pace, but maybe not this much?" Francine wiped sleep out of her eyes. "I slept great."

Everyone was up. Well, all right then. Time to disappear.

"Hungry?" he asked. He walked back to the cooler and pulled out the last of the eggs.

In the distance Alice and Jane were laughing and skipping rocks. He had a few minutes. He threw a chunk of cheese and a chub of salami into a plastic bag and turned up the heat under the eggs.

Nia stood around the stove, giggling. "Did they teach you how to cook like that at guide school?"

He turned the eggs over, revealing them to be uncharred on the back side. "See—not so bad." He doled them out, a spoonful for each, soft and gooey, with streaks of white.

"Goin' somewhere, Dad?" Francine peered into his lunch bag.

"I've had . . ." Campbell caught himself before saying anything more. They're guests, he reminded himself, paying guests.

"This trip sucks," Nia said. "When are we going to have some fun?"

"Do you mind?" He closed his lunch bag and shoved it under his elbow.

"Alone? You going alone, Dad?" Francine asked, her face clouded.

"I'll be fine, kiddo," he replied, doling out more bacon.

"Have anything else to eat?" Jane asked.

"Oh shut—up!" Campbell snapped. They all stared at him, mouths open. He grabbed his bag and ran.

He pushed the canoe into the water and was about to

jump in when he heard footsteps. He turned and saw Francine. "What is it?"

"Paddling alone. Dad? Again? Not the best idea you've had today—or yesterday, as I recall."

"Can't talk now. I'll be back in an hour, tops. You're in charge."

"But hey, wait a sec . . ."

"Gotta go." And without another word he shot into the river and was gone before she could answer.

CHAPTER NINETEEN

~

Monday, 9:00 a.m.

Slaughter River Campground

FRANCINE AND NIA

"*D*ad! You're making a big mistake, no, no, Dad, wait!"

But his canoe shot around the bend. Cursing him, Francine kept an eye on her watch, on the river, and felt like an asshole. At the hospital, no more than six months ago, his face had been pale, his skin cold and clammy, heart monitors tracking his pulse. Now he thought he could do this alone? She waited fifteen long minutes until she couldn't stand it any longer, threw a water bottle into her canoe, and hunted for a branch to pole upriver. She had to keep an eye on him.

Cursing herself for wasting time, she dove under a tree. Twigs and puny branches pulled at her hair. Something scrabbled through the underbrush. Possums would run, so would raccoons, maybe. She remembered the snake.

Startled, she backed up, ready to do battle. But instead of a set of small beady eyes, she saw skinny legs in need of a shave.

"What are you doing under there?" Nia asked.

"I've got to go find my dad," Francine said, gritting her teeth.

"Well, he's not under there," Nia giggled.

"Duh," Francine replied. Maybe later she'd try not to be a jerk. She bent down, and crawled in farther. There, in the dark, was a perfect branch, long and straight, attached to a big limb. She pulled out her Wenger Swiss Army pocket knife, extracted the serrated saw blade, and made a narrow cut, feeling the reassuring grip of metal teeth on soft wood. She pressed harder.

"If you're going paddling, can I go too?"

"Not this time, Nia. Go find something else to do."

Pulling too hard, Francine beaned herself on a low branch, swore, and set the blade in for a deeper cut. She took a deep breath. "Do you mind?" She backed out, the branch in her hand. A little crooked, a bunch of tiny branches, but it would do. She hacked off most of the bark.

"Oh, that's great. We'll fly a flag and signal to them." Nia grinned. "I'll tell the others."

"Don't. Please don't," Francine added. "This is for poling, where I swing the pole over my head, flick, flick, flick stab it into the river bottom, and swing it up again. If you're in my boat, I'll probably hurt you."

"Oh," Nia said.

"Can't help it. It's the nature of the beast."

"Rescue for whom? Your Dad? Those other guys? Do you think they drowned?"

Francine looked at Nia's soft, clouded face. "Tell you what, you can help me load up, and when we come back, I'll teach you how to pole. It's twice as fast as paddling. All right with you?"

"I think I can do that flick, flick now," Nia said, imitating Francine. "I'll get my own branch."

Francine looked at the sky. Clear, but the wind was rising, making for a nasty afternoon if she didn't get a move on. She headed to the boats, reviewing her technique. Nia skipped along behind.

"What are you following me for?" Francine turned and stopped.

"Nothing," Nia said, kicking at sand.

Francine tested her own long branch, set it on top of the seat, dug out her red life jacket and her paddle and a first aid kit, and slipped the canoe into the water. Nia's was better. Shit.

Nia tossed her life jacket into Francine's boat.

"Not today, like I said, Nia."

"I can duck out of the way of the pole. I can paddle. I'll be a big help," Nia grabbed the gunwale. "And when you get tired, I can pole too."

"Ever done it before?" Francine asked, holding the bobbing canoe with one foot.

"Flick, flick," Nia grinned. "Watch me." She swung her own branch over her head and stabbed the water.

"One problem," Francine said. This stupid girl was grating. "Practice, go ahead and do it here, where it's safe. Out on the river, you'll fall in."

"Oh, c'mon. I'm a good swimmer."

"My dad's out there and he has a weakened heart. Let go, and get your stupid crap out of my canoe."

"Then what's he doing out here?" Nia scratched a mosquito bite on her knee. "He should be at a rest home or something."

"I don't care, Nia. Go away."

"You don't care about your dad or you don't care about me?" Nia asked. "The other girls and I . . . we think you're mean. I don't much mind, but your dad is . . . don't you, you know, feel a little guilty? You shouldn't have let him go alone."

"Nia. Let go of the goddamn painter."

"Everybody is deserting us. What if some wolf or bear comes into camp? What are we supposed to use for defense? Our paddles? What if someone gets hurt? We need guns. Got one?"

"I don't fucking care!" Francine climbed in and pushed off.

"Hey! Wait! Francine! No!" Nia ran into the water after the canoe. "You can't leave us alone here!"

"Wanna bet?" Francine turned away. Someday, somehow, she'd learn social skills, but not today.

Shoving her stick into the bottom of the river, she pushed off and slowly and carefully stood up. Taking a wide stance, she braced each foot against the gunwales, pivoted the branch over her head, and sunk the other end into the bottom and pushed off again. She shot forward ten feet. Focusing on her balance and keeping her movements precise, she moved upriver and past the first bend. Fast and slick as snot. Neat.

The bottom was a little muddier than she was used to, but there was firmness there, if she placed the pole just right. The canoe just seemed to fly. Swift and fast and true, the way she liked it. No wonder Lewis and Clark made miles.

There was no place she'd rather be than on the water.

With one eye on the river and another on the canoe, she scanned the shore for the blue of Dad's shirt. Finally she was doing something real, something important. She powered up the river, feeling useful for the first time in years.

She moved past the second bend and into a long stretch where the wind was starting to whip down the river channel, following the river no matter where it went. Carefully she passed a long line of white cliffs and remembered passing them the day before. Swallows took off in a swoosh as she went by.

An hour and a half later she was running out of steam. She'd never poled more than thirty minutes. Every stroke threatened to knock her over. She'd fallen down three times onto the seat, and almost fell into the water twice, twisting her shoulder and barely staying upright. The current was moving, maybe three knots downriver, while wind kicked up one-foot-tall waves at the bow. If she sat down, she'd have to paddle and move half as fast. She leaned into the pole, holding steady with legs that started to feel trembly, and whirled the pole overhead, and dug in again. Dad would be fighting harder with his paddle.

Shoving down panic, she pivoted the pole over her head, and eased past the third bend, hoping he hadn't gone around the other side of an island, as she tried not to think about what might have happened to him. Who would she have to argue with if she lost him? He'd gone so far.

Foop. A gaggle of white pelicans took off right in front of her. Startled, Francine lost her balance, dropped into the boat, and bruised her arm. Balancing carefully, she got back

on her feet, shoved the pole into the bottom, and noticed
something out of the corner of her eye. Looked again. A
green canoe bobbed in a marsh, ten feet from shore. Was it
Dad's? Had he collapsed inside? She shot over to it, hit a
clump of marsh grass with a clunk, grabbed the other canoe's
painter, and tied it to her thwart. Dad's Oakland A's cap was
in the bilge but no Dad.

"Dad?" His life jacket was piled in a heap on the bottom
of the canoe. Had he drowned? "Dad? Where are you?" Oh
God, please no. She scanned the stony beach. If only he was
on land. She pulled both canoes up on shore.

Pacing up and down the beach, she dug through broken
marsh grass and found footprints heading off toward some
shrubs. She followed them, breathless, her heart fluttering.
They led up the sandy shore in a zigzag pattern and onto some
grass. He had to be all right, oh, please, please be all right.

"Dad! Where are you?" She ran to a rise. She raised her
voice again. "Dad!"

"Lewis? Is that you?" His voice was weak and raggedy.
But it was him!

Lewis? What the hell? Buoyed by hope, she crashed
through low scrub bushes. She found him sitting in a shallow
area, leaning against a log, his head in his hands.

She slammed to a halt. She reached one hand out to touch
his shoulder. It was cold and clammy. "You all right?"

He didn't hear her. She bent down, her stomach in flut-
ters. Was she too late to get his nitro? "Dad?" Lifting his
hands from his face, she felt warmth on his cheeks.

His eyes flickered.

She sat back and took one of his soft hands in hers.

"You're lucky I found you," she said, and stroked the back of his hand. "You okay?"

"I found a patch of sun," he said, rolling up one mud-splattered sleeve. "It's warm. I'm just fine." He hesitated. "What are *you* doing here?"

He had a scrape on his chin and a streak of mud on his face.

"Did you see them?" Francine asked.

"I t-t-told you not to c-c-come," he stuttered. "You were supposed to s-s-stay."

"Never mind that." Francine sucked in her breath. "You feeling all right?" He looked so pale.

"Have you noticed how the clouds just kind of hang up there and don't move at all?" He sighed. "I've been watching them for hours."

Francine saw he'd made a cushion of sorts out of dried grass, sticks, and logs. He tipped over a little.

"Here, let me help you." She peeled off his soaking wet shirt. Goose bumps covered his chest.

He sat up straighter, like a soldier. "Lewis said I should wait for him here." He noticed her long face. "Came up here on your own. Really?"

"Of course."

"Lewis?" he asked.

"Dad. I'm not Private Lewis."

"It's Cap'n Lewis. Honestly, Francine, I wonder whether you ever learned anything at that school." He frowned. "I've been reading *Undaunted Courage*."

"C'mon, let's head back." Francine hoped like hell he could make it.

"E.B. and Laura have got to be around the next bend." He struggled to stand. A dribble of spit edged his lips. He raised himself onto one knee, wobbly as hell. "I don't want Meriwether to know I haven't found them. Don't tell, okay?" He grabbed Francine's arm.

"Dad, want some water? Gatorade?" She masked her worry with a smile. She held out the bottle.

He studied it. "Lewis never drank anything green. You sure?"

Francine nodded.

Campbell took a sip, paused, then drank as if he hadn't had any water in a week. He drained most of it and handed it back. A little slop of green swung in the bottom.

"You'll need to rest," he said. "You must be tired, honey."

Honey? He hadn't called her honey since she was five. "Had a bit of a busy morning then?" she said, hoping the sound of her voice would bring him back.

"It took me no time to get here, kiddo." He staggered back to the river, wading in. Francine ran beside him, trying to keep him from falling in the water.

"I can't see Lewis from here," Campbell said. "Cap'n Lewis! Cap'n Lewis! He was right here, Francine, just a second ago."

"Take my hand," Francine said, in a low calm voice. "Sit here next to me, okay, Dad?"

"I searched for them up and down the river, Captain, and didn't see a sign of them."

"You did a good job, sir," she said.

He grinned.

"I'm all right," he said a minute later. "Feel much better now. What's in that drink, kiddo?"

"Sugar, mostly," she said, uneasy. "Electrolytes, stuff like that."

"Man, I feel great now. I'm the bionic man!" Campbell wobbled toward the canoes. "On a mission to Mars. Keep the stars on your right and head off until morning."

He was unsteady like a colt, all legs and no direction. He wove around the beach and tried to push his own canoe into the water. Luckily it was tied to her canoe and didn't go far. He lunged after it and slipped into the water up to his knees.

Francine splashed after him and maneuvered him into her canoe. "Don't get in that one, sir. Meriwether wants you to go with me." He fell into the center with a thunk.

"Come on in, old girl, time's a wasting," he mumbled, climbing up onto the bow seat, churning his paddle up front, and splashing water all over.

She retied the bow of his canoe to the stern of hers and paddled hard, doing her best to keep her weight low to compensate for his weaving around. "Quit wobbling all over. You'll swamp us. Sit still. Paddle slower. Pay attention, or I'll tell the Captain."

"We have hours to go before daylight," he said, "and miles to go before we sleep."

Oh Jesus, Francine thought, and prayed she'd get him back to camp in time.

CHAPTER TWENTY

⊘

Monday, early morning
land

LAURA AND E.B.

The sun caught Laura's face, half-hidden under the tarp, the top of Tucker's sleeping bag nestled under her chin. She sighed, satisfied, dreaming she was still with Mitch, his arm over her, the two of them cuddled up close under the goose-down duvet at her place in Brentwood, the sound of the city far away.

She turned over and felt something odd, something hard, something cold.

She patted around. This was no Dux mattress under her shoulder. This was cold, hard ground. Then she remembered. This was camping. Lumps of leaves and strewn clothing were bunched up around her body. Twigs were stuck in her hair, and a stone dug into the small of her back.

She opened her eyes into a blue-lit world. A tarp hung over her head, casting bluish light over her and a man sleeping beside her. Oh, E.B. His shirt fluttered in a slight breeze.

She sat up with a start. She rubbed her back, dislodging

153

the sleeping bag. She covered him with it. Let him be warm for a change.

E.B. was different. And strange. And new.

She backed out of the shelter, careful not to dislodge the tarp. Her arms were sore and her back ached. Stretching, she felt like she was a hundred years old. Bruises blossomed on her legs from her fight with Tucker. She hoped the bastard was dead.

Coming back and watching E.B. sleep, she relaxed with the sound of his even breathing and wished she could tuck close into the warmth of him. He seemed so solid, so caring, not like any other man she'd ever known. She reached out to stroke his cheek with one slender finger. His eyes flickered open, settling on her face. She pulled her hand back, embarrassed.

He opened his eyes wider, and smiled at her. He worked his hand free of the sleeping bag, extended it in greeting, like halfway between shaking her hand and an embrace. "Good morning."

"Have you always liked the river?" she asked, trying to ease the tension. Birdcalls echoed from the cliffs on the opposite shore. The sun was warm. Overhead crows crisscrossed a clear blue sky.

E.B. sat up. "Were you cold last night?"

"Not a bit," she said. "Thank you for everything." She wrapped her arms over Tucker's stinky flannel shirt and blue jeans that bagged at her knees. She couldn't remember a man ever being like E.B.. If only it were possible. But how long would it last? Until he found out what she did for a living? Of course. Stella was right about so many things.

"I'll make coffee," he said suddenly, flushed with heat, thinking of her beside him. And he hadn't even touched her. Good thing, too. She was so beautiful, her hair across her eyes, looking cute as hell in Tucker's clothes. He knew, if he made even one move, it'd be over. She'd never go for someone as humble as a hick farmer from Montana.

He hoped the coffee was good; it smelled okay. He had pulled two logs nearer the little camp stove to make a bench for him and for her. His hip ached from the fight and he limped a little. Later, he'd face the music, waking up with the sore hip for weeks, but for now, it didn't matter, nothing mattered as long as he was with Laura. He tried not to think about what Tucker had done or had wanted to do to her.

"You didn't answer my question." She handed him back his warm and half-full coffee cup.

E.B., stymied, couldn't remember her asking him anything. Trying not to be rude, he hunted around in his mind for some kind of clue. Farming? His tractor? Her legs?

"The river," she prompted him. He looked as starstruck as some of the guys in the front row.

"You mean, liking it and all?" He felt like an idiot. "Well, yeah, now I do . . ." he faltered. He used to hate the damn river. "It splits my ranch in two, kind of a pain, going around, using the cable ferry, that is, when it's working." Before Berniece left, the river had been in his way. Now it comforted him.

"I never thought a river could be beautiful," she said, watching some ducks land with a whoosh. "Our river in LA's just a concrete ditch. And it's empty most of the time."

"Like that slab of concrete I saw in *Terminator*? I thought that was fake." He scratched mosquito bites on the back of his neck. "Not too many cyborgs in Montana, except for some of the guys hanging out at the Feed 'N' Seed," he laughed.

"I've dated cyborgs." She grinned. Most of them in her club.

"So what do you do back there, in LA?" E.B. handed her an apple. Tried not to stare.

She took a bite. "Entertainer," she said softly. That was true, wasn't it? "Where'd you grow up, E.B.?"

Grease caked under his nails; his hands were coarse as rawhide. He'd never been ashamed of being a farmer before. Her skin was precious and smooth and delicate. He shoved his hands deep into his pockets and mumbled, "I come from Loma, like I told you. Not far."

She leaned back and grabbed her knees. "Kind of like Norman Rockwell? Lots of kids, then?"

"Me? No, no kids. I've got plenty of nephews and nieces, though." Berniece hadn't wanted children; he had. "Rockwell paints a picture of calm and quiet, but it's not really like that. We . . ." he stumbled. "These open skies can fool you. Warm one minute, freezing the next, rain, snow, hail. We have hail insurance for a reason. Temperature can drop as many as sixty degrees in a half day. We get locusts. It's no Rockwell."

He used to love it; now he wasn't so sure. The land, the dirt between his fingers, the warm sky, the endless sky, the scary sky. "We have it all." For the last few months he'd hated everything.

"A tough weather day in LA is rain, lots of rain. Rains like hell."

"I bet you're great up on the stage." That's as far as he was going to go. With a body like hers, yes, anything and everything was possible. To distract himself, he turned off the heat under the little stove and burned himself in the process. No matter. He didn't feel anything except her warmth. "I'm in bed by nine most nights, up before five."

"I dance," she muttered. "The money's great."

"I bet you do," he croaked.

"What do you think? With a body like this, you think I'm a ballet dancer?"

"Uh, no . . ." E.B. stuttered. "Didn't mean any offense."

"Boobs get in the way."

"Of course," he said, stupidly. He had no frigging idea.

"How the fuck would you know?" She threw the coffee at him, splattering his cheeks and nose. "You're a man, so you should know, like, everything?"

"I'm sorry."

"Climbing into your canoe was the biggest mistake I made since I moved to Montana. And that was a doozy. Another state filled with assholes. LA was a lot better than this."

E.B., reeling from the sudden onslaught, wasn't sure where he'd gone wrong. She must be an exotic dancer, then, to be so peeved. What the hell, he'll pretend he hadn't guessed. "Let's get the show on the road, all right? Campbell must be worried."

Working separately, they gathered the tarp, Tucker's little stove, and sleeping bag; threw them all into a duffle bag; and loaded up the canoes. They cast off in silence, the sound of their paddles the only thing Laura wanted to hear.

"I should have never left you alone back there," E.B. said.

"You think?" Laura slid her paddle in. "I had to promise him a little something."

"Him? Tucker? What about the kids?" E.B. was glad she was talking again.

Overhead, a hawk circled lazily in a cloudless sky. Across the way, birds called, signaling distress.

"There were no kids," she said finally.

"You're half his size. You know jiujitsu? Kung fu?"

"Don't ask me about it again, ever." The smell of Tucker's clothes seeped into her skin, making her feel queasy.

"I'll find him."

"You should," she said, lifting her paddle out of the water and taking a stroke.

"I'll have him arrested for assault." E.B. steered them carefully around a bend. "You're all right now."

"Wanna bet?" she asked, looking behind her.

"What is it?" he asked. He'd just had her feeling better, like the calf he had calmed just last week, soft muzzle resting in his hand.

"Tucker's back," she said softly. "And he's gaining on us. He must've found a way to repair the canoe."

CHAPTER TWENTY-ONE

@

Monday, morning
on the river

FRANCINE AND CAMPBELL

"Lewis! Captain Lewis!" Campbell stared straight. "Indians!"

In the stern, Francine froze. Sunstroke. She'd seen it at camp.

"Whoa, Captain, you're going to swamp us. Steady. Steady, I say!" Campbell's voice rose. "No, Daisy, don't panic. Everything's going to be all right."

"You okay, Dad?" Drugged-out people in New York muttered to themselves all the time, but they were bums. This was *Dad*. This was different. "Dad! Hey, Dad! It's Francine." Remembering her training from camp, she put together a plan.

First, get him to a beach. The closest shore was full of bushes, and beyond, marshes lined both sides of the river. Shit. Couldn't pull over there. She rounded another bend and paddled down a long, straight stretch. Mud and more mud. He'd sink up to his thighs, and she'd never be able to get him out. In the distance, maybe a quarter mile away, there was something tan and low. A good beach. All she had to do was get there. Fifteen minutes later she slammed onto the sandy shore, nosing up on it, the empty canoe clunking into hers from behind.

Campbell, startled, flew off his seat onto the floor of the canoe.

"What's going on, Capt'n?" he asked, climbing out. "I haven't received my latest orders. Zack"—he sneezed—"where's Lewis?"

His eyes were glazed, his skin whitish. He held his arms at his sides as if he'd deflated in place.

Francine reached over to touch his hand, slipping her fingers onto his wrist to check his pulse. Weak, but there.

"Give him a sec." Campbell threw off her hand. "He'll be right back."

"Who?" Francine asked. "I don't see anyone." There were no homesteaders' cabins here, no beat-up old ranch roads, no shacks. No one to help her. She tried to remember everything to do with sunstroke. Water, and lots of it. She filled her bailing bucket and poured it over his feet. He snuffled at her, grinning.

"Cool. Feet. Good start, girl. Capt'n says, give the men water, lots of water." He paused. "But maybe not on my toes?"

She handed him the last of her Gatorade. He swallowed it all. She waited and watched him. After five long minutes, he sat up and looked at her, his eyes bright.

"It's a good book, *Undaunted Courage*. Lewis and Clark were fearless," he insisted. "They fought grizzly bears, right here, with their bare hands."

"I see." She thought a sec. "Left their rifles in their boats?"

"You bet."

He still looked a little wobbly.

"Right as rain, Francine."

Campbell shifted; the ground felt hard. "I was only pretending." How could he tell her he'd been hallucinating? She'd worry like crazy.

"Shithead."

"Ever think about Lewis and Clark? Didn't you study them in school? Can you imagine how much moxie it took to do what they did?"

"You scared the crap out of me, Dad." Francine scooped up the bailing bucket and filled it again. "I practically kill myself coming up here, and you think it's a joke? You went all mental. Early Alzheimer's, something like that? You're fooling around?" She pitched some rocks at the beach by his feet. "Just who are you now, Dad? Mickey Mouse? Minnie?"

"Sweet as a summer's day," he said. "How ya doin', girl?"

"You look like shit to me, Minnie Mouse. You hot? Got sunstroke? Better cool off." She dumped the water on the top of his head.

That felt good, Campbell thought, as the cool water dribbled down the back of his neck. Still, she was right. His heart was still beating too fast, and he swore he saw Sacagawea in the field—he sure as hell wasn't going to tell Francine that. He felt ashamed he'd lost control.

He recognized her sad, pinched look. He'd been trying to hide how he felt, all fluttery and out of sorts. Out of body was more like it. He couldn't tell her where he'd been, but it had been scary. He sat down next to her, doing his best to control his trembling hands. "I'm sorry, Francine, I didn't mean to hurt you." God, everything he did was wrong. When was he going to do something right? "Lewis and Clark are my heroes."

"Then you stay here and talk to them. Entertain them, make fun of them. I don't need this shit, not from you, not from anyone." She headed to the canoes.

"Francine, please don't be mad. I'm sorry." He felt a little nauseous.

"You should be sorry, fooling me like that, or trying to. Which one is it?" She pushed one canoe from shore and zipped up her lifejacket.

With her so pissed off already, maybe he should take advantage and tell her about Daisy. How much angrier was she going to get? Scream at him? Probably. With no one else around, this was as good a spot as any. Why had he waited so long?

"Get in. The bow seat," Francine said. "I don't have anything more to say to you."

Up front, and trying not to exert himself, Campbell considered himself lucky. Lucky to be in the canoe, lucky Francine had come to get him, and lucky he felt better. That had been much closer than he'd ever wanted to go. He was sure he could still see Lewis waving from the shore. He'd have gone with him too, if Francine hadn't come and saved him.

"If it weren't for you," he said, "I'd still be back there. Thanks."

She paddled silently, listening.

"This trip hasn't worked out at all the way I promised," he said. "I'm sorry about what happened."

"Look." She pointed to a faint full moon that hung just above a ridge.

Campbell felt a soft breeze blow across his cheeks. Daisy was going to love this. He'd told her about the birds, but she hadn't really understood. And he'd tried to describe the calmness of the river, the peace, the solitude, the open skies. He heard swallows cry from across the river.

"Would you ever believe that? Birds everywhere." Francine laughed, catching her breath. "It doesn't matter what you say. I'm still mad at you."

"I should hope so," Campbell said. He rubbed his sunburned face and watched the water flow around his blade. Maybe he could fix things with Francine after all. That would be some kind of miracle. More than he'd ever hoped for. He couldn't believe he thought he was talking to Lewis and Clark.

Thankful, he slipped his hand into the water and felt it flow by his fingers. "It's just a Class One river." He rubbed his face with his wet hand. "Like a bathtub. Supposed to be, anyway." He paused. "You've done great," he said. "Mom would be proud." His voice cracked a little as he turned to look at her. "As am I."

Francine sat up straighter in the canoe and took a few hard strokes. After awhile she started humming behind him, out of tune as usual. As for him, his stomach was churning as if he'd eaten acid. What had he been thinking? Introduce his mistress to his daughter on a canoe trip? Francine looked so cute in her red life jacket. And now, he was going to hurt her. He couldn't stand it.

"I did nothing you wouldn't do," Francine said.

"Fine vacation we've had together. Lots of adventures." Campbell slid his blade in and watched the shore flow by. He wanted to prepare her somehow. Just, oh please, couldn't he savor the moment a little longer, the moment he'd always wished for? Tomorrow, or tonight, or later when they got to shore again, lunchtime, anytime; just not now. He'd tell her before nightfall. What a weenie. He should tell her now.

Across the way, swallows called out as they circled to their nests. Behind them, the second canoe rode high in the water.

The humming stopped. A cloud of bugs took off for shore.

"Hey, Francine." Campbell scratched a mosquito bite on his neck. "I need to tell you something. Something I should've told you long ago. Something true. Something you're not going to like. I need to tell you about Daisy. Have a minute?"

CHAPTER TWENTY-TWO

Monday, morning
on the river

E.B. AND LAURA

"You must have sunstroke. That can't possibly be Tucker behind us," E.B. said. "Drink more water. Feeling dizzy?" They had to get into shade and quick.

"It's *him*. I just know it's *him*."

"He was good and tied to a tree and our old canoe had a hole in it as big as my thumb."

"Someone must've helped him fix the canoe. Every once in a while I see a fountain of water coming this way. Take a look."

"Maybe it's a different canoe," E.B. said. "Maybe it's the BLM rangers with their motorized drift boats." He thought a sec. "Besides, Tucker couldn't fix the canoe without some fiberglass cloth, epoxy, time . . ."

"All that asshole had was time. For God's sake, E.B., pick it up, will you?"

He turned around carefully. Nothing but scrub brush, endless water, empty fields, and birds. "I don't see anything," he said. Poor girl.

She twisted in her seat. "Look, just there!" A frisson of fear overtook her. It was hard to hold the paddle with her sweaty hands.

E.B. took another look. "You sure you're all right?"

Laura dug her paddle in hard and leaned into a side stroke. "See for yourself."

E.B. grabbed the gunwales as the canoe lurched, tipped, and turned upriver.

"Now! Now! Can you see him now?"

It was hard to see anything for the glare. Something was coming downstream; that was for sure. He picked up his paddle, turned the canoe downstream again, and dug in deep, fast strokes as they picked up the current under them.

"Damn you, E.B.! We've wasted too much time already. Faster, faster."

He kept looking back between taking five, six, seven long, hard strokes a minute. Laura, sweating hard, matched him stroke for stroke. They were about a quarter mile from some trees and bluffs. Just had to get there. Then he'd take a stand.

He squinted against the sun as they flew down the river. He'd done nothing but disappoint her. He went even faster, spray flying off his paddle with every stroke. This time at least she wasn't alone. And he was stronger and bigger than Tucker.

"Why didn't you pack a gun, E.B.?"

E.B. kept his head down and kept paddling. There was nothing he could say. No words would suffice. The river's usually so pleasant. No one out here ever hurt anybody. There's no cause for worry. All of it sounded pedantic and stupid. He churned through the river, keeping his head down and their progress straight and true.

Behind them the fountain of spray grew.

They forced the canoe to go twice as fast as the current, and as soon as they went around the bend, E.B. charged for a tall cutbank, hitting the sand with a resounding clunk. "Go on, climb up. It's safer up there."

She went partway, grabbed a rock nestled in some roots, turned around, and came back down.

"You go on up," she ordered. "I'll hang out here and beat the shit out of him."

"Not you, me, this time," he said, putting his hand out for the rock.

"Not on your life." She cradled the rock like a baby.

She looked wild, half-civilized.

"Then help me unload and make it fast," he said. "We have to hide everything. That's you, me, the gear, the canoe, and the paddles." Together they pulled out bags and boxes and fishing gear and bait and stinky socks and carried it up to a bluff to the top of the bank. Someone had made footsteps amongst the rocks and roots, but they were slippery. Every few seconds E.B. and Laura would lose their footing, and have to grab roots and charge up again.

Laura threw the last of the bags up the steep bank while E.B. was still below. "Can you see any of this shit from the river?"

"Take it a bit farther back, yes, that's it. Good. Now, we hide the boat." She came on down to help him.

They duck-walked the boat out of the river and hid it behind some bushes.

"Pull some branches from the trees and cover the rest of the hull," E.B. said.

Laura moved fast, pulling twigs, branches, leaves, and duff as fast as she could. She peered down the river. Even from here she could taste Tucker's foul breath in her mouth.

"Good, that's it, now." E.B. saw her scratched arms and the fully covered canoe. "Now go on up the bluff."

"What about you?"

"I'll be there in a sec."

A minute later, E.B. looked up at the bluff. She was standing like a sentry. "Get down!"

Laura lay facedown on some tan grass, her head just above the lip of a bank, Tucker's gear well behind her. She didn't like the look of E.B. down by the river, vulnerable and alone.

He examined their footsteps and also the scrape in the mud from the canoe. It led from the water up toward the cutbank. An arrow showing their way, for sure.

He stripped a branch from a tree, and, starting at the water, walked backward, sweeping sand from side to side, obliterating their footsteps and the gouge in the sand from the keel of the canoe. When he was done, he ran up the steep bank, grabbing onto roots to pull himself up faster, and lay down next to Laura, placing one hand on her back. They watched the river together.

The bow of a blue canoe slid around the bend first. Then Tucker came into view, about fifty feet from shore. He was back paddling, keeping even with the bank. Water splashed constantly from his bailer and his paddle. He scanned the river, studying the brushy bank, turning his head from side to side, looking for them.

"Keep going. Keep moving forward. Go, go, farther, farther," E.B. whispered. He held his breath.

Smoke spiraled off a cigarette Tucker held between his lips. E.B. watched him take a few more back strokes, coming toward the shore in a back ferry move.

E.B. closed his fingers around the shaft of his paddle.

Laura studied Tucker, the round rock at her hip at the ready. He was thirty river feet from her and twenty feet below her perch. She could see his stubbly cheeks. He was bailing, studying the shore. E.B., with his hand on her shoulder, gave her small comfort.

Suddenly Tucker stopped paddling.

"Oh, God," she whispered in E.B.'s ear. "I left my paddle on the beach."

"Where?" E.B. asked quietly.

Laura peeled out one finger and gestured to the shore, down near the water's edge. The orange blade was buried in a bush, not visible from the water, but the other end stuck out, four inches of visible blue shaft with a bright yellow handle.

"Let's just pray he doesn't see it." E.B. tightened his fingers around hers.

With a studied look, Tucker put down his bailer, took a drag of his cigarette, flicked it into the water, and pushed off into the center of the river.

Laura, keeping her mouth down on the dirt and trying not to breathe dust, watched Tucker.

"He's heading on," E.B. said.

Laura smiled weakly. Her shoulders ached like the morning after a long night dancing on the pole. She went to lift her head.

"Not yet," E.B. whispered, placing his hand on her shoulder and nudging her gently back down onto the ground. "He could turn around at any time now. Wait."

Once Tucker's canoe had floated out of sight around the next bend, E.B. cleared his throat.

"Let him go on for a bit," E.B. said. "I just can't imagine how you overpowered him."

"Jesus Christ, E.B. Just get me away from that asshole or I will certainly kill him. Or you, if you ask me again."

"Got it," E.B. said. "In an hour he'll be halfway to Coal Banks and long gone."

She stayed down, feeling stifled.

The sun warmed the air. Tucked in behind a pile of rocks, Laura relaxed very slowly. A little. A chipmunk skittered across an open area in front of them, tail high, sniffing the air.

She placed her rock down beside her. "Kind of pretty, isn't it?" she ventured, wanting to believe she was safe.

A hawk circled overhead, eyeing the chipmunk. "Will he be all right?" she asked. The hawk dove. She caught her breath. Heard a cry. The hawk rose and headed across the river, something in its mouth.

"Jesus, that was fast." She felt her heart, banging fast.

"They miss most of the time," E.B. said.

"Jesus. Just a little chipmunk."

"Still scared?"

"Yes," she answered, shivering. She would never forget that cry. "Can we go now?" Even here, on the bluff with E.B. next to her, she still didn't feel safe.

Ten minutes later, they were back in the canoe again.

The sun's beams danced on small wavelets. She wished she could enjoy it.

Hearing the pain in her voice, E.B. tried to lighten her mood. "I'll sing that song from *Frozen.*" He stopped paddling and rested a minute.

"Not that one, I hear it all the time. How about something else?"

"I don't know anything else, and I don't know this one either," he laughed. He couldn't remember any songs after third grade. That's when Mrs. Henderson said he couldn't hold a tune.

"Never mind," he mumbled, "we'll just paddle for a bit. I'll hum it."

"Oh please, no," she said and laughed.

They were gliding near the shore. He could paddle with her forever. She was just as anxious as a wild hare, all quivering and fluttering with nerves. He was big enough, and he'd fought some, but he wasn't a fighting man—but now, he'd take Tucker out with one shot, no problem. He wished he'd brought his grandfather's Remington 34.

Coming around a bend, he pulled back to avoid strainers. The current was fast here. He pulled one, two, three times, just about to pass the last branch, when he felt the canoe stop suddenly.

Had they hit a snag? He glanced back in the water. He put his paddle in again, and then pulled back. Something hooked on his blade. "What the hell?" he turned and leaned over, tightening his grip. And went in.

Under the water strong arms grabbed at his head. E.B. fought back, kicking against the force, and then it was gone.

By the time he came up gasping for air, the canoe was fifty feet downriver, and Tucker was hanging on to the canoe, Laura in it.

CHAPTER TWENTY-THREE

~

Monday, noon
Coal Banks Landing

DAISY

Forty miles away, Daisy was hurtling down Virgelle Ferry road toward Coal Banks Landing, in a 1968 Econoline van driven by a guy named Frank who was hitting every pothole while talking on his cell phone, chewing gum, and stubbing the ends of his Marlboro cigarettes into an overfilled ashtray. "Drop Kick Me Jesus Through the Goalposts of Life" blared over the radio.

Frank weaved back and forth across the double yellow line, getting back in his lane only when they heard the loud wail of a truck hurtling toward them on the highway. Then and only then did he swerve to the right side of the road and his wheels ran along the white line.

This time Daisy gasped. Two inches away the asphalt dropped off. She closed her eyes. The van straightened out. She finally took a peep. Stay straight, please, oh God.

Frank dropped into a pothole, struggling to hold the wheel, and bounced back out again.

Something on the side of the road caught Daisy's eye. She glanced right. A white cross flew by, covered with flowers, then another and another.

"What are the white crosses for?" she shouted, over the din. "Religious fundamentalists looking for converts? Don't you think there's a better place for crosses than the road?"

"Road casualties," he replied, enunciating every syllable, "fatalities." He bumped into another pothole. They flew out the other side and dropped with a bang.

"Could you please, please, please, slow down?" Daisy croaked.

He looked at her and laughed, taking a deep drag from his cigarette and blowing smoke out the side of his mouth.

"Slow down, ma'am? Why, that's heresy in these parts," he crowed, then punched it. The van lurched forward. "The only thing I slow down for is cattle and I don't see any—not yet, anyway."

"Cattle? On the road?" Daisy took another look at the driver.

"Free range," he said and accelerated into a turn.

"That doesn't make any sense," Daisy said. "You'll run into them."

"Sometimes we do," he said. "But then we have to pay for them. It's kind of expensive."

"Could you please slow down a little? I don't want to die out here."

Frank flicked his cigarette butt out the window, balanced his left arm on the windowsill, and steered with his right. "Nah, we're all right."

Daisy was appalled. Was everyone in Montana crazy? She

grabbed the handle on her door, trying to steady herself from slamming into the dash. This wasn't what she'd planned for. She'd had in mind instead a yellow cab driven by some Middle Eastern guy complaining about the weather or the traffic—not this hick who drove as if he were fleeing a fire.

"How much farther to Coal Banks?" she yelled, tightening her seat belt and grasping her purse.

"Not too far—ten minutes, maybe," Frank answered and thrummed on the steering wheel.

Daisy closed her eyes. She could do ten minutes. Heck, ten minutes was nothing. She'd waited five years for this day. Two weeks ago at her place on the Upper West Side, Campbell had said he had something important to tell her in Montana. Something special.

Daisy smiled. At thirty, she was ready to be a bride.

For their reunion in Montana she'd picked her clothes carefully. She was wearing her white Keds slip-ons, white shorts, a candy-apple-red camp shirt, and a broad-brimmed straw hat. It had a wide white ribbon that fell across her shirt. Her extra-large Jackie O sunglasses made her feel cool. She knew she looked great. She opened and closed the clasp on her beaded pink purse, which cost half of last week's paycheck. It was worth it.

"Been to Montana before, ma'am?" Frank asked.

"Nope." She wasn't going to say any more to *him*.

She preferred to concentrate on Campbell. She closed her eyes. The last time they'd traveled together, they'd gone to Hawaii. Back then, Campbell had run the real estate operation for Mechanics Bank on Wall Street and was always doing deals. It had taken months to arrange a getaway. Their first morning there, they'd been sitting on the lanai, watching the surf roll in, when the phone rang. Campbell flew home that afternoon. Watching the surf lost its allure after that. For a whole week, Daisy had slowly sipped Mai Tais and Rum Collinses, waiting to go home. She'd used his Visa until it reached its limit on Wednesday. This trip there would be no goddamn phones. None at all. Good.

"You going on the river, ma'am?" Frank asked, jolting Daisy's reverie. He turned down the radio and smashed another cigarette into the ashtray.

"Uh-huh," she muttered, lost in thought.

"Wearing that?" he gestured with one tobacco-stained finger at her white shorts.

On the river there'd be no phone, no e-mail, and no goddamn truck driver.

"Of course," she answered, fluffing her hair a little and giving her four-inch-wide ribbon a toss.

He scratched his stubby chin. "You have warmer clothes, like a sweater or something? Raincoat?"

"They didn't say it was going to rain," she answered, patting her Land's End twenty-inch carry-on by her feet. "Besides, I've got warmer stuff."

"I bet you do," the driver said, making Daisy feel a little funny.

The brakes squealed as he slowed down, whipped the wheel around, and careened onto a dirt road.

"Hey!" she yelled, reaching out to grab onto anything she could but slamming into the door instead.

"Good thing it's locked, huh?" he said. "We're here." Frank stopped in a cloud of dust that rose over the bed of the truck and floated onto the windshield. "Coal Banks Landing, ma'am." He tipped his hat. "At your service."

He jumped out of the truck, ran around to her side, and opened the door. He held out one grubby hand.

Daisy looked at the picnic tables, empty and forlorn campsites, and two seedy trailers near the boat ramp. A door banged shut.

"I'm sure you've made a mistake," she whispered. She undid her seatbelt and stepped down onto the running board; she looked at the campground, then back at him. She didn't move.

"No mistake," he said. "This is it."

She saw him study her.

"C'mon," he said, gesturing with his hand. "Hop down. You can see the river from here."

She was frozen in place, one hand on the door, the other holding her little purse.

"Hey, lady, you getting out of the truck or not?"

She buried her fingers into his big paw and stepped down, but stayed near the door.

"Excuse me," he said, pushing her aside a little and pulling out her duffle bag. He set it down and walked around the truck to the driver's side door.

"Hey! Wait a minute. Don't leave me here!" she begged, curling her fingers around the passenger's door handle.

He gunned the engine.

"But no one's here!"

"Gotta go," he said, spitting gravel as he sped down the road.

CHAPTER TWENTY-FOUR

Monday, afternoon
on the river

E.B. AND LAURA

*L*aura screamed.

E.B. was gone.

The canoe hurtled down the river, backward. She took a stroke, but something was holding the boat. Had she hit another snag? She looked under the canoe. Five fingers clung to the hull, five inches from her legs. Five fingers reaching up from a man in the water—a man she hated. Tucker.

"Goin' somewhere, honey?" He grinned. Water crashed around his head as he held on.

"You bastard!" She pulled her paddle back and swung at his hands, but he moved them under the hull. She tried for his head, but he ducked under.

She felt him push the canoe toward shore like a kid with a toy boat. When they hit shore, she jumped out and tried to clonk him with her paddle as he rose from the water. He grabbed the shaft mid-blow. "Darling! Sweetheart! I've missed you."

She stood back, weaponless. She took up the horse stance. She'd go down fighting. "You looked pretty good back there, toasting your nards," she said. "Need some sunscreen?"

"I need a gallon, darling, 'cause I'm huge."

"Not from what I saw." She roared with laughter.

"There, there, now, no reason to be rude," he said, coming close enough to embrace her.

"Like I said, Tucker," she said. "I like forceful guys and I think you're terrif."

"That's right, that's what you said!" He spun around. "Was that before or after you hit me? Or tied me to the tree? Oh darling, I love the way you play!"

"Shall we try again?" Laura asked. "You know, finish the job?"

"She's got a sense of humor, ladies and gents! Finish the job! Yes! Let's! The canoe leaked badly, but the kind guys from the BLM patched it for me. So now, my little chickadee, no boyfriend, just you and me, darling. Alone together, at last."

"What's your pleasure, Tucker?" She licked her lips.

He twisted her around, so her back was at his chest. His smoky breath in her ear made her cringe. His hands grabbed her breasts, pulling on the flannel shirt she was still wearing. "You look great in my clothes, honey."

Laura elbowed him in the ribs.

"You know I love that kinky stuff." He backed off a little, then tucked her in closer, holding her arms down. Pressed his hands under her shirt. "Nice," he gasped. "Sweet Jesus, nice. Size of frigging grapefruits. Mmmm mmmm."

Laura twisted her body, held her breath, and pushed him

back. Tucker kept so close to her she couldn't get any purchase. What was that Mr. Lee said? Close combat lessons, Laura, listen and learn. But she couldn't remember any of it with Tucker's face at her throat.

"I'm ready to finish what you began," Tucker said. Holding her tighter with one hand, he unbuckled his pants.

"If you like, I can make you really happy!" Laura said and kicked him, catching him in the crotch. He stumbled. She took off up a slope, tripping over bushes, thorns digging into her feet as her flips-flops flew off.

She tucked behind a rock. He flew by. Panting. She grabbed a big rock.

She squinted at the river, looked uphill at Tucker fifty yards off. And downriver. E.B. was still too far away. But she could reach the river, couldn't she? Hightail it to the water and hide? That's if she could swim, that's if she could run barefoot through thorns. She ran back to the water anyway; anything was better than being a dead duck. She was halfway to the water when she felt a blow and was knocked down onto her stomach.

Tucker's weight forced air out of her lungs. He dug his elbows into her arms and pushed her face into the ground. Sharp pebbles dug into her hips and shoulders. She kept gasping for breath, her mouth gulping dirt. He pulled off her, flipped her over, and crowed, "That's how we do it in Texas, sweetheart!"

He sat there, watching her.

At last her lungs started to fill. She gulped in air and let it out slowly. It was as if her heart had stopped. Everything ached.

"Let's take a stroll, shall we?" he asked. "Unless you want to do it here?"

"In the thorns and rocks? Sure if you want to be a bottom."

He grabbed her arm and dragged her back to the shore. "Not yet."

She searched for a weapon—paddle, rock, tree branch, her bare hands? Tucker squeezed her fingers so hard she thought he'd break them.

"No, darling, no toys. Not anymore," he smirked. His hot breath puffed on her neck as he reached over, pushed her down, and lay beside her.

"I'm not being very ladylike," she whispered. "Perhaps I should ask you about yourself? Where'd you grow up?"

"Don't talk, listen."

She eyed a paddle, just out of reach of her right hand. "I've always preferred men, but I like girls, too," she chattered. "Men love threesomes. With big girls. You like big girls?" She let out a gasp of pleasure as his fingers crept toward her delectables. "Bet you never get enough. Just like me."

Tucker slipped the top of his pants down. He kept his jaw tight, and lay down on top of her, bracing himself with one hand. With his other hand he dug into her shorts.

Out of the corner of her eye Laura noticed a movement from the trees. E.B!

Crack.

Her wind went out of her as Tucker fell on her chest.

"Is he dead?" she asked E.B. as she eased out from under Tucker's unconscious body. A trickle of blood eased out of Tucker's nose. She bent down to sense his breath. Not yet; she leaned closer.

He grabbed her throat and squeezed.

"Asshole," Tucker croaked. "She dies unless you give me your boat."

"Feel like killing someone. Kill me," E.B. said.

Tucker tightened his grip around Laura's throat. "Seen too many films, buddy boy?" He grinned.

Laura's eyes felt like they were being squeezed out of her head. She couldn't speak.

"My little vixen." He pulled her arm and forced her to sit next to him in the mud about six feet away from E.B. "Watch this." With his free hand, he grabbed at her breasts. "Get lost, bud."

Laura wished she had a knife.

"So you think this is a nice way to treat girls?" she croaked. "New way to make me hot?"

Tucker held her head to the ground, and with one leg forced his foot onto her throat. "Get lost, asshole."

E.B. stood back. Walked away ten feet.

"Farther. Farther. Or she doesn't breathe again today."

Laura heard E.B.'s footsteps disappear as Tucker's weight pushed down on her neck. She tried to kick him, but he was too heavy for her. He reached back to slug her. She twisted, reached around above her head, found a rock, and hit him with it. Tucker fell.

Laura rose and pounded one good blow into the asshole's face, then another and another, the rock slimy with blood, her breath heaving. Tucker still struggled a little. She could finish him off. She reached back again.

"Stop!" E.B. yelled.

"Get the fuck out of my way," she cried.

Tucker opened his eyes and stared at her, his eyes fathomless.

She held the rock over his head.

"Don't." E.B. pushed her aside. "Leave it, Laura. Have a little Christ in your heart."

"He never watched out for me before."

"But he's watching you now," E.B. said. "And he says, let it go."

Together they tied Tucker's arms behind his back, bound his feet to his hands, and roped him up good. They tied him into the good canoe and towed the leaky canoe to an island. They covered him with leaves and branches and duff so no one could see him from the water and left him in the middle of the island. Then they bashed the leaky canoe with rocks until they cracked it but good, filled it with rocks, towed it to the middle of the river, and watched it sink.

"Maybe he'll drown out here," Laura said.

"Maybe he will," E.B. said. "Maybe no one will find him until December. Maybe God is watching him too."

"Not on your life," she said.

"You're probably right," E.B. said, taking her hand.

At the water, they stood there watching the river. She was too fidgety to sit still.

"Quit worrying about me, I'm fine," she said, through tightly clenched lips. But she wasn't. She was going to have nightmares about Tucker Claymore for a very long time.

CHAPTER TWENTY-FIVE

~

Monday, afternoon
Coal Banks Landing

DAISY

*H*ey!" Daisy hollered, waving her arms over her head. "Hey! Frank! Stop! Wait!"

He flicked a cigarette out his window, skidded around the corner, and disappeared, blowing up a cloud of sand that came toward her like a scene out of *Star Wars*.

Choking on dust, Daisy turned away. Grit clung to her eyebrows and rimmed her ears. Her once-pristine white shorts were now peppered with dirt. In front of her was nothing but flat, bare ground dotted with clumps of dead brown grass. Rusty barbecues, leaning precariously on their supports, stood clustered beside chipped concrete picnic tables. A small block building with a smokestack squatted in the center of the campground, and off to the side, a trailer teetered on supports. The open door banged in the wind.

Feeling deserted, Daisy knew, just knew, that Frank had made a mistake. This certainly wasn't the Coal Banks Landing that Campbell had described. This place was a dump.

Now, she'd have to walk back to the main road and hitchhike to the proper place.

On her way, she noticed a sign, just near the entrance to the campground, set off to the side, that read "Welcome to Coal Banks Landing." She gasped.

Desperate to see someone, anyone, she clung to her handbag with one hand and clutched the handle of her duffle bag with the other, wishing she was still home, or at least back in Frank's truck heading to civilization. She ran over to the trailer, peered in to see a torn Naugahyde sofa, a sky-blue plastic chair, and a pile of dirty dishes on a counter. Yellow faded curtains drooped from the windows.

"Hello!" she yelled into nothingness, her voice echoing and hanging empty in the air. "Hey—is anyone here?" She felt like an alien. Mosquitoes and gnats buzzed in and around her ears. She tightened her grip on her handbag, stepped out of the trailer into a bright summer sun, and almost tripped on the low step just outside.

This was not at all what Campbell had promised at the Museum of Natural History where he had shown her dioramas of pronghorn antelope grazing among lush and expansive landscapes. As soon as he came in to pick her up at Coal Banks, she'd give him what for.

A twisted US flag banged from a pole, startling her. A crow called overhead, banked, and flew away. Near her feet plastic bags and aluminum beer cans skittered and hopped across dirt. Off to the side and dropping steeply toward the water was a boat ramp. Maybe he was down there. She practiced what she was going to say.

On her way over, Daisy did a mini-clean, eased her fingers

across her eyebrows, smoothed down her hair, and swept dust off the front of her red-linen camp shirt. She dug into the bottom of her purse for her favorite lipstick, Maybelline Coral Red Dream. She might not be a Saks Fifth Avenue girl, but she was no slouch either. As a receptionist at Fanflagen and Neut, she knew her way around. And this was no resort. She tapped her foot. What the hell had he been thinking?

Her sandals flapped against the scored concrete as she followed the ramp down below the level of the campground to where it buried itself into water the color of a macchiato. No Campbell, no one at all. Just marsh grass and a river, moving way too fast. She choked back tears.

Had he forgotten about her? Was she in the wrong place? Wrong time? Hadn't he said Coal Banks Landing, 2:00 p.m. Monday, and made her repeat it three times? No, she was right. He was late. Making her think it was her fault was so much like him.

She squared her shoulders, wheeled her duffle bag over gravel, and headed toward the little welcome building in the middle of the campground where she could at least get out of the wind to wait.

A black smokestack rose six feet above the roof. She stumbled on a rock, hurt her toe, cursed Campbell, entered the vestibule, and, grateful to be out of the wind, opened the door to an inside room where she expected to find a little stove and sink. Instead, she saw an open metal toilet standing in the corner. Flies circled lazily in the dim light. It stank.

"Jesus Christ!" She backed out into the vestibule and heard the whoosh and clatter of wind. She covered her head, crouched down, and tried not to cry.

This was a test. A test to see if she was tough enough to be with Campbell. After five years of sneaking around, what was she going to say? No? She could do this. No tears allowed. She stood up and marched out of the vestibule into a driving wind. Within the hour he'd come for her, and they'd have a great night, and he'd pop the question and she'd say yes. She kicked at dirt. Yes to the dirt and dust, yes to the bleak landscape. Yes, even to his daughter, Francine. Yes to everything. Yes to her new life. Yes.

She placed her duffle bag down carefully on a patch of dried grass to keep it clean, shoved her hat down, and marched back to the campground to check out the last item she had yet to explore—a large sign, set on posts, near the entrance. Posters and maps and fliers clung to the corkboard, held on with not enough rusty thumbtacks.

The words "Missouri Breaks National Monument" ran across the top of the sign. Underneath, a wiggly red line ran from left to right on a rain-streaked map. One hundred forty-nine miles with crazy names: Black Bluff Rapids, Evans Bend, Wood Bottom, Hole-in-the-Wall, Judith Landing, and Slaughter River. The river's route. Wow, it went all over everything, wiggling back on itself like the worms she'd seen in Central Park.

Below the map was a faded photo of two men in Indian buckskin jackets. The shorter guy held a pelt in his hand, the other a rifle. Lewis and Clark. Daisy smoothed the papers in place and studied them. Behind her a truck pulled into the driveway. Engrossed in thought, Daisy hadn't heard a thing.

CHAPTER TWENTY-SIX

~

Monday, afternoon
on the river

CAMPBELL AND FRANCINE

*F*ifteen miles upriver from Coal Banks Francine brushed a mosquito away from her face and frowned. "Daisy? Who's Daisy?" she asked, her face clouded.

"She's a friend of mine," Campbell said, his voice cracking. He took one look at his daughter's sweet face and didn't know what to say. Nothing would be right again.

Across the river a group of huge white pelicans with bright yellow beaks took off. They looked like something out of Francine's Curious George children's books. He wished she was young again and he was still her hero.

"Someone you know in New York?" Francine asked, pulling strong and steady in the stern. "From work?"

"Yes from New York but not from work." Campbell tried to make his voice sound lighthearted.

"Then where? At a movie? Union Square? The sushi place you keep threatening to take me to?"

"We'll go to Uncle Jack's when we get home, if you want,"

he said. "Have some mushroom and salami pizza, your favorite." Oh God, he was in for it now.

Francine was puzzled. "Known her long?"

"Well, it's not important."

"Really? Then why are you all nervous and shit? You're flitting around like a fly in a window."

"She's a nice girl." He took a few strokes. He couldn't lie to her, not anymore.

"Nice? Like girlfriend nice? Or nice like Helen, who runs your office and knows everything? Or Mom's first cousin Bertha? You're kidding, right?"

Down a long, straight stretch of river Campbell saw the blue-green tents of camp. Ten minutes away. He worked his jaws, grinding his teeth while he paddled, an old habit he used to relieve stresses beyond his control. Jesus. What an idiot he'd been. Francine didn't deserve it and neither did Daisy, who at this moment was waiting for them at Coal Banks Landing. A full day away. Alone. Where she'd spend the night, completely unprepared. At least E.B. and Laura had each other. He aimed toward a bluff of marsh grass and bumped harder than he wanted.

"Dad, don't stop here. We're almost there."

"I've got to get out," Campbell said.

"You have to go? Again?"

"No, that's not it." She knew, then? How much did she know? He glanced at his daughter, at her ponytail all jammed under the rubber band. Just the way she liked it. "Are you coming? Want to stretch your legs or something?"

"Nah, I'm okay here." She watched the river flow by between them.

Campbell couldn't remember the last time he'd seen her sit quietly like this.

An owl called, its hooting echoing across the cliffs towering overhead. Seemed to call out to him, *coward, coward, coward.*

"Enough of this shit. Come on, Dad. Get on with it. We need to get back to camp."

"Give me one more minute," he croaked. Now or never.

"Is it trouble with your heart, again?" A turtle laboriously climbed up a rock. "You have to tell me. Is it worse than we thought?"

"You like the river? Beautiful here, don't you think?" He felt terrible. "Francine, my heart is fine. It's just—I'm sure Daisy will like the river as much as you do."

"Daisy who? Your girlfriend?" She sat up suddenly. "She's coming here?"

The turtle extended his head.

"Yes."

"You're screwing her?"

Francine's little body was ramrod straight, jittery with tension.

"And it's not important? Does she know that? How does she feel when you call her nothing?"

"I didn't mean it that way."

"You say what you don't mean. You don't say what you do mean. Anyone home?"

"Francine, I'm not very good at this," he said. "And yes, she's my girlfriend."

She watched the turtle slide into the river, wishing she could disappear too.

"I thought you'd rather tell me off here than at camp."

"You think I care?"

"It was . . . I planned . . . let me explain," he stuttered. "Your mom and I weren't getting along. I was lonely."

"Too good to be true, I thought so." She dug into the ground and picked up a handful of rocks. "I knew something was up the minute you invited me."

"That's not it," he said, searching for something, anything to calm her. He needed to think, sort it all out.

"I don't want anyone else here. With us." Francine threw a rock into the river. "You're the one who said, 'This is going to be a special dad-daughter trip.'"

"I've been trying to tell you about her for weeks. Just never had time . . ."

"You shithead. You know that. You *lied* to me. If I'd known about this charade, I wouldn't have come and you knew it," she said. "Take me home."

"In a few days, I will, I promise."

"I'm not getting in a canoe with your goddamn girlfriend. I'll catch a ride at Coal Banks."

Campbell felt his stomach cave in. "It's out in the middle of nowhere. They don't have taxis. They're just truckers, farmers, there, if you can find a ride. It's a long way to Great Falls, and you can't just get in anyone's car."

"I'll find a way."

"Francine, please."

"You don't give a shit about me," she said, silent now, tears escaping their constraints, pushing over her eyelids. "You never have."

"I *always* have. I've always loved you. More than you'll ever know." Campbell struggled for words.

"Does Mom know?"

Campbell cringed. He didn't feel like answering that question. Too close to the bone. He changed the subject. "You've done nothing but push me away these last years. Always running to Grandpa's."

"For good reason. It's all about you."

"Spending time with a sullen teenager is no fun."

"Being present is what parents need to do. Teenagers aren't supposed to be fun."

"I never wanted to hurt you."

"Right." Francine's tears overwhelmed her eyes. "As if you ever gave a shit."

She stood back from him, a mere few feet away, but it was a distance that felt like a mile. Her skinny little body shook with rage. Was she right? He couldn't stand to see her hurt like this.

"I've made a terrible mistake," he whispered. What an idiot he'd been. "I am so very sorry." He stood away from her.

"When we get home, I'm moving to Mom's permanently."

"Hey, no, please don't . . . I love you, Francine," Campbell stuttered. Their evenings together were the highlight of his week. "Please. Francine, please don't do that."

"Wanna bet?" she said.

Francine moving out permanently so he could keep seeing Daisy was a no-brainer, but losing Daisy would be terrible too. He couldn't do it to either of them.

"It's not that hard, Dad. Just dump her," Francine said, leaning against a tree. "We don't need anyone else on this trip. Not with us, not now, not ever, Dad."

Campbell watched her eyes follow a butterfly skittering around the trees. If they were home, she'd run after it. If they were home, he'd be with Daisy. So now Francine knew everything. Most of it, anyway.

"Well, now, wait a moment." Campbell could see Daisy less, he supposed, but no Francine? No more Dad-daughter nights? No more having her at his side, sitting beside him on his beat-up couch, watching baseball, telling stories about the Yankees, and throwing popcorn at the screen? He couldn't bear it if he couldn't see her. That hadn't been in his grand plan at all.

"Come on, get back in the canoe, and let me think," he said. Paddling always helped him ease into his day, or what was left of it anyway. It was time they got back to camp.

Behind him he could feel Francine lengthen her strokes. That girl was not afraid of anything. At least he had taught her one thing right.

"Full balls out, Dad, only way to go."

CHAPTER TWENTY-SEVEN

✑

Monday, afternoon
Coal Banks Landing

DAISY

*D*aisy, engrossed in the history of Lewis and Clark's Voyage of Discovery, sensed something behind her. "Have you been saved?"

"Jesus Christ!" She clutched her handbag. "You scared the hell out of me." She looked up into the shadow of a tallish man, and saw a narrow, grizzled face in need of a shave. Had he seen Campbell? She wasn't sure if she wanted to talk to him at all.

"Didn't mean to startle you, ma'am." He stepped back, tipped the bill of his maroon Montana Grizzlies cap, and put out his hand. "Good afternoon. My name's Logan."

"Where'd you come from?" Daisy looked at that hand, a much stronger hand than hers, and shook it slowly. He twisted her fingers, letting go when she squirmed.

"I drove here. My little Louisa—my red truck—she's parked right behind those trees. And you? Paddled here all alone? I don't see another car—or a boat. How'd you manage?"

Daisy checked him out—early thirties, dark-brown, curly hair, chocolate eyes she could swim in, a dirty, ripped T-shirt, ratty, sun-bleached blue jeans with holes at the knees, and New Balance tennis shoes with torn, knotted laces. A pocket held cigs. Another country hick? Place was full of them. "Uh, I got a ride," she said, not really ready to make conversation. But perhaps he could help? Somehow?

"You here for the revival meeting?" he asked, sticking a toothpick in his mouth. "Lot of folks in these parts, they're kind of hesitant, but you sure got here early."

"Uh, no." Daisy frowned. She'd seen Mom go to those meetings every week, hopeful, trying to get solace, trying to get some help when she'd been so broke, and all they did was ask her for money. "I'm waiting for my . . ." she hesitated, ". . . my husband." She wasn't lying, was she? Isn't that why she came? So he could pop the question?

"What brings you to Coal Banks?" Logan asked. "What's your name?"

"Daisy," she answered, feeling a little nervous.

"Well, Daisy"—he pulled out a cigarette—"no one who's been on the river before reads that shit about Lewis and Clark." He struck a match on his jeans and lit his cigarette.

"Have you seen anyone out here? Is it always this quiet? My husband, have you seen him? Six foot and change, full head of dark hair, he was supposed to be here an hour ago."

"Nope." Logan peeled a piece of tobacco from his lip. "No one here but us chickens. Can I get you a drink? Something ice cold and refreshing?"

She felt a trickle of hesitation in her spine, the familiar shiver that Campbell had told her to ignore. Squaring her shoulders and standing tall, she followed Logan across the dusty campsite to his truck. A trailer and boat dangled off a hitch in the back.

"Louisa," Logan said and smiled. "Say hello."

Daisy heard mosquitoes zero in on her ears and face. She batted them away but not soon enough. One left a small bump on her lower eyelid that itched like crazy. "Goddamn bugs," she said, reached for her purse, and dug in. She'd forgotten her bug dope? Her Six Ways of Separation bug spray? A natural product?

She peered inside his truck with her good eye. A green cooler with a white lid stood open. Inside, ice glittered in the sun.

Logan slid one of his enormous paws into the cooler. "What's your pleasure, little lady? Coors, Corona, Bud, pop?" He pulled out a Budweiser and cracked it open. The sound of fizz broke the silence.

"Something for the bugs?" she asked, her left eye twitching.

He dug in the cab of his truck and tossed her a small plastic container.

A fanatic label reader, she eyed the small print, 100% DEET. "No natural products?" she asked, handing it back. "I'm not putting any chemicals on my skin."

"Suit yourself," he laughed and slid the container into the front pocket of his blue jeans.

A minute later, her face was clouded by mosquitoes, and her eye was almost swollen shut. Every time she blinked, it itched like crazy. "If it's no bother? Could I have it back?"

"First trip to the river?" Logan laughed and tossed her the bottle.

The bug dope was warm and had been near places she didn't want to think about. She slathered her palms, face, neck, and arms. Mosquitoes disappeared. Maybe chemicals did have a place in the world. She took a deep breath and sighed.

"Feeling a little better?" Logan asked, letting his fingers trail her hand.

She shuddered. Get it together, girl, and now. You are alone. Remember that. "I got a ride from a guy named Frank," she said quickly, wishing he was still around.

"Big guy? Local boy? Drives like a maniac? Face like a racehorse?"

"How'd you know?" Daisy asked.

"Fullback on my football team in junior high."

"Ah." Daisy didn't doubt it. He was a big lump of a man.

"Well, Daisy, how about a Corona?"

"Thank you." Beads of water clung to the ice-cold glass. She took a sip. Heaven. She eyed him over the top of her bottle. Not so bad, really, with those eyes and curly hair. Still, she wasn't sure. His off-putting sense of humor made her wary. Where the hell was Campbell when she needed him?

"Ah, the pause that refreshes." He drained his Bud. "Want another?" He threw his empty on the ground.

"That's the Coke jingle." She grinned.

"Observant little thing. So, beautiful, want another?"

"Not yet," she muttered, scuffling her feet in her now-dusty, sparkly sandals. Campbell didn't like it when she had more than one drink a day.

"My dad used to say a day goes better with beer." Logan dug into the cooler. "Shit. I better not have too many. Tucker would be pissed if I drank it all."

Daisy wrapped her fingers around the cold bottle and watched Logan pack his boat with fishing rods, boxes, and bait. Wouldn't Campbell be surprised if she found him first? He was always begging her to take some initiative. Now was her chance. "Where you heading?"

"Do you mind standing out of the way? I need to back down the ramp."

Daisy stepped toward the water.

"You waiting for a bus?" he asked. "I need more space than that, Daisy."

"I've never been on a boat before, Logan." She batted her eyes.

"Hold on, I need to find my wrench." Logan dug behind his seat.

"Maybe you didn't hear me," Daisy asked. "A ride, Logan. Take a pretty girl for a ride? How 'bout it?"

"Got it!" He tucked himself back behind the wheel, hooked his elbow out the window, and turned to look backward down the ramp.

"My boyfriend, he could be hurt. He's all alone out there on the river." She leaned into the window.

Logan kicked the engine over. A loud rumble filled the air, and he ground the gears into reverse.

Daisy hung on to the door. "Please."

"And what would he think if he got here and you were gone? He'd be one sad puppy, that's for sure."

"Then we'll find him first."

"Hey, little girl, the answer is no. I'm no Boy Scout. I'm here for a reason, to go fishing. There's supposed to be some good sturgeon out there."

"Then teach me how to fish." Daisy couldn't believe she'd just said that. She'd seen "Fishing With Frank" on the Discovery Channel with Campbell and it was disgusting.

"You got to bait your own hooks, Daisy, but tell you what. I'll clean what you catch. Deal?" Logan's eyes twinkled in the late afternoon light.

"Deal," Daisy answered. She wondered about the wisdom of getting into a boat with someone she didn't know. And who drank. On the other hand this was the second time in one afternoon she was doing something new. Campbell would be proud.

Logan backed the truck down the water, released the boat, and drove back up, the empty trailer banging and rattling all the way. Daisy watched with fascination. She could never do that. He came back, holding two fishing poles and a blue Tupperware container.

"For you," he said, tossing her a rod.

Startled, she stood back, grabbing it at the last moment. "Thanks."

"Bait!" he said proudly, holding up the container.

"I'll get my bag."

"I'll be waiting for you." He wandered back to his boat, a cheerful bounce to his stride.

Trying to convince herself she'd made the right decision, Daisy ran up the ramp to retrieve her duffle bag in the middle of the campground. It was still sitting there, on its patch of dried grass, but now it was surrounded on all sides by trucks and trailers and RVs.

In the distance, the flag popped in a breeze. The door to the trailer was propped open with a rock. The hubbub amazed her. Coal Banks had been so empty before. Now that it was heading into late afternoon, all the boaters would be coming in soon. She had to hustle if she was going to surprise Campbell before he came in.

Off to the side, she saw a canopy hung with a banner with the words "Have You Been Saved?" written in green letters on a white background. A man and a woman were setting out chairs nearby.

Daisy knew all about religion, and it was no friend of hers. She knew what would happen if they saw her.

"Going somewhere, hon?" a woman asked, standing in front of her in an enormous, flowery dress. Small blue eyes behind wire-rim glasses, open face, kind smile, brunette hair piled high on her hair with combs and a number-two Ticonderoga pencil.

The woman took a step closer and touched her arm. "Name's Berniece. What's yours?" She tightened her grip on Daisy's arm. "It's never too late to be in His hands."

"I appreciate your kindness, ma'am," Daisy said. "I'm sorry, in a bit of a hurry to go fishing." She looked around the woman, and hoped Logan was still waiting. She started toward the ramp, and the woman kept pace in her sensible shoes.

"Let me walk with you," Berniece said.

"I'm fine, really," Daisy answered.

"There's no understanding the ways of the Lord," Berniece whispered. "But I bet He doesn't want you going in that boat." She stood her ground, ample chest heaving.

Daisy narrowed her eyes. What else did this biddy know about her? Too much already. She craned her neck, trying to look down the ramp.

Berniece took a step closer. "Oh, he's still there," Berniece said, tightening her grip. "He's waiting for you. But go with him and you'll be sorry."

"Leave me alone."

Berniece panted in Daisy's ear. "You can do what you want, honey," she puffed. "It's a free country, of course."

"Damn right," Daisy said, hands on her hips. She tapped her toes. Logan was undoing the ropes between the boat and the shore.

"But before you get in that boat, it would be prudent to heed my warning," Berniece whispered. "If you go, you'll never come back."

"You're just a jealous busybody," Daisy replied. "I'm going, whatever you say."

Vroom! The engine burst to life, propeller blades churning water. Logan peered down, adjusted something.

"You'll wish you hadn't," Berniece said, her voice low.

"Get offa me!" Daisy cried and pulled away.

Down at the bottom of the ramp, the engine noise dropped to a soothing rumble.

"Hey, Logan!" Berniece yelled, her voice echoing off the distant cliffs. "You hear me, Logan? You hear me now?" She yelled louder. "Thomas at the police station told me you'd be paroled soon. Three times a charm, don't you think? Ready to take your troubles to the Lord?"

CHAPTER TWENTY-EIGHT

&

Monday, afternoon
on the river

E.B. AND LAURA

"*W*here'd you learn to handle men like that?" E.B. asked.

Laura wouldn't say. They were moving slowly, E.B. paddling, while Laura, dawdling along in the bow, barely taking a stroke. He kept talking about geographical features of the landscape, but she didn't care. Not while Tucker was still alive. Not when someone could hear him scream. He was as slippery as snot and twice as nasty. She'd never escape him just like she'd never escape that asshole Harry who was probably still waiting for her in Fort Benton. Here in the godforsaken wilderness she was a whopping big target, about to be brought down.

She'd been lucky. So far. But sooner or later she'd have to answer for her sins. She tucked her legs up to her chest and stretched her back.

"Laura?" E.B. asked. "You okay?"

"My hair's such a mess. All this wind and sun." She hoped

he'd take the hint and change the subject. He didn't need to know her history; he didn't need to know a thing about her.

What could she tell him about why she had to take self-defense classes? That she often had to walk to her car at three in the morning? That Stella was robbed at gunpoint and almost kidnapped even though she'd been armed? What it felt like to be examined, studied, eyeballed by men who moaned? How the place smelled rank?

How 'bout she tell E.B. about how customers stuffed money in her thong; the aggressive ones who snapped the nylon and tried to grab a peek, the ones who tucked in tenderly, and the others, gentle and shy, who just threw money on the stage? How much should she tell him about that? How much money she made? Or the way that money helped her buy a nice place in Brentwood? Then what would he say?

If she told him, he'd look at her as if she were dirt—except the part where she bought a house. But she wasn't pieces of things; she was all those things. Her success and dancing fit hand-in-hand like her feet in well-fitting Manolo Blahniks or Christian Louboutin high heels. Smooth as sunshine and twice as nice.

She deftly steered the bow away from a branch floating a few inches below the water, peeked under her arm back at E.B., and waved. He looked kind of cute. Endearing. Sweet. Kind of wonderful. Until he found out her history.

"What'd you do, pump iron? Pull cars with your teeth?"

"I work out at a gym five days a week. Sometimes more." She laughed. That much was true. Worked out to the point of tears, of throwing up. All the girls did, but she did it more.

She could tell him that, at least. Her shoulders hurt. The fight with Tucker had taken it out of her.

"Bet you can bench-press one hundred and fifty pounds."

"Not quite. I took a couple of self-defense classes from this guy. It was no big deal," she muttered. "Think it's going to rain?"

The silence between them was something she could hide in.

She took a few strokes. Big deal? Those fights with Tucker were a huge deal. She flicked a mosquito off her knee. She heard her instructor Sifu Lee's voice in her head. "Work on your hitting," he used to say, "harder, harder." Was that hard enough, Sifu? I knocked him silly. She wanted to thank him and tell him he was right, but he could have taught her more. She dropped her hand into the river. She needed to dip her feet in there too; they hurt.

"Women around here—they don't beat up men," E.B. said.

He sounded worried. Like wondering what kind of woman she was.

"I'm not a friggin' Amazon, if that's what you're worried about. LA's a tough place to live—and to work." She heard a whoosh. A bunch of birds, bigger than the sky, rushed over her head. "Quick. Cover your head. They'll poop on us." She ducked.

"Those are eagles, bald eagles. Ever seen one? Don't hide."

She could hear the smile in his voice.

Laura peered up into the brilliant blue sky. "Jesus. They must be six feet, wing to wing."

"River's full of them."

"Beautiful white heads and black wings. Hey—did you see that? With a smidge of yellow at the tips of their beaks. Like makeup. And they're not bald at all. Who would've known?"

"Exactly."

"When did we start on this trip? That was . . . just yesterday? This place is—I've never been anywhere like this before, 'cept Griffith Park, but that's in LA. You can drive there."

"Thought the river would grow on you," E.B. said, taking a long stroke.

Laura watched one of the eagles soar and land in the top of a dead tree. She wondered if it had a nest there and whether it was full of chicks. What would it be like when they took their first flight . . . would they feel the same way she felt on the river? When they dropped and suddenly took flight? Or would they just fall?

Behind her, E.B. felt like he'd just started the trip. There was never enough time. He wanted days, weeks, months. With the river. With her. He wanted to remind her that she hadn't wanted to come at first, but that seemed harsh. Telling her how beautiful she was, how capable and vulnerable and wonderful and different, was too scary, even for a big guy like him.

"Hey, watch out. You're steering us into the reeds."

With a deep stroke, E.B aimed them away from the marsh and toward the center of the river again. He'd been staring at her again. Lost someplace he hadn't visited in a very long time. He wondered how he could get closer to her.

He was a little afraid of her, of her power. Laura was stronger than Ms. Fitzhugh, the girls' coach at Loma High, who looked like a semi, bench-pressed two hundred pounds, and made all the boys jealous.

He let the canoe glide toward shore. They had an hour or two before Hole-in-the-Wall campground, where he thought the others would probably be waiting. It was a big spot with a broad view of the river. Campbell would be pacing and nuts with worry, but after all this time he could wait a little longer. E.B. couldn't hurry, not now. Not when he was with *her*.

They pulled up on the sandy shore, sat down, and he slid his eyes over in her direction, then looked away.

He'd seen those women with their kung fu moves on TV, but what he couldn't figure out was how Laura had managed to subdue Tucker twice. She sure didn't look that strong. "Laura, you thirsty? Comfortable? Need anything? Feeling all right?"

"Fine, for the moment, yes."

To Laura, E.B. had an easy way to him, a solidness, something she'd never seen amongst those sleazy men in LA. Going home in a few days was going to be hard. She didn't want to change their fragile peace, the tingle she was starting to feel when he was near.

"You paddle well now. You're a quick learner," E.B. said.

"Thanks." She looked at her dusty toes in her flip-flops that had gone through so much with her on the river; she was amazed she still had Beth Ann's little shoes.

"You live in Hollywood? Beverly Hills? Beautiful downtown Burbank?"

"Heavens, no. Brentwood." She peered at the river below, moving steady, the color of a macchiato. Her favorite drink.

He followed her eyes. "In winter, when it's forty below, when you walk on the snow, it crackles like Styrofoam."

"What makes you so blue?" Reading men's faces was easy, falling in love with them was hard.

E.B. smiled awkwardly. "I'm all right."

"Not just a bad harvest, then?"

"What brought you to the river?"

Tell him about Harry and his thugs? Hell, no. "I needed a change. A guy told me about the big skies in Montana." That much was true. "I came to Great Falls. And then Campbell—he was very persuasive." So were Mike and Harry, she thought. "Campbell said you needed a partner. I didn't know what to expect." She laughed. "What makes you happy, E.B.?"

"Happy?"

"I thought so. You're the saddest person I've ever met."

His struggle for words touched her heart.

"It's a ton of work to run a ranch," he said finally. "Your work, does it take a special skill?"

"You've got to do something in the winter, aside from stare at the walls, I bet. I saw a ton of churches on my way over from Great Falls. You one of those fundamentalists, Holy Rollers? Speak in tongues?" she asked.

"Me, no. Never been my style."

His face clouded. She'd hit a sore spot.

"Does performing make you nervous?"

"I bet you were an altar boy, always kissing up. Cute."

"Presbyterians don't have altar boys," E.B. said. "I was just asking. I'm not judging you."

"That's what they all say."

"Must be hard, every night, performing sometimes when you just don't feel like it."

"I talk too much. My best friend Stella always says so." She spun on her heels. "It's a job, E.B., just a job."

"But you never told me what kind of performer."

"Does it matter?"

He gestured for her to climb in the canoe. "Not really."

"So you understand."

"Yeah, of course. If you don't want to tell me, it's okay."

Everybody in LA understood. Why would a country hick mind? Maybe he was all right, after all. "Then why do you keep asking?"

"Just forget it . . ." E.B. said. "Let's just go. Campbell has got to be crazy with worry."

"Well then, E.B., I'm a pole dancer, best dancer in downtown Burbank." She grinned.

"I figured something like that . . . with . . . your . . ."

"With my what?"

"Good looks," he stumbled.

Laura knew better. She knew what was coming.

"Is it difficult? I've never been, but guys say . . . You wear anything?"

"Of course. More interesting in what I do wear. I always have *something* on. Pasties, my butterfly thong. And my Christian Louboutin Lady Page pumps. Real classy shoes. Expensive."

"Does your mother know?"

"I support her. What do you think?" She paced the shore. "What part don't you like? Five hundred dollars a night? Make that much a day? Didn't think so. My body? That's your problem." She climbed away from him, stood very still, and hooked her fingers under the bottom of Beth Ann's top. "You want to see your problem? Supported me since I was fifteen when my father left. If you had these, would you be ashamed?"

"No, no, please don't." E.B. covered his face with his hands.

She lifted her shirt up to her elbows. "It takes work for this body. People pay good money. Hey E.B. Here's a look— for free."

"Please, don't." He backed up. "I'm so sorry."

"Stared you down, didn't I? Got special skills, don't I? What about you? If I had wanted to tell you, I would have. And you dare judge me. I thought you were different." Suddenly she climbed into the boat and pushed off.

E.B. stood, stunned. By the time he came to his senses, she was twenty feet from shore, moving away fast.

"Wait! I screwed up. Laura!"

He dove in, heard nothing but the beat of his own heart, and kicked hard, then harder. When he came up for air, she was forty feet away. He had to reach her before she gained the center of the current and was gone. He swam hard, forgetting about his breathing, giving it his all, kicking and stroking as fast as he could. When he heard the scrape of a paddle on the hull, he popped up just below the boat and slowed her down. He slid his hands up until his head was above water.

"Hey, you, you with stars in your eyes," he gasped. He draped one hand over the bow. "Stick around. Come on, be reasonable."

"Will wonders never cease." Laura splashed him. "Find out what I do for a living, then, boom, you think I'm a hooker."

"Let me get in the boat." Hand over hand, he moved down the hull until he was opposite her. He leaned down on it and almost tipped it over. "Water's warm," he said, tipping the canoe a little more.

"Let go! You're going to dump me!" She leaned back and raised her paddle.

He tightened his grip and pushed down harder. The top of the gunwale kissed the water. "Go ahead. Hit me, if you like. I'm a good target. Unless you'd like to come in? We both could use a bath."

"I've already been in today, or don't you remember when I saved you?"

The current moved both of them downriver fast.

"Give it up, E.B." She paddled over and over, not giving in.

"Then you'll forgive me?" he asked, spitting water. Waves broke over his face, but he held on. The sun grazed the hills opposite, painting them rose.

"You're a nuisance, Ezra Benson."

"You could say that again," he said. Pulling the canoe, he swam toward a muddy bank. Thirty feet away and closing fast.

He felt something soft under his Tevas. He stepped into knee-high water and sank up to his thighs. Pulled the canoe closer.

"And what do you want now, river monster?"

"You. C'mon, get out a minute."

"No."

He tucked the top of the hull under his arm.

"So you can swim. Good for you."

"I couldn't care less about what you do for a living." What would Mom say? Not if she met Laura, not if she saw what he saw.

E.B. could feel the warmth of her body, the touch of her skin, the beat of her heart. He looked at her and imagined holding her. God's little sense of humor was working over-time today. He moved in closer, breathing in her scent. "I care about you, Laura."

"Right. As if." Dad used to say that when she was five, and disappeared when she'd been ten. Had Stella been right? That there was someone out there? The right one?

He reached out and touched her arm with his muddy fingers. A rivulet of mud ran down her hand, staining her leg and dribbling on her toes. She gazed at globs of mud on the nail polish on her toes.

"So?" she asked.

He rubbed her arm with the back of his hand. "Want more? I've got plenty." He leaned into the canoe.

"No. Not now! You're all muddy!"

"All the better." E.B. got up on one knee and climbed in, mud and water streaming off his body, his hair plastered over his forehead, eyes closed for a kiss.

"Don't even try it. E.B.! No! Stop!" She pushed him back, mud sliming her hand.

"Can't stop me now."

"Wanna bet?" She dabbed a dot of mud on his forehead, marking him.

Without another word he leaned forward and kissed her.

CHAPTER TWENTY-NINE

Monday, afternoon
Coal Banks Landing

DAISY

"Go back to church where you belong, Berniece!" Logan yelled. He turned back to Daisy with a smile. "You coming, honey?"

Daisy's resolve was dissolving. Berniece seemed so sure of herself, but religious people were like that. So who was the better risk, the lunatic fat lady or the man in the dirty T-shirt and ragged blue jeans? Neither.

She threw back her shoulders, pivoted her duffel behind her, and headed for the shade of a tree that overlooked the river.

Logan motored away.

Damn him, and damn that big fat lady. It would have been great to see Campbell so surprised. Take the initiative indeed. Damn them all.

It was about four. The slight breeze earlier in the day had built to a stronger wind that flicked leaves over her head and tossed twigs onto the ground. Families and children called to each other over the crowded, busy campground.

Daisy scanned the river, the boat ramp, and started asking other canoeists about Campbell. No, no one had seen a man six feet, with sandy hair in a group like his. She went back to her post, ahead of the campground, on a little spit of land. There, she'd see him first as he rounded the bend. She waited for hours as shadows crossed the canyon walls and made their way slowly down to the water.

When the last canoe came in after 7:00 p.m., it was downright chilly. Daisy paced, trying to keep blood moving, her fingers and toes stiff and cold. Dusk dropped like a shroud. Campers lit lanterns while children turned on flashlights and giggled by firelight. Daisy tucked her little sweater around her and shivered. "I'll take care of everything, sweetheart," Campbell had said back in New York. Even the damn toilet shelter would be better than this. Daisy paced the shore, trying to stay warm, looked at the little families fifty feet away, and her heart just caved.

Over the sound of the wind, she heard a man singing, and concentrated. Yes. It was the same one! "I've Touched the Hem of His Garment," that old hymn from Mom's church choir! It felt as familiar as her favorite sweater. Mom!

Daisy, torn, wandered toward the sound. It was the most comforting thing she'd heard all day. She found a small gathering singing "Come, Ye People, Come," and walked up close enough to see them. She hid behind some trees.

Children and adults were praying over a table covered with plates of blackened hot dogs, baked beans, buns, bowls of pickles, and potato chips. Oh God. She was so hungry. Something caught on her ankle. She lifted a paper and glanced at its headline, which was hard to make out in the twilight. "Have you been saved?"

She balled up the flimsy paper and allowed the wind to take it away. Religion hadn't been Daisy's savior; it had been her ruin. In her senior year of high school, Mom had donated her college fund to the church. Pissed off and unable to control her anger, Daisy had taken up collecting butterflies. Driving pins through their crunchy bodies was deeply satisfying, even though it made her high school friends wince.

Now, she returned to her spot beside a tree, by the bluff again, near the river, and kept her eye on some butterflies flicking around a bush. One of these days she'd show Campbell her collection. He'd be proud. She had forty-eight boxes tucked in the back of her closet.

Trying to cheer herself up, she practiced what she was going to say when he popped the question. How long should she make him wait before she said yes? Five minutes, ten? Make him squirm? An hour? She worked out his every move, the twinkle of his eye, the slow smile crossing his face when she'd say yes.

"What are you doing over here in the bushes?" a woman asked.

Daisy jumped a mile.

"You all right, honey?"

In the flickering shadows from a smoldering fire, Daisy couldn't see who it was at first. Someone large, wearing a long coat with big red buttons.

"Don't be scared. It's just me, Berniece."

"I'm fine," Daisy sputtered.

"I'm so glad you didn't go out with that Logan." Berniece

clucked her tongue. "It's cold and lonely out here, Daisy. Want to join us in the revival tent?"

"Me? No." Daisy backed up. Mom had ended up in a mental hospital from talking to people like this.

"Hungry? Thirsty?"

"No." Daisy paused a moment. "No, thank you."

"It's just us girls. Me and Marcy. We'd love to have your company."

"Can't. Sorry. I'm waiting for someone." Daisy stuffed her hands into the pockets of her sweater.

"Marcy and I—we've been worried about you." Berniece smiled. "Wait with us. You must be freezing. Honey, whoever he is, he's not coming now."

Daisy felt like Berniece was walking inside her head. "Leave me alone."

"You got a tent? Marcy says you're all right, but I can't stand to see someone suffer. The Lord God, He doesn't want anyone to suffer either, sweetheart."

Daisy stepped to the edge of a campsite. Behind her, flames crackled and sparked as someone threw a log on the fire. Weren't there any cops or rangers out here to keep this lunatic from bothering her? "I'm not your sweetheart," she said, her voice faltering.

"But you're God's and He cares for you and He loves you."

"To take me to the promised land! Yes!" Daisy hissed. "But not now," she said, her mouth taut, her voice a rasp. "I'm not ready."

Berniece's face fell.

"Now, would you mind?" The last time she'd seen Mom, it was at the mental hospital, where she was working a rosary, while the Ativan made her forget Daisy had even been there.

"The Lord God works in mysterious ways," Berniece murmured. "Honey, you'll be with us tonight, somehow, I just know it. Lost lambs always run at first, until they learn to follow the shepherd. You'll be much happier. I promise. God will take good care of you, you'll see."

"I'm not a lost lamb. I'm fine on my own!" Daisy yelled back. She knew Berniece was lying. Her back hurt and her legs were stiff and freezing. Campbell was nowhere in sight, and she hadn't had anything to eat since that goddamn two-day-old muffin at Kennedy airport.

"It's my nature, I guess," Berniece cooed. "Cornelius says. Everyone needs the Lord sometime."

"Oh, bunk."

"Cornelius thinks he has to work hard to earn a place in heaven," Berniece explained. "But I don't think so. God's already reserved a place for him."

Behind her, Daisy could hear chicken crackle on a barbecue and smelled hickory as it sizzled and popped. Oh God, I've got to stay strong. She willed her backbone to stay straight. "No thanks," she said, her voice weak. Is this the way it started for Mom too?

"My mission is to save souls. And yours needs saving. I can tell."

"Can't you see? The preacher is waving to you." Daisy squinted in the dark. She couldn't see diddly-squat. Wouldn't recognize Campbell if he stood right next to her. Where was he? Drowned? Lost? This was no time for her to lounge around and eat.

"Owe no man anything but to love one another: for he

that loveth another hath fulfilled the law. Romans thirteen-eight," Berniece intoned.

Daisy stood straight. She hadn't gone to church all those months for nothing. "Blessed are those who hunger and thirst for righteousness, for they will be filled. Matthew five-six," she recited and watched Berniece's eyes grow wide.

"If anyone thirst, let him come to me and drink. John seven-seventeen," Berniece said with a smile.

"The end of all things is near," Daisy grinned. "Therefore be clear minded and self-controlled so that you can pray. One Peter four-seven."

Berniece backed up, her mouth contorted. "You don't have to. I mean, I was just trying to help."

"Better start praying. Now." Mom's training had come in handy after all. Daisy thought of other verses; she knew so many.

The fat lady left.

CHAPTER THIRTY

~

Monday, late afternoon
land

CAMPBELL AND FRANCINE

"You've still got that cruel streak, Francine," Campbell said. "Knock it off."

"This is like *Groundhog Day*, Dad. You know, like the guy had to wake up literally, like, fifty times acting like an asshole until he finally figured it out?"

"Chill out." He hoped he could get her back before they returned to New York.

"As if. Whatever." She slammed her paddle on the water.

"You don't have to be that way," he said.

Six baby birds paddled like hell after their mother, who was heading into the grass. Would the mother ever wait for them? "Just drift, please, Francine, give me a sec." A sec to gather his thoughts, a sec to get his heart beating normally again. He took a deep breath, then launched into new and unexpected territory. "Look," he turned around, faced her. "Daisy is my business, not yours."

"Be that way. See if I care."

"You asked me to spend more time with you. I will." He took another breath. "You told me that I've been less than thoughtful about inviting her without asking you first." So far so good. "That was the wrong thing to do."

"Less than thoughtful? You think?" Francine spat. "You dissed me, Dad."

"Yes, I did." He took a long stroke and watched the water flow off his blade. "Now, would you be so kind as to listen for a few minutes?"

"More shit about Daisy?"

"No."

She placed her paddle across her lap. "I'm here."

"So." Campbell hoped he could bring her around. He pulled them into some rushes and held on to the tall grass. "Do you remember when you were little and I had to teach you how to cross the street?"

"I'm gonna drive next year. Get a grip."

"Yes, of course, I knew that." Where did the time go?

"And?"

"Growing up so fast. Too fast."

"It happens." Francine's voice was sharp. "What did you expect?"

"So, soon you'll be going on dates." He watched a duck land across the river and slid his eyes over to Francine, hoping he was on solid ground.

"Me? Someone's going to want to go out with me?"

"You bet." Campbell moved carefully onto a log. "Of course they will."

Francine turned aside. No one would want to go out with her, of course. Her world of horses, Descartes, and Grandpa was just too weird. She wasn't even pretty, not like the other girls. Not like Hannah. All the boys wanted to go out with her. "As if." Francine stared at her hands, then started picking at one of her fingernails, still caked with mud, short and stubby, just like she was.

"They will. Because you're beautiful."

Francine blushed. Too much time with Dad and she was going soft. Still.

"So let's make a deal."

"Like Hannah's father? He's going to buy her a car when she turns sixteen?" Francine grinned. "A sixty-six Camaro would be good, fire-engine red." She hummed a little. "Glass packs."

"Not that kind of deal."

"Ah, c'mon, I already know how to drive."

"No. Stop chattering about a car."

"What kind of deal?" She narrowed her eyes.

"If you go out on dates, can I go on dates too?"

"This is a trick question. And if no one asks me out?"

"Then I stay home with you. I always loved watching ballgames and *Friends* reruns with you. But I'll bet you'll be going out."

"That's a stupid sitcom. I always told you I hated it."

"Something else, then. I don't care. We'll make a bet. Grandpa taught you how to bet, didn't he? Ten bucks?"

She shook her head.

"No? Twenty?"

Francine looked down at her skimpy chest. No bet was going to make any guy like her.

"All right, let's talk real money. A hundred bucks? You can spend it on whatever you like."

Hm. This was starting to get interesting. "Maybe." She could use a hundred toward a new iPhone.

"So, okay, that's settled. But our deal—there's more to it."

"What more? Two hundred?" This was getting better by the minute.

"Nope. Something different." He folded his hands together. "You want to do something with me? Say, a weekend in the Pine Barrens?"

"I've been there and I ride alone."

"I can learn."

"To ride horses? With me and the guy? That's just too weird. Unless you want to buy another horse? I know a nice colt, fifteen hands, needs just a little training."

"No, we don't need another horse. And no, I wasn't going to spoil your fun."

"Then what?"

"This is the deal. You have a date, I have a date. I've made mistakes. And so have you . . ."

Francine ignored the last part. But the first? She wasn't sure who this guy was. He looked like Dad, he sounded like Dad, but he wasn't the same. "You've made mistakes? You think?"

"Uh-huh." He placed his hand on her arm.

She frowned. She'd been stellar. Well. Mostly. She looked at him. This was new ground for both of them, worth a shot.

"But we start over. You want your old man around, I'll be around. And that's a promise." He thrummed his fingers on his paddle. "And if you're busy, I still have a life. Deal?"

Francine mused. "Daisy's not going to be so happy, being second." She slid some wisps of hair off her forehead. "No matter what, you're still not putting her sorry ass in our canoe."

"Not if you don't want to." He placed his hands on his knees. "We have three more days on the river. Down to Judith Landing. You can paddle with me, or I can get you a solo canoe. You don't have to be in the same boat, or even the same tent, or the same campfire, or the same anything with her."

"As if I'd ever allow any of that." Francine wasn't altogether sure, but somehow she felt better.

"If I want to see her, I will, but she will be second, as you requested." He shifted closer to her. "Okay?"

"Easy, Dad, easy." Francine waved him away. "You're embarrassing me." Her eyes were watery—too much sun? Sunscreen? She pulled out her shirt ends. Man, where did all this water come from?

"Deal?" he asked. He lifted his paddle. "What do you say?"

"Let's get a move on, Dad. It's getting late. And yes, we have a deal."

They pushed off from the reeds. Campbell dug in, his strokes strong and sure. He was smiling. She knew it. He always went faster when he was happy.

⌒

CHAPTER THIRTY-ONE

Monday, late afternoon
land

E.B. AND LAURA

S till feeling the softness of that kiss, E.B. reached for Laura and felt only air. He opened his eyes. She was sitting at the opposite end of a log.

"Enjoying the day?" he asked, tongue-tied. "What are you doing over there? You don't like guys who are soaking wet?" He moved a little closer.

"Good thing it's a warm day, huh," she said, eyeing him and sliding a bit farther away.

What would she say next, *it's not you, it's me?* Was it that he needed a shower? "Everything okay?" He didn't think he stunk that bad.

"Don't you think we should get going? We haven't seen Campbell since yesterday."

Crushed, E.B. thought he had been doing pretty well. Considering. Considering, what? That he had the manners of a country boy? Had he forgotten something? He'd been polite and thoughtful and taken his time. She'd been giving him signals all day. Was he that dense?

"No, I'm fine. Just a little tired, that's all."

"I bet." Couldn't be. He had had that feeling. That great feeling.

"How 'bout a drink? You thirsty? Hungry? Cold?" He was babbling, but he didn't know what else to do. The day after tomorrow she'd head home to Great Falls or LA or East Podunk, or some such godforsaken place.

"I know, I just know there's someone's hand in it," she said suddenly.

"Someone's hand? Whose hand?" Had he missed a step? "In what?"

"It's beautiful here, don't you think? I bet you don't even notice. The best views are wasted on people who don't even bother to look."

"But I do," E.B. answered, trying to look at the hills in the distance, but his eyes kept drifting to her. A hand in it, indeed. He'd pray again, if that was what it took. Thank God for *that* view. He liked that part about no other humans in sight. He scooched closer.

Then he remembered. Oh God. He was a married man. What if Berniece was back at home, in the kitchen, a spatula in her hand, her white apron flour-dusted, a large pot of stew simmering on the stove? What would she say? Are you dreaming? Sun get to you? You, a Montana farm boy, with someone like that? Get real.

Was he mad?

"Being out here, doesn't it make you want to believe in something bigger than yourself?" Laura asked.

"Uh, uh," E.B. answered, tongue-tied. "All I know is my tractor, winter wheat, summer wheat, the weather, uh, oil changes, spark plugs, you know, stuff," he lied. In December, on the darkest day of the year, probably in the middle of a blinding blizzard, he'd remember this fine summer day and the way her hair flew in the breeze. Even if that kiss had been a mistake, she'd returned it. Or maybe she did that with all the guys she met?

He leaned back on his elbow, admired the line of her chin, her blue eyes, the body he couldn't help from wanting. Then he told himself, no, not for me. Not for this farm boy.

"The cliffs rise like a dream from the river. It looks as if a majestic hand brought them there, carved out of earth. And it's so quiet."

"I guess. Never thought about the land in that way." What a liar. What would Mom say? Shame on you. The land had his blood in it, his grandparents, his soul, his faith every spring when he worked it with his tractor and prayed for a good crop.

"My brother says it helps him to pray," Laura said, "but I don't. How 'bout you?"

E.B. was silent. He used to enjoy the feeling of being part of something whole. Once.

"You know, pray?" she asked.

"Pray? Don't know how," he muttered. Shut up, you fool, he told himself. Don't spoil this dream.

Laura stretched her legs.

E.B. tried not to tremble. Or moan.

"There are so many churches here. I saw them along the road from Great Falls. And announcements about revival meetings. Religious country, not at all like LA." She eyed the shore. "I'd think, to you, God would be a comfort—with the weather and all."

E.B. searched for a way to change the subject. Baseball? Fashion? Life in LA? All that was anathema to him.

She sat up. "Oh come on. You must've been involved in church at some point."

"I never said I wasn't."

He looked at the moon peeking through the trees. He knew only too well that feeling of belonging to something bigger than himself, and he missed it. Even on those twenty-below days when they bundled up and went to church and he just wanted to stay in bed. "God doesn't take vacation, why should we?" he'd say to Berniece. Now, he knew better.

"Most farmers are fools." He pitched a few pebbles into the river. "They think they can go out drinking every Saturday night, and on Sundays dress in their best, wipe their boots by the front door of the church, and be saved." Some farmer's wives too, he thought bitterly. Damn you, Berniece. He stood up and paced under the shade of a cottonwood tree. Blossoms drifted onto his arms and onto Laura's shoulders. She looked like she was wearing a wedding dress.

"What's the matter with you? Don't you like the land? Can't you see what I mean?"

"I couldn't say."

"Bunk. You're making that frown again. Didn't you grow up with faith? Churchgoing Christian? I bet you are. Or were."

"I couldn't say." Of course he could. He had planted deep, prayed, kneeled, spent nights out here, on his horse Tessa, for days, talking to God. It wasn't the talking about God he minded. It was the other. It was that goddamn preacher who destroyed his family. He threw rocks into the water.

"Hey, you're splashing me," Laura said. "I didn't do anything to you."

"You asked. So I'm telling you." He threw a rock at a tree, heard a resounding thunk. "Around here, everyone's religious—from great-grandparents down to pesky two-year-olds. Religion is born in you, fed to you like mother's milk, from your first day to your last."

"I knew it."

He picked up a blade of grass, chewed on it, and let the wind blow it away.

"You must have been lonely since you left the church," she said.

"Lonely? Not really." Lonely as hell. Lonely in that big house, no other voices breaking the silence that crawled over him like a bunch of ants and never went away. He wasn't going to tell *her* that. Hell no.

"When I was a boy, I didn't know any different. I loved stroking the smooth pews on a warm day, watching flies make squares in the air, seeing sunlight streaming through the windows, and I would fall asleep during the sermons sometimes, while outside it was so cold and the wind blew a hundred miles an hour. Learned a few things, I guess. Gave comfort." God, if this is a test, I'm failing.

"Doesn't sound so bad to me, I've never had that."

"Well, it was."

"Then why do you look so sad?"

He paused a moment, disarmed by her comment. "We . . ." he stopped. "We did what we were supposed to do."

"We? Who's we?"

"Church dinners, Scout suppers, Bible meetings, choir—endless events helping the elderly, the homeless, the children. All good things. Always cooking. We, she . . . always cooking, always involved." Once he started he couldn't stop.

"She?" Laura whispered. "You mean like church ladies? Your mother? Aunt? Sister?"

He marched back and forth. "I did my part, Laura." His voice was clear and cold. "And it was nothing. Not worth a damn."

"Girlfriend? Wife?" she asked, her voice quiet.

"Because then we got a new preacher." E.B. paced. "Stanley Cornelius the third. He got the congregation all riled up. We're Lutherans, for God's sake! Not used to that kind of thing. Neighbors, best friends, pillars of the community jumped up, fell down, waved their arms over their heads, and cried like babies. 'It's the rapture!' some of them said. 'It's a gift from heaven! God's finally listening!' Even the old men with gnarly hands and curled-up backs, those old guys had tears running down their faces."

"Like those Pentecostal preachers—like on TV? Like the one who's coming here?"

"She left." E.B. took a breath. "One day she made a tuna-noodle casserole for a church dinner, packed a case of fresh chokecherry jam in the back of her Buick, and took off."

"Your girlfriend?" Laura asked.

"'I'm joining the preacher,' she said. I never saw it coming." He threw his paddle into the canoe. "Let's go."

"That preacher—he must be something."

"You'll have to ask her. She was—I mean—is, my *wife*. She's the one who ran off with the preacher. My wife. Berniece."

CHAPTER THIRTY-TWO

⌒

Monday, evening
Coal Banks Landing

DAISY

nce the sun went down, a chill settled over Coal Banks Landing that Daisy couldn't shake. The cold seemed to delve into her bones and settle there. She crouched down behind some bushes and trees, hoping to get some shelter, but now the bushes and trees were alive with the sounds of frogs croaking, twigs snapping, and animals moving. She hoped they were small.

On the other side of the bushes, Daisy heard mothers call for their children, the clink of barbecues and coolers being put away, and families getting ready for bed. She wanted to be with them, to be home again, back when Mom was all right, back when she used to tuck her in, her soft kiss bright by Daisy's cheek, the hall light on all night. Now she was all alone. Campbell wasn't coming now, tonight or maybe never. She held back tears.

Another hour went by. She wrapped herself up in a little ball, as tight as she could get. Her feet were freezing, her rear end had gone numb, and her fingers, clenched around her legs, had frozen up on her. She was sure she was going to die and no one would ever know.

Something howled, a deep wail that echoed across the canyon walls. Whatever it was, it was coming into camp, and she'd be the first to go. She cried helplessly, loud, convulsing sobs. Her voice rose with a wail. She tried to muffle it and buried her face in her hands.

A few minutes later, she heard footsteps close by and stayed very still.

"You okay, honey?" someone asked. "You don't sound so good."

Daisy kept her head down.

"You can't stay out here. You got that blanket, Marcy?"

Someone, another woman, wrapped a blanket around Daisy's shoulders and cooed, "Poor, poor thing. Out here alone, no coat, no nothing. "What's your name, dear?"

Daisy wasn't going to say. Warmth enveloped her body, whether from the blanket or the people, she didn't know or care. Strangers' hands tucked the blanket around her.

"You think you can walk?" the first woman asked, and Daisy, stiff with cold, tried to straighten her legs. Strong arms, on both sides, helped her up. Stones and twigs dug into her bare feet.

"My shoes," she said, her voice cracking. Hands surrounded her and slipped on her shoes.

"Lift your feet, great, it's bumpy, careful, stop, left, good."

"She's nearly frozen to death, poor thing."

A few minutes later, Daisy sat in a camp chair near a warm fire in the campground, a cup of hot tea in her hand.

Three faces surrounded her—a tall, thin man in a dark coat, a thin woman, and Berniece.

"Hi, Daisy," she said.

Daisy nearly spilled her tea.

"Berniece, Marcy, make up some more hot soup," the man said. "You're half-dead, child." He came over and whispered in her ear. "Don't worry. We aren't going to hurt you." His voice was soothing, like honey, or warm maple syrup on a cold day.

"What time is it?" Daisy croaked.

"Midnight, I think. We're glad to have you with us. You remember me?" Berniece asked.

Daisy stared into her tea. "Yes." She wasn't going to tell them anything.

"Better now? Want something else? Some soup?"

"Yes, please." Daisy's stomach ached with hunger. She'd be careful with this bunch, have something to eat, and disappear, though where, she had no idea.

The man tended the fire, breaking up the logs with a stick, making hot coals sizzle and pop, mesmerizing her.

"Time to go in, dear," one of the women said a few minutes later, beckoning Daisy like a close friend.

"I'm not sure." Daisy looked from one to the other in the dying light from the fire.

"You have those biscuits ready, Berniece?" the woman called out. Twenty feet away, bright lights poured out from an RV.

Biscuits?

"My goodness, Daisy, I haven't properly introduced myself. I'm Marcy. I'll help you every step of the way. Need a hand?"

"Yes, please, I'm starved." Just like Mom's biddies at her church suppers. She didn't have to believe to eat, did she? She stepped up onto a milk crate, took Marcy's hand, and was soon inside.

The RV held two bunks and a small galley kitchen. Faded sky-blue curtains drooped from the windows. Two thick red wool blankets were stacked on a settee.

"Come along in, little sister," Berniece intoned. "We're all friends here." A pot of chicken soup simmered on the stove.

Daisy took a seat on one of the settees and eyed the stove.

"Just us girls here, honey." Berniece gestured to Marcy, who was plumping pillows. "How 'bout some soup?"

"And put out some biscuits, Berniece," Marcy said.

"Oh God, yes, please." Daisy took a bowl, inhaled the aroma, and took a sip, trying not to slurp. As if. She'd down the whole thing in one gulp if it weren't so hot.

The man stepped inside. He was wearing an old-fashioned frock coat with worn silk lapels, a bow tie, and scuffed black shoes. A preacher, Daisy thought, just like at home. He went to shut the door, but Berniece put up her hand.

"Not yet," she said.

He stepped back out.

Daisy felt relieved. At home, she avoided clubs and groups and gatherings for the same reason. She sipped her soup hurriedly.

"Where are you from?" she asked, trying to fill the silence.

"We'll make introductions after. That all right with you, Daisy?" Marcy slid onto her knees beside her.

Berniece and Marcy nodded and muttered beside Daisy.

"It's okay, sweetheart." Marcy smelled like roses.

Daisy was eyeing biscuits cooling on the stove, when the man stepped back inside.

"Douse the lights, Berniece, and light the candles. God wants to welcome this new child in His own way," the preacher said, his deep brown eyes staring into Daisy's.

Well, heck, she'd been through this before. In tenth grade. Some kind of ceremony with Mom. Right after, she'd caught a train to Park Slope, and spent the afternoon fooling around with Conrad.

"Okay," Daisy replied, wondering whatever had happened to Conrad. Hadn't he joined the marines?

"You'll never be in our way, sister." The preacher straightened his tie.

"Didn't say I was," Daisy said. Before, with Mom, she'd pretended she was somewhere else. That took concentration. She closed her eyes. Conrad's place had been nice.

"You were out there for quite a long while, alone," Berniece said.

Yeah, but that was before. Before she got the heebie-jeebies, before she almost froze to death. Jesus, didn't they have any more soup? She held out her bowl.

"The girls told me you didn't have a jacket or a tent. Good thing we found you." The preacher sat down too close to her.

"I've always loved chicken soup." Daisy scooched down the settee, hoping not to offend. Ah, a fresh bowl. She hummed. The women at Mom's church were the same way, courteous and not insistent. It used to make Mom happy that Daisy came to church at all.

But in the middle of the night, Mom used to pace the house, worrying her. "I just don't think you're completely with us, girl," she used to say. Daisy sure as hell wasn't going to tell her about Conrad and what they did Sunday afternoons in Park Slope. That was when she decided to hold Mom's hand during the sermons and started memorizing gospel. And telling Mom how much she loved the Lord.

The preacher draped a scarf over Daisy's neck. For the first time in hours, she was warm. Even so, she kept her eye on the open door. She wished she knew where Campbell was. Was he safe out there on the river? If only she knew.

"Roll out the prayer rug, Berniece." The preacher took Daisy's cold hands in his warm ones, making her tingle. Oh God, how she missed Campbell. She closed her eyes.

When she opened them, the RV was bathed in soft light from six pillar candles, flames sputtering from the breeze from the open door. She sat up, letting her eyes rest on the preacher. His soft brown eyes tended hers, caressed them, enveloped them, and held her captivated. The corners of his eyes crinkled with delight and softness and warmth and she smiled.

He reached for a leather-bound and worn Bible hung with colored ribbons. Like Mom's. He reached for her hand, then trailed fingertips up and down her arm.

"I'm okay here," she said, cautious. Mom's preacher never made her feel like this.

"Lay the prayer rug under her feet, Marcy. We are not here to put the fear of God into you, my daughter," the preacher cooed, "but instead to show you only wonder, peace, and gratitude. Is that all right with you?"

"Can I have a biscuit?" Daisy asked, handing over her empty bowl of soup.

"We can do this any way you want," the preacher said with a gentle voice, a velvet voice. They rolled out a little rug near her feet. Their voices were easy, gentle on her senses.

"Our God is not an angry God," the preacher recited, and Daisy was glad for that. Not like the minister at Mom's church who loved that hellfire stuff. He used to make the whole congregation gasp and tremble.

"Biscuit?" Daisy asked. "Please?"

"The Lord Jesus Christ knew this full well, how deceptive and wicked men's hearts are," the preacher said.

"I haven't had anything but this soup all day. Could you please hand me just one biscuit?"

The preacher frowned. "Not now. Can't you wait five more minutes?"

"Oh gosh, I've waited all day. Nothing since breakfast," she paused. "I'll be a much better parishioner if my stomach isn't rumbling so much." She'd fool them.

"At the very gates of Heaven, sinners are turned away," the preacher recited. "Seems like a simple enough request. Marcy?"

Daisy popped half of the biscuit into her mouth.

"Better now?" Marcy murmured. They surrounded her.

"Have any sins to confess, my daughter?"

"Not that I can think of." Daisy wolfed down the rest of the biscuit.

"Everyone has sins." Marcy patted her on the hand.

Daisy pushed back, but Marcy's hand was stronger.

"It's so much easier if you just confess," Berniece murmured, patting her on the shoulder. "You'll feel so much better."

Daisy recoiled from their hands. People at Mom's church knew better than to come that close. "Don't touch me. Please, don't touch me."

They retracted their hands in unison, and gave each other a knowing look.

Just like the blue-rinse set at Mom's Chapel of the Ascension.

"When God comes into your heart, it will change your life forever," the preacher said.

"Well, you know, I've been down this road before. Didn't work for me then and doesn't really work for me now," Daisy said.

"I told you she was a hard case, Cornelius," Berniece huffed.

"Leave this to me," the preacher cooed. "Feeling better, Daisy? Warm? Not so hungry anymore?"

Daisy nodded. "Yes, thank you."

"Then listen for a few minutes. Can you do that? And help us, now?"

His eyes were like stars, dancing, pulling her in. How could she disappoint him? Church had certainly given Mom a lot of comfort. Maybe she'd been right after all. A little bit anyway? Would Mom have gone around the bend without them? Daisy wasn't so sure.

"They should never have touched you," the preacher reported.

"Damn right," Daisy answered, standing up, her legs vibrating with tension. Mom had looked so sad when they'd taken her away.

"The Lord will protect you."

"Protect me? Ha! That's what they said about my mother and look what they did to her!"

"Oh dear," Berniece muttered.

"That must've been terrible for you." The preacher's voice was soothing. "How old were you?"

"What difference does that make? The church made her crazy! They took her to the mental hospital. All she could do was mutter verses from Mark. She died last year. Hardly anyone went to her funeral. What kind of a God would take my mother away?"

"Sister," the preacher said. "The Lord doesn't want to hurt you. We're just trying to save lives here."

"Didn't do such a good job with Mom," Daisy declared, feeling smug. Bunch of charlatans. What the hell did they know?

"Things happen," the preacher said, his voice honey, molten gold, beseeching her. "If you are standing on the right hand of God, you will be fine." He took a breath. "Maybe He wanted your mom to come home."

"I needed her."

"Of course you did. I know how much you loved her."

"I should never have let her get so involved."

"The Shepherd looks over all his sheep, and he watches over your mother, and he's watching over you too. He loves you."

"Right. A righteous God does not take mothers from children."

"It's not a question we can ever answer," the preacher replied. "My daughter, all my daughters, please, can we pray with Daisy? Give your sister here some comfort?"

Marcy and Berniece came around Daisy and, without touching her, sat with her. She could feel their heartbeats in unison with hers.

"It wasn't your fault, Daisy. It wasn't anyone's fault. Put your faith in the Lord, sister, and you will be watched over."

She sniffed and closed her eyes a second. Could it be true? Not her fault? How could he be so sure? She was sure, wasn't she? Hadn't she tried? Hadn't she done everything? Tried to forbid her to go to any more meetings? And still she went.

"The Lord loves you, Daisy, and forgives you," the preacher intoned.

Somehow Daisy was on the floor. How did that happen? Forgive? Me? God forgives me? But if it wasn't my fault, what would He forgive me for? Her knees hurt. She pushed herself up on the couch again, relieved no one kept her down. The breeze through the open door was freezing.

"Having faith doesn't mean anything but comfort from those who love you. Through good times and bad. We will never leave you the way your mother left you," the preacher murmured.

"Could you please close the door?"

"Let us pray for Daisy."

"Amen." Berniece and Marcy rejoined.

"You're loved, my daughter. No one here wants to give you anything but love."

Could it be true? It couldn't be. How could she be so confused? Everything was so messed up.

"God, come and ease Daisy's pain," the preacher prayed.

Daisy's eyes spilled with tears, a gasp erupting from her

throat. The preacher's hands were on hers. She held on tight. She felt as if she'd been touched by grace.

"We are here, Daisy. Marcy, Berniece, myself, God—we are all together. No one is lonely, cold, tired, or hungry anymore."

Daisy hugged Berniece, then Marcy.

"We are all sinners. Yet we are in the family of the Lord."

Daisy leaned her head on Berniece's shoulder and felt her arm around her.

"Sister Daisy. Is there anything you want to ask Him?"

Daisy sat up with a start. Something was wrong. "Campbell? He's . . . my fiancé." She started crying again. "He's lost. Out on the river. He was supposed to be here by three," she said. "Oh God, you've got save him!"

"I'm sure he's fine," the preacher said.

Daisy sniffed. "I couldn't stand it, if . . . if . . ."

"He's in a cozy tent, missing you," the preacher whispered. "I promise." He put his hand on her knee.

"How can you be so sure?"

"Just wait and see. Don't you trust in Him? That He is watching over Campbell just the way He is watching over you? Don't you feel comfort?"

Daisy wanted to believe. She had to believe. "Are you sure?"

"Of course. Now are you ready to make God your savior? My daughter, Daisy, we all love you. You have entered the Kingdom of Heaven and you have been saved."

Daisy blinked back tears.

"We're here, Daisy, watching over you, like your mother is, like Campbell is. God has brought us all together. Now, will you pray with us, Daisy? Pray for your mother's soul. Pray for Campbell?"

"Please keep him safe," she said, and bowed her head.

A few minutes later, she opened her eyes; the door was closed, and she felt like she was home with Mom. Comforted. Watched over. Not lonely anymore.

"Marcy, make up some of that chamomile tea. Berniece, give me a hand here, please." The preacher wrapped a blanket around Daisy. "We thank you, God, for our new sister here. Oh dear, she is still so cold. Warm up the stove again, Berniece."

But Daisy wasn't listening. She was imagining she was standing on the shore, in the morning, watching Campbell come toward her, in his canoe, his hair flowing in a breeze, unsure how she was going to tell him she'd found a home with the Lord.

CHAPTER THIRTY-THREE

~

Monday, earlier that day
on the river

E.B. AND LAURA

"You're married?" Laura spat. E.B. had been decent, useful, kind. *Of course* he was married.

"I was . . . I am . . . I mean," he mumbled, "Berniece . . . it was her idea. She walked out on me."

Laura picked up a couple of rocks and pitched them into the river. "Same shit, different day."

"I haven't filed, yes, that's true," E.B. muttered. "Haven't been sure. It's been two months."

"Save it." Laura stared at the river, embarrassed. When would she ever learn?

"I'm not that way."

"Right." Hadn't she even wondered once why he was being so kind? "Seems simple enough to me. You make googly eyes at me, you flirt with me, you kiss me, you're married. What's different about you? I see that shit every night, E.B."

"Hey, wait a sec. I'm a farmer. I go to town twice a week.

241

Who am I supposed to flirt with, the checkers at the Park 'N' Shop, the little old ladies at the welcome center?" He stood next to her, staring at the river, feeling her disappointment. "It's been a long time since I kissed a woman I liked."

"I've heard it all before." From the men at the club, trying to pull her aside after a show. Those others at the stage door, leering at her. Goddamn Harry. The friggin' thugs. She jumped up and ran down the shore. As long as she kept running, no one could tear her apart.

"Slow down." E.B. followed her for a bit, then stopped. "I don't think Berniece is coming back."

Laura heard a plaintive tone in his voice she needed to ignore. She charged up a hill and scrambled over a pile of rocks. It couldn't be true; it would never be true. No decent man, ever, now or in the future. The only men who wanted her were the unavailable kind. Or the ones who tried to force themselves on her.

E.B. leaned on the rocks, below her, poised to follow.

"Stay there," Laura said. She needed time to think.

He waited.

"So, I'm supposed to trust you? Now? Why?"

"Laura," E.B.'s voice echoed across empty canyons. "You have every right to be angry. Listen to my side of the story. Then judge."

She crouched under the shade of a cottonwood tree. "This better be good."

"Berniece and I." He took a breath. "We've known each other since high school. There aren't that many women in these parts. Our families thought it would work out. And it did, for a while. That is, until she found the Lord."

"Don't come any closer." All that sweet talk. Why should she believe him?

Suddenly the leaves overhead started rustling. The wind picked up enough so that she started to worry about branches falling. She moved back toward the beach. E.B. kept his distance, which was a relief.

"I thought you were a churchgoer." Laura turned to face him. "I knew it."

"Was. I was. She is. Hell, she's so involved she *lives* with the church." He held very still.

"You string me along, the whole time knowing you'll be seeing her."

"What? I'm not seeing Berniece. What are you talking about?"

"Your wife. Yes," Laura said. "That's right, they said tomorrow. Coal Banks Landing—isn't that where we're going?" Laura would tell Stella everything, down to the same old piece-of-shit ending. The wind started to whip up waves on the river.

"Too much time in the sun and you're delirious," E.B. muttered. "Come on, let's get going while we still can. We've got to catch up with Campbell this afternoon."

"Tomorrow night at Coal Banks. Should be kind of cozy, don't you think, you, me, and Berniece?"

E.B. stepped too hard into the canoe, making it wobble. "Maybe it's not them."

Laura climbed in and pulled back on her paddle, hard. "Think I'm making this up?"

E.B. placed both hands on the gunwales as thunder cracked opened the sky. "Jesus," he said suddenly. "We gotta get moving."

Laura looked at his eyes, then glanced up at the darkening sky. Wind shot down the river, making whitecaps. "We going out in that?"

"Yes! Any minute now! Get moving! Paddle hard!" Dark clouds that had been hanging over distant cliffs were now overhead, banking over the river and growing thicker all the time. "It looks like it might hail."

Pings of water peppered the river, making circles grow.

"Faster! Faster!" he cried.

She could feel him paddling behind her, speeding up, faster and faster as she matched him stroke for stroke as he steered them into the main current, into the whitecaps. The temperature dropped about ten degrees. Her whole body shivered with the cold. She glanced at the shore as it sped by. It cooled off even more.

In a minute marsh grasses bent nearly double as gusts of wind ripped across the water. The wind shifted again, this time into their faces.

"Come on!" he shouted over the wind.

Rain was coming harder now, dampening her shirt and covering the river. "Hurry! Hail out here can kill you."

Her hands, wet on the shaft, twisted when she took a stroke. Tightening her grip and getting down on her knees, she helped him power through another bend.

"Hole-in-the-Wall campground shouldn't be far," he called, his voice fading in the howling and rising wind.

Laura kept her head down and concentrated on her stroke. The boat felt like a part of her now. Heavy rain poured down the back of her neck and under the thin fabric of her shirt. Thunder rattled overhead. Lightning cracked in front of the canoe, illuminating very briefly some shelters on a bluff. The black clouds and rain came back obliterating everything. She pulled harder into a darkness, unaware of which way to go.

The canoe slammed into shore. Hail opened above them like machine-gun fire.

"Run!" E.B. shouted. "They're some shelters up there. Run like hell!"

CHAPTER THIRTY-FOUR

Monday, afternoon
Hole-in-the-Wall Campground

E.B. AND LAURA

*L*aura charged up narrow paths overgrown with weeds while rain and hail pelted her head and shoulders, growing harder with each minute. At the top of the bluff she ducked inside a three-sided log shelter. Grateful to be under cover, she watched ice balls hit and bounce off the ground, while the rattling over her head sounded like machine-gun fire. Where was E.B.? She was about to head back outside to find him when she heard the sound of pounding feet cracking ice.

He was breathing hard and soaking wet when he barged in.

"I stopped to get Tucker's stuff. Change quickly. Hypothermia's no joke in cattle country. I'll turn my back. The hail should be over in a minute or two."

They stood at the open wall, staring at the storm. The wind blew up, bending little sapling trees so their tops touched the ground. Hail pummeled the clearing, blowing up splatters of mud and ice. Booms cracked overhead.

Digging into the plastic bag, Laura noticed only enough clothing for one. "E.B., you wear the clothes this time; I'm all right."

He lifted a strip of marsh grass off her arm. "I'm used to it. This is still your turn. Go on, go change." He stared at the forks of lightning fracturing the sky. "Hope this hail doesn't ruin the crop," he shouted over the din. "Last year we lost everything."

"It's like the sky's splitting apart," Laura said, mesmerized by the storm.

"Hells bells. The insurance company will double my premiums if it lasts much longer."

Laura turned to the back of the shelter, peeled off her clothes, pulled Tucker's stinky sweatshirt on, and hid her underwear behind one of the benches. The hoodie was as big and dry and soft as her bed at home. She searched the bag for more clothes. E.B. was still in his wet things. Now what? All she found was the old sleeping bag.

"We were lucky." He paced back and forth across the open doorway. "Hail as big as this can dent cars and give you one hell of a headache." As if on cue, several chunks of ice, the size of golf balls, bounced inside the shelter and came to rest at his feet. "Between the hail, the locusts, too much or too little rain, it's a miracle we have any crops at all. And this stuff is small. I've seen them as big as my fist."

"What would we have done if we hadn't found the shelter?" Laura asked above the din.

"Crouch down in the mud with the canoe upside down on top of us and pray."

"I thought you didn't believe in God," she said.

"Warmer now?" he asked a second later. The rain and hail stopped. Sunlight illuminated the ground, making mist rise from the cool, wet earth.

She nodded, grateful for his care, grateful for the sun. What would Stella say? Out in the storm with a sweet man and you're not taking care of him? "You're shivering. Take those wet things off, and wrap yourself in Tucker's sleeping bag."

E.B. backed away. "No thanks."

"What did you tell me? Hypothermia kills, you said. What, are you immune to the cold? Take off your clothes and put on the sleeping bag. Get on with it, E.B." She wasn't going to lose him—not now.

Laura watched clouds separate and drift away while E.B. changed. Taking care of him felt right. In a few minutes, he stood beside her, looking funny with the bag around his middle. He grinned.

"Thanks."

His presence was solid, warm, comforting, direct—in a word, wonderful. She longed to touch him.

He pointed out a narrow ridge way across the bluff, where a hole went right through the rock. The moon, rising, hung just inside.

"Hole-in-the-Wall, with moon," he grinned. "It's something, isn't it?"

She nodded. Something was the way she felt with him so close.

"Watch," he said and pointed. "Not up there, down at the ground."

A squirrel ran across the bare clearing. The shadow of a

hawk crossed its path. The squirrel bolted up the shelter's walls and dove under the eaves, chattering loudly.

"Lucky. Like us," he said, putting his arm around her shoulder.

She tingled all over.

"There's more," E.B. said. "Watch."

But Laura wasn't looking, not where he was pointing. She had heard something, something different. This was no swish of a hawk or the cry of a mouse. This was a boat.

"E.B.! He's back. It's him. It's Tucker!"

"I can't hear anything."

"It was the clink of paddles. I told you we should've killed him." Laura looked out the empty door. "We're caught here, just like that poor mouse we saw before."

"It could be anybody."

"You can stay and wait for him." She looked out at the barren campground with its pathetic little trees. "But I'm leaving."

"You want me to run in this?" he asked.

"Sometimes, E.B., you make me crazy. I can't wait any longer." She took off.

He caught up with her on a farm road, the ratty sleeping bag tucked around him awkwardly, her nearly tripping in her flip-flops.

"Avoid the sand," E.B. said. "And for God's sake, don't trip in the prairie-dog holes. Follow me!"

She dashed between bushes, over a pile of cast-off logs, and up into the hills, following his footsteps. Weeds scratched her legs, and thorns dug into her feet. She kept slipping out of the flip-flops, and held them as tight as she could with her toes.

At the top of a narrow rutted road, E.B. stopped in a small clearing.

"All right. We can see everything from here." He caught his breath. "You okay?" A white wooden shack stood nearby. Broken windows sparkled in the sun. "Get inside."

"Shit. I've lost one of my shoes," Laura said. "I have to go back and get it."

"And risk him finding you?" E.B. nudged her across the porch and toward the door of the shack. "Not this time."

"What is this place?" She hesitated. It looked dusty, worn, history written in its broken floorboards and leaning windows.

"It's an old line shack, built by one of the early ranch hands. Now, hush." He waved her inside as he kept his head back from the window. They stood between an ancient white stove, a metal cot, and a wooden chair. "Best to stay low. Now wait. Crouch down, and be quiet."

"Can you see him?" she leaned over his shoulder.

"What do you want to do—be a target? First you leave your shoe, and now you peer out of the window. Come on now! Get your head down!" He pressed his hand on her shoulder.

"Hey! Let me up."

"Stay there."

"Can you hear anything?"

"Not yet."

"It's disgusting down here!" She perched a foot from the wooden floor. She wasn't going to go any lower. "The floor's covered with trash and little brown pellets." She held her bare foot an inch above the floor.

"Mouse turds, Laura. Try not to breathe in too deep."

"Let me up!"

He pressed harder on her shoulder.

"Someone's coming up the road," he said. "Stay still."

She froze, hands suspended above the floor. She needed a weapon. She searched the shack. The chair was too far away and the bed too heavy.

E.B. moved back from the window.

Laura's head was level with the bottom of an old chipped white enamel stove, the word Elmira written across the front. On the top was a small cast-iron skillet. E.B. closed his hand around the handle.

She heard the crunch of gravel. She didn't dare move. If Tucker attacked E.B. again, she'd find a way to slam his head into the stove.

E.B. lifted the skillet.

"You'll kill him with that," she whispered, seeing a tight concentration in his eyes.

"That's the point, isn't it?" He held the pan over his shoulder.

Laura watched him, her breath shallow and quick.

The crunch on gravel stopped. Laura held still.

Silence permeated the shack while a gust of wind rattled the windows.

Two more footsteps. Where the hell was Tucker? Just outside the door? Behind the shack? Could she surprise him from here? E.B. tapped her shoulder to keep her low.

She held still.

Another crunch on gravel.

Silence.

A footstep rung on the wood porch just outside the door.

Laura closed her eyes and muttered, "God, please, please, *oh please.*"

E.B. cocked his arm, tightened his mouth, and held his breath.

"Hello?" someone called from outside the shack.

That goddamn Tucker, trying to lure them out. Laura braced her legs.

A man's fingers appeared around the doorjamb. "Anyone there?"

E.B. lifted his arm higher.

A swing of arms and a pair of tan zip-apart pants appeared in the doorway. "E.B.? You in there?"

E.B. hesitated. "Campbell?" His hand stopped in midair.

Campbell stepped in and when he saw the skillet, his eyes went wide. "What's the matter with you? What are you trying to do, kill me?"

"Don't sneak up on people like that," E.B. said.

"What are you guys playing at, cops and robbers? Cowboys and Indians? E.B., put down the goddamn pan."

E.B. relaxed his arm.

Laura stood up and felt the urge to pee. More relieved that he wasn't Tucker than that he was Campbell. Thank God! She wanted to rush over and hug him, but he looked as though he'd been through the wash. His face was sunburned, and his eyes were surrounded by dark circles. "Let me explain."

"Save it. We've all been worried sick," Campbell said. "Where the hell have you been?"

"Here, there, in the river, on the river, a bluff. We got mugged," Laura said.

"Mugged? Out here? What, by a bunch of owls? A pussy-cat? Wolves?" Campbell's face clouded.

"Campbell, you were supposed to wait for us," E.B. said.

"Two days I've been out here looking for you! Killing myself paddling upriver! You must've gone on the other side of an island or something."

"We holed the boat on a snag." Laura's words came out in a rush. "That was the beginning of it. E.B. went inland for help, someone took pot shots at him. Meanwhile, while I was waiting by the river, this guy came . . ."

"I said, save it." Campbell looked them both over. "You're wearing men's clothes, Laura. And E.B., a sleeping bag? Don't tell me you went swimming, while I was going crazy looking for you? Jesus Christ."

"But it's true," Laura said. "There was this guy . . ."

"I understand. Everything." He studied the two of them. "Kind of cozy, don't you think? Couldn't stay in the shelter cabins, eh? Benches a little too narrow?"

"That's not it at all," Laura said. "You're missing the point. Try listening for a change."

"I don't care. E.B, you don't abandon people on the water. You of all people. Christ. It's a stupid Class I river."

E.B. looked like he was stifling a smile.

Campbell ran his fingers through his thinning hair, as if to pull out the rest of it. He strode out the door. "I'll tell the others you're here," he said bitterly, and marched off, his sandals crunching gravel.

Laura, fuming, watched Campbell's figure shrink as he walked across the broad bluff.

"You in trouble?" Laura asked. "I can tell him everything. Not your fault."

"It's all right," E.B. said, smiling now and stepping closer to her. "Once he sees the canoe, he'll figure it out."

Laura wedged her one bare foot near E.B.'s and held him tight, their breath in unison. He was so warm. She wanted to tell how she felt.

"It was so peaceful out here for a moment," he said, leaning against the doorjamb. "At least it wasn't Tucker," he murmured, placing his arm around her shoulder. "Feeling better now?"

Laura rested her head against his chest.

"I suppose we'll have to tell Campbell everything," E.B. murmured.

"Everything?" Laura came closer, her mouth even with his.

"I wouldn't do that, if I were you," he mumbled.

"After all we've been through?" she asked, pressing herself onto him.

"I'm not very good at this."

"You weren't so bad the last time," she said and kissed him.

CHAPTER THIRTY-FIVE

༄

Tuesday, morning
Hole-in-the-Wall Campground

E.B. AND LAURA, CAMPBELL, FRANCINE AND THE GANG

"*T*ime to get the show on the road. Ready, every-body?" E.B. asked. Campbell and Francine launched first, Francine in the stern. They drifted while Alice and Nia launched. Kris and Jane were arguing about who should be in the bow until E.B. gave them a shove and they were off. In a few minutes all the canoes were swept up into the current, everyone paddling hard except for E.B. and Laura. They were sweep, a position E.B. had requested. A position where he could dawdle as much as was allowed, which was not nearly enough.

He had taken over the leadership role from Campbell, who was beat. All E.B. wanted to do was to turn around and head back upriver where it would be just him and Laura and the birds and the boat and the water dancing. He watched her expertly sweep her paddle through the water. She'd turned out to be a great canoeist. Time was falling away like the water on his blade, each stroke bringing him closer to the ranch and farther away from her.

He was years and miles away from driving the combine, the deep gumbo mud that caked onto his tractor wheels, the seat hard under him, the constant buzz of cicadas, dust filling the air, the empty kitchen with the one wooden chair at the table.

Laura was the first woman he'd let get under his skin, into his heart. He felt vulnerable and delicate and guarded, a new sensation. He tried to memorize the look of her face, the wide set of her eyes, the joy in her smile, the curve of her jaw, the tenderness of her ears.

His feelings about Berniece had become as pale and ragged as the gingham kitchen curtains she'd always loved that now hung lifeless against the cracked kitchen window—while Laura was the coolness of night on the prairie, the sound of the coyote, the breeze through the cottonwoods. He took a long stroke and eased by a marsh. Funny, he'd never been the romantic sort before. He took another look at Laura. Just today, just the rest of today.

Last night, they'd sat around the campfire over a well-deserved dinner of pasta, pita bread, and boxed red wine. E.B. told Campbell about Tucker, some of it anyway, and reminded himself to tell the BLM rangers about the guy tied up on an island near the Marias River. Campbell described how Francine had poled upriver and saved him, a real hero. They had a few more toasts until darkness set in hard and it was time to turn in.

Campbell had shared his tent with Francine, and E.B. and Laura shared another. E.B. had slept well, next to Laura, whose warm, even breathing made him dream about her and what could be. Until about 4:00 a.m., when his dream involved Berniece, who was back in the kitchen, scolding him. He had woken in a cold sweat.

Easing down alongside some tall rock formations, he held the canoe steady and skimmed his fingers along the rock. Smooth as his homemade kitchen table at home, which he'd sanded and sanded until it shone. Berniece had admired it, and Laura would too, if she ever saw it.

"The cliffs—they just get bigger and bigger," Laura said, interrupting his thoughts. "Hey," she said, pointing ahead. "We're falling behind."

"It's okay. We're sweep. We're supposed to be last."

"Makes me nervous," she said.

"A lot?" he asked.

"Not really," she answered, humming to "Can't Fence Me In."

E.B. clasped his lips hard. Dream on, bud. Not for you.

"Great day, after all that hail." She turned back and smiled at him. "I washed my hair with the girls last night—and bathed in the river. The water's so murky you can't even see your hands. I was so grubby. Hey, E.B., when I started on this trip . . . I rushed into it . . . I didn't know . . ."

"Anything?" he asked.

"Just about," she laughed. "Nothing about the river, that's for sure." She paused, took a long minute to clear her throat. "You think those guys are still waiting for me in Fort Benton?"

"If they are, I'll arrest them. I'm deputized."

"No shit."

"No shit, Sherlock. The police chief, Erik Sorenson, is my best friend from high school."

"Small town."

"Loma, Montana, population, 92."

She laughed. "Brentwood, California, population, 51,343." She was sure she'd seen the police chief at one of her shows. "You go away to college?"

"Great Falls."

"You a traveling man, E.B.," she laughed.

E.B. fell in love all over again. "Anyway, soon we'll pass the cable ferry, then around the bend it's the long reach to Coal Banks. It's not far."

"It's so peaceful here." Laura dragged her fingertips through the water.

E.B. felt like he'd been out in the sun too long.

"It's just . . . I didn't know. In LA, where I grew up, my brother kept bugging me to go camping, but I told him I wouldn't sleep on the ground. If only I'd known." She took a long look at the sky, at the river reaching beyond, calling her. "It's as if my heart has been broken open."

E.B. smiled and kept his thoughts to himself. He was busy capturing magic.

"It's strange, how I feel. Like the land crawled up and captured my heart," Laura said.

"It's the river," E.B. whispered. Words jumbled around in his mind. Nothing sounded right. "Laura, I . . ." He paused. "I've had a good—no great—time paddling with you." How much did he have to say? He thought he knew how she felt. And yet. He'd had the same feeling about Elizabeth Nowell in high school, but when he'd asked her out she'd creamed him

with a no and a snort. Same answer from her best friend
Molly. Years later, convinced he'd never get married, his
mother suggested Berniece. It was convenient and easy and
she said yes. He pulled over to shore and watched Laura stand
up, her long legs going on forever.

He tried not to stare.

"It's beautiful," she said, looking out onto the river.

Your legs? She noticed him staring? "Uh . . . sort of," E.B.
mumbled.

"You're kind of quiet today. Cat caught your tongue?"

E.B.'s heart felt fragile. "As a kid, I loved to wander, explore arroyos and ridges with Sparky, my mare. Get up early
before dawn and watch the sun rise. Head out to the barn,
help new life see light. Then I got too busy." He waited for
more sweet words to come into his mind, but there weren't
any. Just Berniece, standing in the wings. Waiting for him.
"There are times when the weather is just brutal."

"I didn't like Montana when I first came." Laura sat down
and leaned her cheek on her knees. "But it kind of grew on me."

"It can be a tough place anytime of year, mosquitoes, heat,
cold, rain, hail." Damn why couldn't he just stop talking?"

Somehow he was falling and couldn't stop. What could
he say to her? I don't want to live here without you? Please
don't go back to LA?

"What's got into you? Don't you like it at all?"

"That's not what I meant," he sputtered. "I used to love
the land, but that was a while ago." He wasn't sure if he fit
here, anymore, or anywhere. Just with her, somewhere with
her. Anywhere with her. "I just don't feel the same way about
the land that I used to. Not your fault."

She threw a bunch of rocks in the river. "If you hate it so much, why don't you just leave? Say, move to LA, see how you like traffic, crowds, high costs, crazy-ass people looking for handouts?" She climbed back into the canoe, shoved off, and turned around slowly. "I was just trying to tell you, to show you, how much I've come to love the land and you went and ruined everything. Why is it that you have to ruin everything, E.B.?"

CHAPTER THIRTY-SIX

≥

Tuesday, afternoon
Coal Banks Landing

DAISY

The sun crested a hill, flooding the campground with light. A few children played Frisbee on the lawn, their high-pitched cries and laughter filling the air. Campers, lost in dreams of fishing or canoeing or just sitting on the bank, watching the river, eyed the children and went back to swapping stories and sipping coffee. At the back of the campground, Daisy stepped outside the RV and blinked back grateful tears.

She'd had only four hours of sleep, not at all what she was used to, but it felt like eight. After spending the night with Cornelius and Marcy and Berniece, Daisy's knobby knees still ached from kneeling on the floor of the RV, but she didn't care. She hadn't felt this happy since she'd won first place in spelling in third grade at PS 60.

It was Tuesday, Daisy's second day at Coal Banks. She sighed and stepped down onto long grass, the damp blades cool against her toes. She was wearing Marcy's canary yellow dress, one with forget-me-not blue flowers that climbed up her sleeves.

"Forget-me-nots for a day you'll never forget," Marcy said. Marcy was a lot skinnier than Daisy, so the dress bunched and gathered in places where it wasn't supposed to, but this didn't bother Daisy in the least. Her other clothes were just not right anymore.

"The good Lord doesn't want to baptize you in anything other than a dress," Marcy said. "Both God—and Cornelius—just love pretty girls in pretty dresses. Don't you?" She placed her hand on Daisy's shoulder. "You look beautiful, Daisy."

Berniece, standing on Daisy's other side, tied a ribbon in Daisy's hair. "Let's get going, girls, we have God's work to do."

Daisy stood between her new best friends. A little nervous now, she wasn't quite sure what was next. The three of them ambled, slowly, down to the river. She hoped the water wouldn't be cold.

The preacher meandered in front of them, a Bible in one hand, his black hat in the other. Daisy watched his white hair flitter in the breeze. He was reciting prayers, just as he had in the middle of the night when he had taken her, his baritone voice soft in her ears.

"Let us pray together." Cornelius took up his place at the riverbank. The four of them stood silent for a few minutes. Crows called from across the river, swung up into the air currents, and took off in a rush of wings. Down below, Daisy, feeling like she, too, could fly, felt herself guided to the bank. Marcy and Berniece stood beside her, while the preacher waded into the water behind Daisy. Her toes felt mud.

He cleared his throat and began. "Ready, my daughters?" They nodded.

Daisy bowed her head and hoped she'd never have to tell Campbell all the details of her conversion, the "how." She'd been so tired, so comforted by the soup and biscuits and RV and warm soft arms around her, that she let Cornelius slip it in, just a bit, and she had felt so whole, so welcome in His new world. She blinked against the bright sunlight, and stepped into the water. Oh, it was warm.

"Hold your nose, dear," Berniece murmured.

In the river, up to her knees, Daisy felt Berniece's and Marcy's arms behind her. As they leaned her backward, she suddenly felt apprehensive, like they might intend to drown her.

"It's okay, honey," Marcy coaxed, placing one hand under Daisy's back and feeling her tighten up. "It's only for a second, now."

The preacher held out his hands in prayer.

"Do we," Cornelius asked, "all of us—Berniece, Marcy, and all members of this extended family—promise to guide and nurture Daisy by word and deed, with love and prayer, encouraging her to walk in the way of Christ and his peace, and stand up for God's justice in this world?"

"We do," Marcy and Berniece said in unison.

"We give you thanks, O God," the preacher bowed his head, "for your nourishment and sustenance of all living things with the gift of water. I baptize you, Daisy, in the name of son, the Father, and the Holy Ghost."

In one swift motion, Daisy was underwater, and in a second back up again, gasping and sputtering.

"Welcome to your new family, Daisy," Berniece whispered.

Daisy blinked into a new day. She felt so fresh, so new. Had all her sins been washed away, even that latest, littlest one?

"We thank you, O God, for the water of baptism," the preacher continued. "Through it we cleanse of our sins and are reminded that all good things come from God, especially the gift of life."

"Daisy," Marcy whispered. "Welcome to the world of the Lord."

Daisy looked up and felt their love wash over her. Cornelius's eyes danced. She still loved Campbell, and didn't feel guilty in the least. "Give yourself to the Lord," Cornelius had said. That part had been easy. Now, she felt a bond with the man standing beside her.

Above, the sun hovered over the ridge. She heard the slap of waves by her feet, and understood, for the first time, why Campbell loved the river so. He would be proud of her taking this step to their new life together. Wherever he would live, she would follow him. She would tend to him and care for him the same way Cornelius was caring for her. Maybe, someday, Campbell would come to accept the Lord. But for now, she basked in the light.

"Sisters, meet Daisy." Daisy beamed, and Cornelius presented Daisy to Marcy and Berniece, and she hugged them all. She was filled with love and happiness, standing on an altar with God. And soon there would be Campbell. Eventually he would come to love them all just the way she did.

Ten minutes later, wet hair still plastered down her back,

damp dress clinging to her a little more than she wanted, Daisy stood outside the preacher's RV and looked at her new sister Marcy, working at the stove. The girls had asked her if she wanted to change, but Daisy wanted the moment to linger as long as it could. She wasn't cold in the least. She fingered a locket Marcy had given her, warming the metal heart in her hands.

"Would you like more biscuits, Marcy?" Daisy asked, and pulled out a tray from the oven in the back of the preacher's RV. They were plump, fresh, warm and inviting, right out of a Pillsbury can, but people love 'em, Marcy said. Since the baptism, the three of them had prepared and browned six dozen biscuits and placed them on a table covered with a blue-and-white checked tablecloth. They were almost ready for the throngs that would assemble once Cornelius had finished his sermon.

Daisy had taken a few trips to the ramp to see if Campbell had come in, but as it was still early, she'd come back to help set up. Now, with the latest batch of biscuits out of the oven, she ran back to the ramp and checked again. She couldn't wait to introduce him to the preacher.

"Quit running around like a banshee, Daisy. He'll get here soon enough," Berniece said, pouring hot coffee into coffee urns.

Daisy stopped short, too excited to stand still. "What am I going to say?" With the biscuits cool enough, she set them on a tray. "Gee, sweetheart, my love, you were gone all night and I found the Lord?"

"You mean after you hug him?" Berniece placed the urn on a table outside. "Or before?"

"He won't be all that happy I converted." Daisy worried her hands.

"You know men." Berniece giggled. "He'll be as excited to see you as a boy on his first date. Just you wait."

"He always says I flit from interest to interest." Daisy carried out the tray of biscuits. "First it was skating, then ballet, then yoga. But Berniece, this just fits, this is me, now."

"Campbell might not want to be converted right away, Daisy."

Daisy almost dropped the last tray of biscuits. "He has to."

"Like I said, honey, men need to be led," Berniece said. "Give him time."

"Campbell's wonderful," Daisy said, feeling delirious. "He'll talk to Cornelius. You'll see. Then we'll talk about our future, together, wherever that may be."

"Uh-huh." Berniece smiled and disappeared inside the RV.

Daisy, feeling unsure now, went off to search for Marcy. She found her just outside the trailer, setting out coffee cups.

"Hey, Marcy? What should I say to Campbell?"

"Just tell him about the Lord's undying love, honey."

Daisy gave her a hug. "You always say the right things."

"Now, darlin', hurry up with that coffee. Cornelius likes his hot."

Daisy saw a flicker out of the corner of her eye. "Just a minute." She scanned the river. A flurry of water sprayed the air. She stepped up to the edge of the bluff, flushed out a family of quail, held her hand over her eyes, and squinted in the late-afternoon light.

"Oh, my God." She held her hand to her mouth. "It's *him*."

There, in the front of the red canoe, right there, was the man she'd been waiting for all day and night, the man she'd caressed, held, and coveted for five long years, the man who was about to propose, and he was right there, paddling slowly, scanning the shore, looking for her.

"Campbell!" Daisy shouted. "Campbell!" Cornelius had been right after all. The Lord *was* watching over him. She ran across the campground and sped down the ramp, her heart full with Campbell, with Cornelius, with the light in the sky, the ripples near shore, the afternoon light in her eyes.

"Yes, yes, yes!" she shouted, as people nearby clucked their tongues. As she ran, she forgot about the way she'd wept last night, the way she'd been welcomed into the RV, the way she'd let Cornelius come close. All that could wait. Did Campbell have a ring in his pocket? Would she make him squirm until she said yes?

~

CHAPTER THIRTY-SEVEN

Tuesday, afternoon
Coal Banks Landing

CAMPBELL AND DAISY

From the water Campbell waved and expertly steered toward the ramp but couldn't come in. A bunch of people were gossiping and blocking his way. Not wanting to lose his turn, he cursed as wavelets banged the hull of his canoe against the concrete ramp under the water. He was about to say something to the other canoeists but decided against it. Daisy would hear him. Francine, of course, would cheer him on.

At last, the people moved away, six carrying each canoe. What a bunch of weenies. He could carry his alone over his head. He pulled in, secured the vessel, and was ready to unload when Francine jumped out of the canoe and took off for the campground. Disappointed, but not surprised, he unloaded, moved the canoe out of the way, and was ready to help someone else come in, but Daisy took his hand.

"They can do it, my love, no more. Walk with me," she said.

He followed.

As soon as they were out of earshot, she grabbed him by the waist and gave him a big hug.

"Oh God, Campbell, yes, yes, yes!" She blinked back tears.

"You okay?" he asked, smoothing back her hair. "Sweetheart? You're crying. Please don't cry."

"They said you would be fine and here you are! I never believed them. Oh Campbell." She buried her face in his shirt.

Same cornflower-yellow hair with a yellow ribbon. Same slender body. "Daisy, my sweet love, why are you wearing a dress?"

"Oh?" she asked, looking at the bodice and giving him a big smile. "This old thing? It's Marcy's."

"It must've been cold last night," he said, feeling like a fool. "What did you do to stay warm?"

"What happened? How come you're late?" Daisy's words came out in a rush.

"Everything's all right now, now," he said, thinking she'd been out in the sun too long. He bent down and kissed her.

A truck, backing up at the top of the landing, was beeping. The driver's engine rumbled, the truck and trailer jangling and clanging behind Daisy.

Campbell, in a rush, pulled her out of the way. "Didn't you hear that?"

"Hear what?" she shook her wet hair. "Campbell, I thought you'd drowned."

"One of the canoes broke apart. Hey, sweetheart," he asked in his quietest voice, his gentlest tone. "Honey, who's Marcy?"

"She's a nice girl."

"Why are your clothes all wet?"

"Before I met Marcy, Campbell, it was horrible. The driver you hired to bring me out here—he drove like a maniac." She pulled on his sleeve. "I was alone for the longest time. Then it was quiet, no one here at all. Then this guy Logan wanted me to get in his boat. And I would've gone, to find you. I was about to, until this lady Berniece . . . You'll like Marcy."

"She's the one who saved you? I'd like to meet her."

"She's real busy right now."

"But I'd still like to. Making friends. That's hard for you," he stammered, "and I'm real proud."

"I paddled upriver," Campbell said. "To find E.B. and Laura who had fallen behind. Strained my heart, but I'm fine, sweetheart." He wouldn't tell her about his collapse and his dialogue with Captain Lewis. "There was a lot of wind and current. I wouldn't have made it without Francine."

"Francine? You didn't tell me *she* was coming," Daisy said.

The ring dug deep into Campbell's front pocket. He couldn't do it, not today, not tomorrow, maybe in a few days, months, maybe whenever. Maybe never. He had to give Francine time to adjust. "She's cool about you," he said. Telling her like this wasn't at all what he had planned. "Sorry about that."

"You should have told me," she said, turning her back.

"I'd planned on telling you earlier, much earlier." He braced himself for the outburst.

Daisy, thinking hard, turned back around. "God moves in mysterious ways, His wonder to behold." Any other time, she'd have been devastated. The preacher had told her that the Way would be long and it would be hard. She remembered his soft hands and gentle touch. She didn't think she wanted to tell Campbell any more about Cornelius. Should she ask Campbell about the ring? Wasn't it the guy's job to propose? Would he kneel inside the tent or ask her, out here, in front of everyone?

Campbell looked at her with a soft grin. "You fall in the water?"

"Sort of." What would Berniece say? What would God say? Hadn't she promised not to sin?

"Daisy?" Campbell asked. "You seem a little preoccupied."

She pressed her hands together. God had saved her, a heathen; He could save Campbell too. He'd be so happy once he understood the True Way. But how was she going to break it to him? "Meet me in fifteen minutes, across the campground, will you, sweetheart? And then you can meet both Marcy and Berniece?"

"Why don't we go together? I just need a minute to wash up," Campbell said.

"I told them I'd be right back." Daisy leaned over and gave him a kiss. She knew it wasn't a regular kiss, just a small tight kiss, a grandmother's kiss.

Campbell looked startled. "I'd love to meet them," he stuttered.

"Be right back," Daisy said and took off.

CHAPTER THIRTY-EIGHT

Tuesday, afternoon
Coal Banks Landing

LAURA, BERNIECE, AND E.B.

E.B. pulled a long stroke as they eased around a cliff face in Tucker's canoe while pelicans grazed the water, lifting off with a whoosh. Cows munched contentedly along the hillside. The land had never looked so beautiful. Laura's long blonde hair flew in a slight breeze. In a few hours she'd be heading back to Fort Benton, where she'd leave for LA, and he would die again.

He took another stroke, passed a stand of trees, and saw, beyond, the glint of cars. Already? Coal Banks Landing? How did they get here so fast? People, cars, and tents would be populating the small campground, making a racket, disturbing his little bit of peace. And Berniece would be there. Damn. Any other day, any other summer, for God's sake. God's little sense of humor, working overtime? It wasn't fair.

A few minutes later, Ken, the owner of the canoe company, grabbed their painter and frowned. "You're late."

"You weren't supposed to be here until late afternoon," E.B. protested.

"I have a busier day than expected," Ken snapped.

E.B. watched Laura climb out, grab her hat, and hand her paddle to Ken. Even though her face was tanned, her eyes bright, and moisture beaded on her upper lip, she looked tense. Did she feel the same? If he told her how he felt, would she call him a fool?

"Pack it up, E.B.," Ken said. "C'mon. Everyone's ready."

Had it really only been two days? "We ran into a snag."

"Whose canoe's this? And where's mine?" Ken asked.

"Long story."

"Some snag," Ken grumbled.

"Some man."

"I heard. We've already contacted the BLM."

"E.B. was great," Laura said.

Ken gave her a funny look.

"I see." Ken looked at E.B. "Berniece is here and she's been asking for you."

Laura disappeared.

E.B.'s stomach turned over.

He walked away from Ken and Campbell, away from campers setting up tents, away from children fishing from the bluffs. Away from everyone. He needed time to think.

Laura stood behind some trees, leaves fluttering in the breeze. She had no business keeping E.B. from seeing his wife.

What would Stella say? Leave him alone and walk away? "But Stella," Laura would reply, "it's not that easy." "No?" Stella would answer. "Why not?"

Hell's bells. Shit. Laura could follow E.B. and see what Berniece looked like. He'd told her the truth, hadn't he? She stayed fifteen feet behind him and wandered into a crowd where people swayed to a hymn, their eyes closed.

She swept by farmers in overalls who gave her long looks like the guys at the club, and by women, a little plump in the middle, who stared as she went by. People reluctantly shifted as she moved in. All of them in rapture under a lazy afternoon sun. Somewhere in front of the crowd, a man was preaching.

"Was it the blowing of trumpets that fell the wall?" he asked. Everyone stood silent, listening, except for Laura. She kept moving, following E.B. as he skirted the edge of the crowd.

She stepped around children, their hands clutching their parents' trousers and skirts as if the preacher's words would blow them away. Ahead, E.B. moved on and she keyed in on his bobbing head.

"Their faith was obedient," the preacher said, his voice a whisper.

Laura slipped behind a tall man with a broad back wearing a green-and-black flannel shirt. She felt a frisson of fear. Tucker? Here? She stopped and glanced again. Not him. She stepped by, relieved.

Now, one row back from a clearing, she peered between two sets of shoulders and saw a preacher in a black frock coat and dusty shoes patrolling across half-dead grass. E.B., however, had disappeared.

"Their faith was venturesome," the preacher said, pacing.

Two women in dresses stood sentry behind him, their hands in prayer, their faces kind and illuminated with an interior light, their bodies vibrating with energy.

Laura scanned the crowd for E.B.'s brown hair.

"Their faith was patient."

The crowd murmured its assent.

"We can do some incredible things through Him." The preacher gestured and implored, holding his hands up to the sky and then out to the audience. His words rose and fell in a cadence in tune with Laura's heartbeat. "It was an incredible leap of faith to cross that River Jordan."

Is my incredible step of faith here? Laura wondered. When I find E.B., I'm going to tell him everything.

The women beside her, their bosoms heaving with passion, fanned themselves with their hands, unclipped their brown-leather bags, and opened coin purses. Men jangled change in their pockets.

Laura weaved closer to the front, nudging people out of her way.

"The people marched in faith and that march of faith felled a fortress," the preacher said, his voice vibrating in Laura's head.

The crowd seemed to simultaneously sigh, and rose up on its tippy-toes, as if to get closer to the Lord.

The preacher's voice rose higher and stronger, hitting a crescendo. "Brothers and Sisters, do *you* want to fell a fortress?"

Good question, thought Laura.

The crowd seemed to move forward in a rush as they called back. "Praise Him!"

Where was E.B.?

The preacher put out his hand. "Do not worry. You are in God's hands now!"

Feeling a pull, she leaned forward, like she was about to

fall, into the river, not the Missouri, but the Jordan. Regaining her balance, she ducked around a tall man in a twenty-gallon cowboy hat and spotted E.B. He was still walking, away from the campground, but a large woman was trailing after him, tugging at his elbow. She was round, pink cheeked, and dressed in a light pink housedress with loose petal sleeves. Laura could have picked her out of a crowd. Pretty dress for a farmer's wife.

"Sin has to be paid for!" the preacher called.

"Amen!" a few responded from the crowd.

Laura stepped behind two large men, her face hidden by their hats, and listened to E.B. and Berniece. She could hear them better than she could see them.

"The Lord has delivered you to my side," the preacher intoned.

"How have you been?" Berniece asked.

"It's a perilous undertaking!" The preacher's voice boomed over the gathering.

"You look a little thin. Have you been eating right?" Berniece asked E.B.

She sounded like a mother, not a wife, for Chrissakes. Laura noticed that she was clenching her teeth.

"What is it?" E.B. asked. "I dropped all your stuff off at church a month ago."

"Treat a stranger like a brother or a sister!" the preacher commanded.

"There was this girl," Laura heard Berniece say. Her words tumbled forth. "She was freezing, weeping, barely making sense. She kept muttering a name. Campbell, I think, took a while to understand her. Marcy and I spent hours warming her up and understanding who she was. So we knew you were coming." She paused. "Marcy and I, we baked a cake."

Laura saw Berniece tuck even closer to E.B. To E.B., maybe Berniece smelled like horses, barns, earth. Wet damp earth. Laura probably smelled like sweat. She kept her arms at her sides.

"Berniece, not now," E.B. said. "Call me, leave a message, send me an e-mail, tell me the story another time. I have got to go."

Berniece clutched at his arm.

E.B. grabbed her hand. "Berniece. Leave me be."

His hand was on top of hers. Right there. Laura shivered.

Berniece cleared her throat. "Cornelius said I could borrow his truck, bring it back tomorrow."

"For what?" E.B. asked.

Laura dug her heels into the ground.

"Please, just listen. Only take a minute," Berniece pleaded.

"But, if you're saved!" the preacher shouted, "you can . . ."

"Amen!"

"Praise Jesus!"

"You can walk with God."

Berniece leaned closer to E.B.

Laura leaned into the farmers in front of her.

"It's you, not him I want," Berniece said, her mouth warming his ear. "I'll be back tomorrow," she said, "in time for supper. Meatloaf and mashed potatoes, still your favorite?"

↫

CHAPTER THIRTY-NINE

Tuesday, afternoon
Coal Banks Landing

LAURA, E.B., AND BERNIECE

*J*t couldn't be true, Laura thought, watching E.B. and Berniece. Oh Jesus, he was so close to her.

She wound around the farmers in front of her, marched right up to the two of them, and planted herself a foot away, just a little too close for their comfort.

"*There* you are, E.B.," she said, full of warmth and light. "The whole crew's been looking for you. Everyone's waiting." She glanced over at Berniece. Her face was flushed, and she scrolled her eyes from Laura to E.B. back to Laura again. Laura pierced Berniece's steely gaze with her perfect Hollywood smile.

Berniece shot E.B. a sharp look.

E.B., surprisingly, just stood there, with a big smile on his face, beaming at Laura. It took Laura aback a bit. Was this a big joke to him?

"Do you mind if I talk to my husband privately, miss?" Berniece asked.

"Gee, I'm just the messenger," Laura purred. "But E.B., Ken's waiting, says he's got another party to load."

"Right," E.B. said, smiling now at Berniece. "I've got to go."

"Give us a minute, if you please," Berniece said, sounding officious. "Tell him to wait. My husband and I have personal things to discuss." She closed up the distance between them and slipped her arm through his.

"If you don't mind? Just give me another few minutes," E.B. suggested. "Then I'll help him load the van."

Berniece shot Laura a look of victory and grinned.

"I'll tell the others." Laura turned on her heel. The sound of Berniece's voice reverberated in her head.

She walked like she was heading to her car at 3:00 a.m. She forced herself through the crowd, trying to move fast enough so that no one would see her reddening eyes.

Back at the shore, she watched the Missouri move by. It was dirty and ugly and mean on its thousand-mile march to the sea. What had she been thinking, busting in on a husband and wife and all their shared history? E.B. was as slippery as all the men she'd ever known.

Out of the crowd, she looked back, at the preacher, at the man who had pulled her in so strongly, just like she pulled in the guys at the club. He was just a man, an excuse for a man, his beard no longer full but scraggly, his arms pins on a wooden body. His words were just a seduction, an act, just like hers. She was just like the preacher. He was another charlatan, just like her. God was just another word for liar.

Damn that Berniece. E.B. deserved better. She remembered his face near hers, the way he tucked her in their only sleeping bag and how he had been cold all that night. And how his mouth had felt on hers, tentative, lovely, smooth, open. And how he had looked with Berniece, shoulders slumped, body aching.

Laura made her way back to the van, climbed inside, and sat next to E.B.'s backpack. Stella had been wrong. She always said that there was a man out there, who wanted to love Laura, who wanted to take care of her, and her him. I had come so close, Stella. There would be no one, ever, Laura knew.

She tucked her nose to his pack and sensed the smell of him. She held it for a moment while outside the van campers and canoeists milled about the campground, happy, catching fish, playing Frisbee, setting up tents. And beyond, the preacher was collecting his flock of lost souls, while she watched the river flow on by, wishing she could turn back time and once again lace her fingers through E.B.'s.

CHAPTER FORTY

CHAPTER FORTY

Tuesday, afternoon
Coal Banks Landing

CAMPBELL, DAISY, AND MARCY

Campbell watched Daisy walk away, her hips swiveling under the poorly fitting yellow dress, her white sandals slapping the ground. He turned to the pile of gear at the ramp and imagined her soft hands in his, her sweet mouth, so eager, the scent of her skin. A minute later, he dropped everything and took off after her.

He crossed the campground. At the far end a group of people were listening to a man in a black coat marching around and speaking loudly. Someone was preaching. Here?

"Leave the door open to worship," the man's voice said.

A shudder went over the group of people. Men tucked in closer to their wives, their mouths slack, murmuring "amen."

Campbell checked out the rest of the campground. Children played and a few people were asleep in lawn chairs. No Daisy. He turned back to the group.

"Put yourself in an attitude to receive the Truth," the voice continued.

Truth, my ass. Campbell laughed, moving forward through the crowd.

"Adulterers are wicked and God abhors them," the preacher said.

Adulterers? So, what else was new?

"You have sinned in the eyes of the Lord," the preacher said, his voice rising.

A man in tan shorts and a brown T-shirt elbowed Campbell by mistake. "Sorry."

"Seen any short blonde girls?" Campbell asked. The guy looked like he was on safari.

"Check with the preacher, over there. He's got a whole harem," the man said and slipped away into the gathering.

"Our God's not a punitive God," the preacher continued. Beyond him, Campbell saw a girl with blonde hair, but when he stepped closer, he found that it wasn't Daisy at all, just a middle-aged woman in overalls, shouting from the sidelines, stabbing the air with her cigarette.

"Sinners, you know who you are!"

Off to the side, Campbell noticed E.B. talking to a woman, and beyond, a flash of yellow weaving through the crowd. Daisy! He followed her, making his way to the front of the gathering, where the preacher paced back and forth, pounding on a Bible. Husbands wiped sweat off their foreheads, glanced at other guilty men, and tightened their grip on their wives.

In front, beside the preacher, two tables sagged with two coffee urns, piles of biscuits, and foam cups in stacks. Behind, an RV stood in the shadows of a cottonwood tree. Two women, wearing dresses, stood on opposite ends of the tables, their hands clasped, eyes down. Then his gaze fell on a third, eyes open and radiant, pacing from RV to tables, carrying cups. A girl with an ill-fitting dress, a girl he would recognize anywhere. Daisy.

Stung, Campbell waited, not sure what to do next.

"Do I have an 'Amen'?" the preacher called out and the crowd answered all at once. Men dropped their heads into their hands and women wept.

"What a bunch of Philistines," Campbell muttered under his breath. The crowd dissipated. His ears rang a little bit with the sound of the preacher's voice. He walked up to one of the tables and stood behind a couple waiting for Daisy to pour their coffee. They strolled away, speaking in hushed tones.

Campbell stepped forward and leaned over the table.

"Coffee, biscuit?" Daisy asked.

"What are *you* doing here?"

"Bet you're thirsty after all that packing." She held out a cup of coffee. "It's good. Just made it."

"Sweetheart, no. Put it down," he said, his voice holding more pain than he wanted.

"It's just coffee, Campbell. It won't hurt you. Take it." Daisy pushed the coffee across the table.

"You don't need to do this, Daisy. Come with me, now."

"Biscuit?"

Behind Campbell, someone coughed.

Campbell didn't move. "Daisy, please."

A man nudged Campbell in the back. "Hey, buddy, make up your mind or step aside."

Campbell slowly turned, steaming, his mouth two inches from the farmer's face. "Wait your turn, buster."

"Hey! I thought this is God's place, a place of worship." The farmer grabbed his wife's hand. "Let's get out of here, Betsy, before he starts a fight."

Campbell gave them a dirty look and held his ground.

"Campbell, please," Daisy whispered.

"Give me a minute," he argued, turning to the people around him. "Can't you see? The preacher's a charlatan. You all know better. Now, get on home and get a life."

They scattered.

"Now, look what you've done." Daisy's eyes filled with tears. "Campbell, come on. Don't be such a jerk."

"Daisy, what are you doing? They've got you all twisted and confused. You know better."

"They were there for me last night. Where were you?" She looked behind him, hopeful, and waved to some other people. "Next."

"Daisy, come on."

She went back to pouring coffee and handing out biscuits.

"Had a tough day, Campbell? I'm not surprised," a woman in a red dress pressed her slender hand on his shoulder.

He spun around. "How do you know my name?"

"I'm Marcy. Glad to meet you." She held out her hand.

Campbell hesitated. "Thank you for being kind to Daisy." He wanted to yell at her, take her by her scrawny neck, and hug her too. "Where did you find her?"

"I'll tell you when we're done serving—or better yet, ask Daisy to tell you. She looks happy, doesn't she?" Marcy adjusted the high neckline on her dress.

He had to admit, Daisy did look radiant. He walked

around to her side of the serving table, and touched her arm. A biscuit fell out of her hand onto the table.

"Come back in fifteen minutes, please, Campbell. I'm busy serving the Lord here."

"This man bothering you, ma'am?" one of the farmers said, biscuit crumbs in his long beard. He placed his meaty paw on Campbell's arm. "The lady asked nice."

"Get your hand offa me!" Campbell yelled.

Everyone went silent. Campbell scanned the crowd. Most stared at him.

"Come on. You hate these kind of people, Daisy," Campbell said.

"Serving the Lord. His wonders never cease," she answered, her voice shaking.

"We can talk, over here, by the river, all you want. I'm with you, everything's okay now."

"You bet." She grinned.

"You don't have to if you don't want to," said a man across the table.

"Come *on*." Campbell ignored his rising anger.

Daisy turned to the next person in line.

Campbell saw strain in her eyes.

A woman, opposite Daisy, gray haired and wearing oversized glasses, leaned on the table. "Honey, he's upset. Take him to the Lord. He's ready." She turned to a boy. "God moves in strange ways, Fred," she said, and patted his blond head. "Let's go find your mom."

"The Lord is ready to receive you, my son," a preacher stepped up and murmured low in Campbell's ear.

"Not for me, not today."

"Treat him gently, Father. He needs you the most," Marcy said, stepping close to the preacher.

In the distance, a horn blared. Campbell forced his eyes into the preacher's. "She gets confused easy," he said.

"Hey!" Daisy interrupted.

"Son," the preacher said. "The Lord can help you. Relieve your pain."

"Back pain? Heart pain? He didn't do much for me while I was in the hospital last year," Campbell spat.

"But you're here, aren't you?" the preacher asked. "Be thankful. He doesn't save everyone."

"Come on, honey," Campbell said to Daisy. "Let me introduce you to E.B. and Laura. They're nice people."

"God-fearing?" Daisy asked. "Thought not." She stepped away from Campbell and toward the preacher. "Take good care of him, Father." She kissed Campbell on the cheek. "You boys work it out." She followed Marcy into the RV and slammed the door.

"Daisy! Daisy! Wait a sec!" Campbell yelled.

"Resistance to God's word is futile, my son." The preacher sidled up beside him. "Give it up, Campbell, and welcome the Lord."

"You should be ashamed," Campbell turned on him. "Preying on a weak soul in her moment of need."

"Have it your way," the preacher said, and entered the RV. Once again the door slammed shut.

"Daisy! Daisy! Come out, please. We can talk about this!" Campbell put his ear to the door and listened.

He heard sobs. Was it her? Were they hurting her? Twigs cracked behind him. There were more? He turned.

"Dad!" Francine was hurrying toward him. "I've been looking all over for you! Ken's leaving!"

Campbell pounded on the wall of the RV.

The preacher cracked the door. "Lost your way with the Lord, Campbell? Ready to confess?"

"Let me talk to Daisy," Campbell urged in his most patient voice, the one he used when deals were going sour and they needed a little more time.

"Dad!" Francine came into the clearing.

Campbell looked from Francine, to the preacher, and finally to Daisy. Her face was riddled with tears. "If you so much as hurt her—"

"Campbell," Daisy interrupted, "if you love me, please let me go."

"God has brought us a new sister," the preacher said. "Let us give thanks."

"What do you do, screw them all at once?"

"The Lord is my shepherd, I shall not want," Daisy recited.

"Daisy! My daughter's right here. She wants to meet you." Campbell waved Francine over.

Daisy didn't move.

"Say hi to my daughter Francine, at least."

"Are these the people who took care of you last night?" Francine smiled. "My dad was so worried. Thanks."

"Hello, Francine," Daisy said in a small, scared voice. "Would you like to meet Berniece and Marcy?"

"Time to go," the preacher declared, nudging them both away from the door.

"Not yet," Francine said, and shoved her way inside.

"Give us a sec, all right?" Campbell sidled in beside his daughter.

"Say, you guys been traveling all over? Which place did you like best?" Francine asked.

Daisy grinned.

"I'm Cornelius," the preacher said. "Please, now, give us a little time. Adult time."

"Have it your way, asshole." Francine backed out.

Campbell stayed inside. "Now, Daisy, please, listen. We'll catch up with them in a few days. There's a name for this, Stockholm syndrome. Of course you want to be with them, but a simple thank-you is enough. Gentleman, ladies, where did you put Daisy's clothes?"

"Honey, no, please, stop. I'm so sorry." Daisy covered her face with her hands.

Campbell stepped close to her. He could feel her sweat. Smell her fresh scent. "Darling, don't be crazy. Just give me your hand."

"I can't! I can't! Marcy, Berniece, I tried. Cornelius, do something. He is suffering so. Campbell, it won't hurt anymore if you just say yes."

Marcy and Berniece gave her a hug.

"Daisy, I have the ring right here in my pocket."

Campbell watched as Daisy looked to him, then at the women, then at the preacher, and then turned her head to gaze at the bright sky outside the RV. Finally she dropped her eyes and stared at Campbell. "Not today."

"Listen to the lady," the preacher said and pushed Campbell out of the RV.

Campbell slipped onto the dirt and stood up. "Daisy, you're making a mistake."

"Not this time," Daisy said, and slammed the door.

The RV burst into life, tires squealing, exhaust pipe pumping out smoke.

It roared away, bumping and thumping down the road, spitting gravel all the way.

Campbell watched it drive away.

"Guess no double dates for a while, Dad," Francine said, standing beside him. "Guess it's just us chickens now."

CHAPTER FORTY-ONE

Tuesday, late afternoon
Coal Banks Landing

E.B.

E.B. walked back toward Ken's van, shaking his head. God had some sense of humor—have Berniece show up at the campground at the same time he was about to talk to Laura. And now he had only an hour to talk to her in a van full of people. See how that's going to work, God. Gee, thanks.

A blasting horn from across the campground startled E.B. from his fresh misery. He sprinted the rest of the way, words tumbling around in his mind, and found Ken behind the wheel of the van, leaning out the window, his elbow on the horn. "A dollar late and a dollar short," Ken spat. "Jesus, E.B., where the hell have you been?"

"It's a beautiful day, don't you think?" E.B. forced a smile, climbed inside, slipped by Kris and Jane, and settled in to the vacant seat next to Laura. She was leaning toward the tinted window, her face obscured by her hat. "You okay?"

"I could use a shower."

E.B. counted heads. "Hey, Ken, what about Campbell and Francine?"

"They wanted to stay out a few more days, head down to Judith."

"Too bad I didn't get to say good-bye." E.B. thrummed his fingers on his knees.

"Prettiest part of the river, I'll say," Ken said and punched it. The van bounced and rattled on the dirt road, pebbles pinging the undercarriage. Driving from the dirt road onto the highway, he hit a bump and everyone felt a thunk and flew back in their seats.

"Slow it down a bit, won't you, Ken?" E.B. asked.

"I wouldn't be in such a hurry if you hadn't been so late."

"I can call, tell them we're on our way." E.B. reached for his cell phone.

"Don't bother. We didn't get that tower Verizon had planned. All the farmers made a big stink at the last planning meeting and everyone caved. You among them."

"That wasn't me, that was Berniece."

"Oh."

"Build the goddamn cell towers everywhere, Ken, that's what I say." E.B. hoped Ken would stop talking so he could say something to Laura.

"You don't say," Ken said.

Ken was silent at last.

E.B. leaned toward Laura. "You seem kind of quiet. Everything all right?"

"You're squishing me."

He gave her a few inches of seat space, even though it jammed him against Jane, who pushed back. "Better now?"

"A little. Thanks," Laura said.

"If you like," he muttered, "I can give you a local's tour of Fort Benton. Town's full of history. It was a trade route in the nineteenth century for buffalo robes and all points north. People would take a paddle wheeler from St. Louis, and once they got here, they'd shift to the stage. A lot of trips up the old Whoop-Up Trail into Canada."

"Whoop-Up? Why did they call it that?"

"Damn if I know. But would you like the tour? We even have a museum."

"I have to spend the morning calling the DMV."

"We have a little one here, off Main Street."

"In California."

"But after?" E.B. asked.

"There is no after," she said, and tucked her head inside her hat.

Ken banked around one turn, then sped into another.

"Ken! You're driving like a maniac!" Laura looked a little pale.

"All right, all right," Ken sputtered and slowed down to fifty-five on the turns.

Laura felt grubby. It was stuffy in the van, she felt like a sardine, and E.B. kept leaning on her. She wondered if Stella had Fed Ex'd money and clothes.

Stella would like E.B. Another married man? How could she have been so stupid?

She wished she had a cigarette, if she still smoked, or a drink, like an ice-cold margarita or mojito. She wondered how Mom was. She'd been gone too long.

"If you give me an hour or two, I could show you my

place," E.B. said. "My Bassett hounds—Sierra and Skyler—love everyone. Bet they've been rolling in manure again. You like dogs, Laura? Cats?"

"Stella will be glad to see me," she said. "I've missed her."

"No big skies in LA," E.B. mused. "No fantastic sunsets, either. Montana is a little wilder than LA."

"Oh, I wouldn't say that."

"What's the matter with Montana?"

"Lunatics."

Ken slammed on the brakes. "Goddamn antelope!" The weight of the trailer bumped into the back of the van and made everyone jump.

"See what I mean?" he said. Several tan animals jumped off the road and leapt into fields nearby.

"I thought they were deer," Laura said.

"Country's full of them," Ken said. "If you look across the fields, you'll see more. They make for great hunting."

E.B. pointed out the window. "Check out the hollows, they're gathered there. Go on, take a closer look."

What looked at first like piles of dead, tan grass turned out to be animals, groups of them, resting near fence corners, lots of them, a tumble of legs. Some lying down, others keeping watch, fawns curled up, their long legs folded beneath them. Their black noses the only sign that they were there. Laura stared, her eyes moist. "They're so pretty. For God's sake, how could you shoot them?"

"Everyone in Montana hunts. It's a rule," Ken said. He downshifted into a turn. "Except E.B. He doesn't drink or party or have any fun, do you?" Ken snickered. "He's a dull boy. You want me to take you hunting, Laura?"

"You want me to take you shopping, Ken?"

"Sounds worse than death, that."

"Pretty much the same in my book." But he had a point. If she could learn to be a better shot, that would help, wouldn't it? Keep assholes like Tucker away. And Harry. What if he was still in Fort Benton, waiting for her? She cringed against the window.

"They don't have big skies in LA," E.B. said suddenly. "Just cars, traffic, and smog. Nor prairie dogs," he added. "Nor foxes at the water, nor wolves howling in the night. Nor frigging antelope."

"Ken, watch out!" Laura shouted.

Ken was passing a truck, but a semi was coming up too fast. He careened the van back into the proper lane, making everyone shudder and scream.

In the din, E.B. turned to Laura. "How you doing?"

"Couldn't be better. I'm covered with bug bites, I'm sunburned, and I stink."

"My kind of gal."

"You have a warped sense of humor."

"That's not what I—"

"Hold on everybody." Ken turned off the highway and dropped down a narrow two-lane road. Across the way, mountains rose above a narrow river canyon. A small town sprawled below.

"Fort Benton," he chirped.

"About bloody time," Kris grinned. "I need a beer."

Laura saw the little houses, the brick buildings, and the river beyond, lined by willows; the sun's final rays illuminating the cliffs.

"You and Berniece getting back together, E.B.?" Ken asked. "She seemed awfully eager to talk to you. Me, I wish I was married." He laughed, downshifted as he turned left down Front Street, passed the steamboat, and slowed down as he paralleled the river bank.

"Laura, before you leave, give me a minute, won't you?" E.B. asked.

She stared out the window, trying to ignore him. She felt the hurt in his heart. What about hers? Can't see you tonight, it's the kids' birthday, in-laws coming, or some other such excuse.

In a minute they passed by the Banque Club restaurant, the Pioneer Inn, and on the river side, the grand historic downtown hotel where she'd stayed. The last place where she'd felt safe. It was such an itty-bitty town.

"The Union Hotel," Ken said, proudly, slowing down even more. "You see there, the Mandan, the riverboat, just beyond? I'll show you around as soon as we get unloaded."

Campbell slammed on the brakes as a mother pushing a double stroller and holding the collar of a black Labrador walked carefully across the street. He picked up speed once they were across. A minute later they reached the landing, where he slowed to a stop. The landing where Laura had started her trip, two days and a lifetime ago.

"This is it," Ken said, got out of the van, and stretched.

From her window Laura checked the streets and side-walks for Harry or Mike or Bart. No men lurking about except for one, a guy with a cane. The man turned, took a long look at her, and tipped his ball cap. Pale face, crooked little smile, sparse, white hair.

"Can I take you out for a drink? You deserve it," Ken said, offering a hand.

"Not tonight, I'm grubby and tired and just beat," Laura said.

"We're staying in the same hotel. I can meet you in the lobby, in a half hour, if you like," E.B. suggested.

Laura looked at him, at Ken, at the scraggly characters climbing out of the van, at Beth Ann's torn, ragged, filthy shorts on her mud-spattered legs. She checked out the view across the water, the bridge beyond, the tall elms casting shadows, and felt the cool breeze coming off the river. Pretty or not, she had to go.

"You'll feel better after a shower," Ken said.

"I'll feel better when I'm home," she said and marched off to the hotel.

◠

CHAPTER FORTY-TWO

Tuesday, early evening
Fort Benton, Union Hotel

LAURA AND E.B.

*L*aura shut the door to room 306 and threw the bag of clothes, cosmetics, colognes, and cash Stella had sent onto the bed. She peeled off Beth Ann's stinky clothes and underthings one by one and dropped them into a steamy little heap on the wall-to-wall carpet, slipped into the bathroom, and stopped, stunned. Oh my God. Clean hot and cold water out of the faucets seemed like a miracle. She jumped in the shower and washed her hair two times with the hotel's collection—Aveda moisturizing shampoo and Lush Carnation Vitality liquid soap. Reluctantly, she stepped out, smelling like roses. Feeling like spring.

Tan lines showed on her upper arms—a farmer's tan, just below her biceps. Her upper thighs were darker too, with a sharp line where the hem of Beth Ann's shorty-shorts had been. Scratches crisscrossed her slender calves. Mitch wouldn't care for her tan. Screw him. She was proud of her sun-kissed skin. Proud of those scratches and nicks and bug bites. Proud of her strength on the river.

Two bruises, the size of a quarter, bloomed just above her right ankle, and one the size of a fist darkened her upper arm where Tucker had grabbed her. She hoped he was in jail.

She arched her back and did a few stretches. Things were tightening up fast. She'd have to double her exercise regimen for a bit. Back home, she'd attend the rest of Mr. Lee's self-defense classes and then take the next session.

She stared in the mirror, looking for new tiny lines around her eyes, and saw a sparkle and a vigor she'd never seen before. She grinned. Alive, yes. Healthy, yes. Worried about her future, yes. In love? Yes! Requited? No.

But one thing she knew for sure. As soon as she was back in LA, she'd move on. The hell with Mitch and the Flying Horses Club. The hell with any club. She could do better than that, any day. That's what she'd learned from the broad Missouri.

Tucking fluffy towels the size of bed sheets around her, she ran a brush through her clean hair, letting strands fly, then pulled back the heavy brown window drapes and gazed at the river and bridge just outside. Down at the patio there were no men there, at least. She hoped the thugs had given up at last.

Light glinted off the water, and cottonwood tree leaves fluttered on the opposite bank. The last rays of sunlight poured through the window. She loved the slowness of the river, the caramel color of it, the way it bumped and curved around the bridge supports, gathered itself together, and moved along on its way. She opened and closed her palms, examined her broken nails, the nicks and calluses on her fingers, and missed the familiar touch of a paddle in her hands.

E.B. Oh E.B.

She wouldn't see this view in LA, and she wouldn't see him.

At home out her kitchen window, there would be nothing but smog. And on her kitchen table little Betsy Finnegan, her calico, curled up on a stack of newspapers, motoring. Nearby would be a stack of paper takeout containers. Even with little Betsy beside her she'd still go home to the loneliness that made her stomach ache in the middle of the night. And in the morning she'd tell Stella about the Missouri, and the man she left behind.

Outside, on the bridge, a young couple was leaning on the railing, his arm around her back, her hand on his shoulder, their heads tipped toward each other.

Oh Jesus, E.B., what have I done? Laura couldn't bear it.

She pulled on the clothes Stella had sent—a silky white sleeveless top, a pair of oatmeal shorts, and her Manolo Blahnik jeweled kidskin sandals with long straps. Jewels decorated the strap across her chipped and faded fire-engine-red toes.

Halfway to the door, she stopped. The shoes didn't fit right. The knots dug into her skin. She took them off and threw them in a corner.

Wiggled her toes. Better.

She slipped off her sleeveless top, too white, too clean, too silky, and yanked off her white shorts; they were too bright against her tanned skin, and when she pulled on Beth

Ann's smudged dirty shorts, they felt like pajamas. Her top, stained with sweat, felt like a second skin. Later she'd find a Laundromat, and return the clothes, clean and folded, to Beth Ann, who had been nothing but kind.

She felt so much better now, so much more Laura-like.

Poor E.B. She'd heard what he'd said in the van and she'd let him go without a word.

Ready at last, she ran out of the hotel room, slammed the door behind her, and flew down to registration where a young woman was standing behind a mahogany counter pecking at an iPhone.

Laura glanced at her nametag. "Hey, Brenda? Can you please tell me the room number for E.B., uh, . . . Ezra Benson?" Her legs were trembling. What if he changed his mind? Gave up on her?

"Sorry, ma'am," Brenda mumbled, not looking up. "Hotel policy, we don't give out room numbers."

"I know he's here, Brenda, please. It's Mr. Ezra Benson. He checked in right after I did." Laura leaned closer to Brenda's iPhone and looked down on it. Playing Candy Crush. Of course. "Brenda? Help me out here." What if he'd headed home to Loma? To Berniece?

"I'm really sorry, but it's policy." Brenda twisted the ends of her hair. "I could get fired. Maybe you can call him on your cell?"

"I don't have a cell phone, obviously I would've tried. Come on, be a sweetheart."

"I can't. I could lose my job."

"Brenda, please. His room number. You see"—Laura leaned way over the counter—"I'm his ex-wife," she whispered, "and his mother's sick. She hasn't talked to him for years. Brenda, are you really going to keep a son from seeing his sick mother the day before she dies?"

"I'm sorry," Brenda sputtered, going white. "Oh God, you could've told me . . . here it is, room three-oh-one. Oh, please tell him I hope she gets better real soon."

"Of course, and thank you."

Laura tried the lobby phone, but there was no answer. Maybe he was in the shower. She ran upstairs to the third floor, down the hall, and banged on his heavy mahogany door. No answer. She put her ear to the door, but there were no sounds. He was either on his way to the bar to have a drink with Ken or heading home.

Laura flew back downstairs, out of the double doors of the hotel, and into the evening's last rays of sunshine and saw the bridge, right there, bigger than life. A figure stood on it. Someone tall. Shadows hid his face. Right height, though, right hair. What if it wasn't him? What if it was one of the thugs? Or worse, Tucker? She stopped in her tracks and took a deep breath. She broke into a run, almost mowed down a white-haired woman walking a small dog, and ran up onto the bridge where wooden boards thumped under her pounding flip-flops.

The man was standing halfway across the bridge, beside the trusses, staring at the water, his back turned to her. As tall as Mike, and as thin. She tightened her hands into fists. She slid up near him, every part of her body ready to fight, breathing hard, and touched his arm.

He turned around, his eyes red-rimmed. "Yes, miss?"

"I'm so sorry, I thought you were someone else."

"I met my wife here, forty years ago, and since she's been gone . . . I make the trip myself, you see, all the way from Havre. On our anniversary."

"I'm so sorry," Laura sputtered.

"Twenty years ago, to the day, and I still miss her. Could you give me a moment, please, for us to be together?"

"Yes, of course," she said, and walked back across the bridge.

Three floors above, in room 301 of the Union Hotel, E.B. pulled back his drapes and stared at the brick wall of the back of the hotel's other wing. Still, no view. He'd asked them for one—his one and only splurge on this whole trip—and they'd given him an inside room. As soon as he dropped the drapes, the telephone rang. He ignored it. Reception again asking for his credit-card number? They'd kept getting it wrong and the machine hadn't wanted to take it. Ken wanting a drink? After he'd made a fool of himself in the van? No. Whoever it was, they could wait.

He had just come up the stairs from seeing Laura run away from him, when he'd been trying to explain, trying to make it right. He shouldn't have bothered. He needed a drink. That goddamn Berniece had screwed everything up, again. Mack from the Feed 'N' Seed was going to meet him at the Banque bar, across the street. He'd go there right after his shower.

He scrubbed and scrubbed in the tepid water till his skin was sore, washing away sunscreen, mud, river water, sweat, and Laura's scent. He came out and dried himself with a washcloth like he'd learned in the service. He felt better, sort of, but hollow inside. Why was he wasting time trying to get clean? He'd just go back to the ranch and cover himself in filth like he always did. He threw on his dirty pants, hoping that Jack's lazy son Frank had at least turned the front two acres. But the rest of the place? It would take more than a week to catch up.

He stared at himself in the mirror; not too bad for thirty-six, but there were more crow's-feet around his eyes from lack of sleep, new strain lines across his forehead, and his hair stuck up again.

What he deserved from spending the night out without pad or covers. He hadn't had to make Laura so damn comfortable. Just his luck to fall for some girl and get his heart broken again. When would he ever learn? He thought for a moment of going to her room, but couldn't stand the thought of her turning him away again.

His hands missed the familiar feel of a paddle. He would do anything to be back on the river again, even with Laura complaining, her voice in his ears. Throwing on his sweat-stained blue shirt, he noticed that his arms and face were darker now, but his chest was still a fish-belly white. A farmer's tan. He was proud of it too. Four generations of Bensons behind him and they all had looked the same under their clothes. The history of the land etched into their skin, something Laura hadn't understood at the start. What could he expect from a woman who thought nature was an empty parking lot? He gave her credit, though, for coming around, learning to love nature as much as she had. Wistful, he knew she wouldn't like LA so much now that she'd been to Montana.

He walked down the landing to the lobby, past a clerk jabbering on an iPhone, past the wrought-iron windows and millwork of reception, out through the double lobby doors, and into the oblique light of dusk. Across the street, the sign Moose Drool beer in yellow neon blinked in the evening sun.

He took a glance at the river flowing by. The river he loved, the river he'd turned to for solace after Berniece left, the river that had broken his heart, then mended it. He ambled over toward the walking bridge—the first bridge ever built across the Missouri in Montana. It had seen even more history than his family and looked golden in the light. A small mist hung above the water, rising off the river and drifting in the breeze. Shafts of light and shadows crossed the river and the bridge.

Three figures walked out of the shade. E.B. stepped up onto the bridge, the wooden boards laid when his great-granddad was a boy. The last rays of sun hit him square in the eyes, and he held up his palm to see who was walking toward him. A three-year-old boy was skipping around, despite calls from his parents to slow down. A family he'd never have.

Out of the corner of his eye, he noticed a figure just beyond the glare, half-hidden in the shadows on the center of the bridge beside the trusses, watching the river in silence and stillness. Was it Mrs. Guthrie, one of the little old ladies of Fort Benton, out for a stroll? He couldn't tell.

He walked a third of the way across and thought about the river, how it started in Three Forks, then over the falls, and here sinuous and curvy, a moving ribbon of water on its way across, easily, a thousand miles or more to empty into the Mississippi River and then into the Gulf of Mexico.

Maybe he'd been a little too hard on himself. He'd had a pretty good trip, met someone wonderful, and let his heart crack and open again a little, since Berniece had left months ago.

Maybe it was a good thing, God's little lesson, teaching him to be humble. He leaned against the railing, watching the mist. He felt thankful for a little romance, a taste of romance, and he gazed into the water and relived the image of Laura in his mind, her hand on his shoulder at camp, the sound of her voice, doing everything he could to memorize every detail.

The smell of roses drifted in the air. It was so real that it made him feel a little dizzy. He felt something, a hand on his arm, probably Mrs. Guthrie's. She was always eager to tell him something. His imagination was working overtime, and he couldn't believe the scent of roses was so real, so Laura-like, and he couldn't remember if Mrs. Guthrie wore roses, but she was so close, and he was happy for a few minutes, and he could pretend she was Laura. He closed his eyes.

And then he heard her voice.

"I've been looking for you," she said.

E.B.'s eyes flew open. Hoping didn't make it so. Of course, she was here to say good-bye. He turned to her, flushed with heat. The river was suddenly so far away, his hopes flowing away with the current.

"All ready for LA?" he asked, trying to keep the tremble out of his voice.

"I guess," she said, standing a little too close.

For a second, he felt like she was vibrating.

"I didn't mean anything with Berniece," E.B. said suddenly, throwing the first idea he had into the air.

"I tried calling you," Laura said, facing him. "Room three-oh-one, correct?"

"That was you?" he asked, unintentionally revealing he had ignored her call.

"I thought you'd left for Loma."

"You didn't change," he said.

"Neither did you. These clothes feel like pajamas," she said, scraping one shin with her foot.

"One and the same, the city girl and the country hick," he said, turning to her and smiling.

"I don't know much about living in the country," Laura said, flicking a leaf into the river. "I usually go to bed just before dawn."

"That's when I get up." He laughed. Had she said "living in the country"? Did she want to? He stayed silent a moment, not noticing the shadows lengthen, darkness seeping down from the hills, bats taking flight, nor the whoosh of pelicans coming in for a landing.

"Winters are tough here on the plains," he said.

"Not so bad," she said.

"And who told you that?"

"And early dawn, when the light is clear and pure?" She squeezed his hand.

Just keep talking. E.B. wrapped his fingers through hers.

"I don't know how to cook." She paused. "But I can learn."

E.B.'s heart filled his chest. He felt her arm on his shoulder, on his back, and gathering all of her, her scent and her soul and her voice and the sound of her laughter, all into him, and he held her, tight, for the longest time.

He kissed her soft mouth, the mouth that came into his,

the body that pressed against his, the warmth that emanated from her body. Her back was so smooth under his rough hands, her breath warm in his ear.

"If we keep doing this, you're going to miss your plane."

"I canceled my reservation," she said.

Below them, a family of mergansers came out from under the shadow of the bridge and started across the river, mom in front, paddling slowly, while behind her, ten babies paddled hard, their eyes eager, one behind, working to catch up. Far off an owl hooted as shadows lengthened, the bridge disappeared into mist, and E.B. and Laura kissed, until it was too dark to see, and he guided her, arms entwined, back into the hotel and up to room 301.

fini

A C K N O W L E D G M E N T S

Many many thanks and love to master writing teacher James N. Frey for yelling "more conflict, more conflict." For friends and writers who have seen this manuscript develop over the years: Inga Silva for her compassionate and kind support, Jeffrey Philips, Cara Black, Elaine Taylor, Margaret Cuthbert, Dorothy Mack, John King, Brooke Warner, Muncie Morger (Fort Benton), Mike and Meredith (Fort Benton). Last, but not least, for Stu, for taking me to the river in the first place.

ABOUT THE AUTHOR

photo credit: Meghan Roberts

SUSANNA SOLOMON, a writer and electrical engineer, lives in Marin County, where she has run her own engineering consulting firm for more than twenty years. Her books include two short story collections, *Point Reyes Sheriff's Calls* and *More Point Reyes Sheriff's Calls*, and her stories have appeared in *Foliate Oak Magazine, Meat for Tea – The Valley Review*, and online in the *Mill Valley Literary Review* and *Harlot's Sauce Radio*. An avid outdoor enthusiast, Susanna has backpacked in Yosemite, Glacier National Park, Point Reyes, the Bernese Oberland, and the Gasternal in Switzerland. She's walked across England on the Coast to Coast Trail, and has canoed extensively on the Missouri River in Montana, the Jacks Fork and Eleven Point Rivers in Missouri, and the Russian and Eel Rivers in California. She now spends her free time studying Tai Chi and Tai Chi sword and swimming in Tomales Bay, which is ten minutes from her home.

SELECTED TITLES FROM SHE WRITES PRESS

She Writes Press is an independent publishing company
founded to serve women writers everywhere.
Visit us at www.shewritespress.com.

Center Ring by Nicole Waggoner. $17.95, 978-1-63152-034-1. When
a startling confession rattles a group of tightly knit women to its
core, the friends are left analyzing their own roads not taken and the
vastly different choices they've made in life and love.

In the Heart of Texas by Ginger McKnight-Chavers. $16.95, 978-1-
63152-159-1. After spicy, forty-something soap star Jo Randolph
manages in twenty-four hours to burn all her bridges in Hollywood,
along with her director/boyfriend's beach house, she spends a crazy
summer back in her West Texas hometown—and it makes her question whether her life in the limelight is worth reclaiming.

Conjuring Casanova by Melissa Rea. $16.95, 978-1-63152-056-3.
Headstrong ER physician Elizabeth Hillman is a career woman who
has sworn off men and believes the idea of love in the twenty-first
century is a fairy-tale—but when Giacomo Casanova steps into her
life on a rooftop in Italy, her reality and concept of love are forever
changed.

Peregrine Island by Diane B. Saxton. $16.95, 978-1-63152-151-5. The
Peregrine family's lives are turned upside-down one summer when
so-called "art experts" appear on the doorstep of their Connecticut
island home to appraise a favorite heirloom painting—and incrimi-
nating papers are discovered behind the painting in question.

Size Matters by Cathryn Novak. $16.95, 978-1-63152-103-4. If you take
one very large, reclusive, and eccentric man who lives to eat, add one
young woman fresh out of culinary school who lives to cook, and then
stir in a love of musical comedy and fresh-brewed exotic tea, with just
a hint of magic, will the result be a soufflé—or a charred, inedible mess?

Wishful Thinking by Kamy Wicoff. $16.95, 978-1-63152-976-4. A
divorced mother of two gets an app on her phone that lets her be in
more than one place at the same time, and quickly goes from zero to
hero in her personal and professional life—but at what cost?

CPSIA information can be obtained
at www.ICGtesting.com
Printed in the USA
JSHW020508250621
16243JS00001B/62

9 781631 523618